FRANK BAKER

THE TWISTED TREE

I0633415

VALANCOURT BOOKS

The Twisted Tree by Frank Baker
Originally published in Great Britain by Peter Davies in June 1935
First U. S. edition and first Valancourt Books edition 2021

Published by Valancourt Books, Richmond, Virginia
http://www.valancourtbooks.com

ISBN 978-1-948405-90-4 (*trade paperback*)
ISBN 978-1-948405-91-1 (*trade hardcover*)
Also available as an electronic book.

Set in Dante MT

For
SYDNEY
where he is . . .

THE TWISTED TREE

FRANK BAKER was born in London in 1908. From a young age, he had a deep interest in church music, serving as a chorister at Winchester Cathedral as a boy from 1919 to 1924. From 1924 to 1929, Baker worked as a marine insurance clerk in the City of London, an experience that he later fictionalized in *The Birds* (1936). He resigned in 1929 to take on secretarial work at an ecclesiastical music school where he hoped to make a career of music; during this time he also worked as a church organist.

He soon abandoned his musical studies and went to St. Just, on the west coast of Cornwall, where he became organist of the village church and lived alone in a stone cottage. It was during this time that he began writing; his first novel, *The Twisted Tree*, was published in 1935 by Peter Davies after nine other publishers rejected it. It was well received by critics, and its modest success prompted Baker to continue writing. In 1936, he published *The Birds*, which sold only about 300 copies and which its author described as "a failure." Nonetheless, after the release of Alfred Hitchcock's popular film of the same name in 1963, *The Birds* was reissued in paperback by Panther and received new attention. Baker's most successful and enduring work was *Miss Hargreaves* (1940), a comic fantasy in which two young people invent a story about an elderly woman, only to find that their imagination has in fact brought her to life.

During the Second World War, Baker became an actor and toured Britain before getting married in 1943 to Kathleen Lloyd, with whom he had three children. Baker continued to write, publishing more than a dozen more books, including *Mr. Allenby Loses the Way* (1945), *Embers* (1946), *My Friend the Enemy* (1948) and *Talk of the Devil* (1956). Baker died in Cornwall of cancer in 1983.

By Frank Baker

FICTION

The Twisted Tree (1935)*
The Birds (1936)*
Miss Hargreaves (1940)
Allanayr (1941)
Sweet Chariot (1942)
Mr. Allenby Loses the Way (1945)
Before I Go Hence (1946)
Embers (1946)
The Downs So Free (1948)
My Friend the Enemy (1948)
Lease of Life (1954)
Talk of the Devil (1956)
Teresa: A Journey Out of Time (1960)
Stories of the Strange and Sinister (1983)*

NONFICTION/AUTOBIOGRAPHICAL

The Road Was Free (1948)
I Follow But Myself (1968)
The Call of Cornwall (1976)

* Available from Valancourt Books

"Sorrow on the acres,
Wind in the thorn. . . ."

A. E. COPPARD

"For man goeth to his long home. . . ."

ECCLESIASTES

Book I

THE THORN

CHAPTER I

TOWARDS the end of April a black east wind that had kept old people indoors and chilled the hands and hearts of young ones, ceased as suddenly as it had begun, and left the clouds grey and heavy for rain. Upon the crusty earth the rain fell vigorously, and copses that were black suddenly burst into speckles of green. Men and women reflected this change. Narrow eyes that had glowered through a backward spring began to gleam with incipient humour. Lips that had moved only to utter some fractious cynicism moved now with pleasantries.

For nearly two days the rain continued to slake the parched countryside. With evening of the second day the storm slowly abated and a strip of faded gold struck into the surly clouds huddled above the sea. As it broadened, misty arms stretched down from it, striking in the motionless water a luminous path to the horizon. With the cessation of both wind and rain the evening was strangely quiet. Thrushes and blackbirds who had rejoiced to sing in the rain, ceased when the rain stopped. Silence found silence, so that lambs were half afraid to call to their mothers, and children who had been playing were filled with a desultory air of lassitude.

Like a dancer poised on nervous feet, the world was waiting. And representative of the world at that breathless moment of transition was Tansy Penderil, who, with a questioning smile, stood by the gate of the farmyard. In a deliberate day-dream she studied a ship moving sluggishly in water that seemed to be thicker than mud. She did not think the ship was moving until suddenly its muddy shape was transfigured into a radiant messenger tipped with fire. It had moved into the sun's path. Tansy followed it as it slowly moved over that shimmering course and became once more a laboured toiler in a sluggish sea. Why didn't it turn its course, she asked herself, and steer towards the sun?

She went through the tin shed at the back of the house and

thus into the kitchen where her father and brothers were having tea. Her father looked up, his dark eyes like beads in his swarthy head. "Come to tea, child!" He spoke kindly and the words rang pleasantly in her ears. Yet Tansy understood it as a command, not a request. Years ago, when she had pushed her younger brother Joe in a dung-heap, her father had said, "Come and be thrashed, child," in exactly the same tone. Tansy always obeyed, conscious that it was simply easier to do so. There was never time to attempt to defy authority. Joe was the same. Both of them respected their father and unwittingly ignored their mother, a patient creature who had yielded all her life to her husband Nicolas. Only Andrew, the first-born, seemed to have carved his own identity—perhaps because he inherited more of his father's capacity for rigorous control of those under him. Emmeline, his mother, from the moment twenty-six years ago when she had first been courted by Nicolas and had been totally unable to say nay to him, had realized when she saw her first baby that here was another Penderil to whom she could never say nay. Nor had she. To her family she became an automaton, albeit a perfectly happy one. Nobody was unkind to her. She was often overlooked—but then, she asked herself, when there were so many important things to concern them, how should they worry about her? Yet on rare occasions Emmeline would have her own way. Neither Nicolas nor Andrew could then withstand her. Nicolas had first realized this side of her nature when, with Tansy yet unborn, she had insisted on the naming of the child. She and Nicolas had been walking along the Penth valley one Sunday evening in July. Passing a stream over which errant montbretias hung their fiery heads, Nicolas had pointed to a thick growth of bright flowers clustered like yellow buttons above the nettles and brambles.

"That's a fine flower," he remarked, never anticipating the quick flight of her fancy.

"Yes, it is that," she replied. "And I'll tell you what, Nicolas, 'twould make a pretty name for a maid!"

"Why, what's it called, then?" he had asked.

"It's called Tansy, a sweet name to my thinking. And I tell you, Nicolas, if this child turns out to be a maid, us'll call her Tansy."

"A silly name for a maid," he had growled, yet aware of a

dominating tone in her quiet voice, new to him and somewhat disturbing.

"A handsome name I say it is. There isn't another maid in the town called Tansy, nor in the world for what I do know."

"The neighbours will laugh," he mumbled, but somehow quite ineffectually.

"Let them!" she retorted. "But see here, Nicolas, you'll promise me here and now that if it be a maid she'll be called Tansy and nought else."

So it had been, and Emmeline, seeing Tansy in her arms, suckled the child with a sad tenderness, endowing her in those quiet moments with a great many of her own cloudy dreams. At twenty, Tansy's face was like that of a dreamer waking reluctantly from an uncharted sleep. Looking at her, one was conscious of the desire to answer questions that she could never ask. Her slate-grey eyes converged to a deep centre of static blue, the unbroken colour of the sea on a summer day. Her cheeks were flushed like those of a child conscious before its parents of wrong-doing. In her somewhat ascetic features lay a sense of design, a balance which was the paradox of the quickening spark in her apparently immobile eyes. She was tall, with a straight smooth body and active limbs. She rarely appeared to hurry, yet she gave her companions a certain sense of speed. Her speech was abrupt and metallic, pitched low, and, like her eyes, possessing an undertone of tremulous energy.

Looking at her as she stood in the doorway, her father had a sudden vision of some distant episode in his life. Groping down, he went back to that moment by the stream-side when Emmeline had given Tansy her name. The picture disquieted him for no obvious reason, and again he repeated, though with less certainty, "Come to tea, child." And added, with forced solicitude, "You'll be getting hungry."

Tansy slid on to the long bench by the side of her brother Joe, who smiled at her ingenuously. She thought it was very close in the kitchen, and that the sounds of her family munching their food were very much like the sounds of cattle munching hay in the long sheds. The clock struck six. Nobody spoke. They were hungry, and the business of the day could wait till their hunger was stayed. Tansy wanted to be outside where the sun strove to strike light into a sullen world. A struggle went on inside her; she felt that she stood on the brink of something, although she could give it no name. She only knew she wanted to be outside. Then she remembered something that could lawfully take her out.

"Mrs. Noggs's cream——" she began, then hesitated, wondering whether it would convince her father.

"Well?" he encouraged.

"She have company and wanted cream for tea. I'd forgot. Reckon I'd better go." She rose and went into the dairy, a lofty lime-white passage adjoining the kitchen.

"But you'll have your tea first?" called her father. "Joe can go," he added. But Joe, catching a faint appeal in Tansy's voice, pleaded a game of football in the field.

Humming nervously, Tansy hurriedly spooned some cream into a basin. Then she went quickly to the door and got outside before Nicolas could say anything. As quickly she walked along the lane. She was filled with a nervous buoyancy that carried her on almost against her will, for she knew that in hurrying away from the farm she had displeased her father. She went down a steep, rocky path leading into the Penth valley, a place solemnly retrospective with tottering stacks and shafts of mines that had been silent for a century. At one end of it lay the sea, a shiftless mirror of the slabbed sky. As Tansy walked on, she smelt the luscious scent of the new gorse springing to little flames of gold. With a sudden swirl a yellowhammer, as bright as the blossom, arose from a clump of it, so that Tansy was tempted to imagine a world where flowers flew into the air and birds grew upon bushes. "What a pretty singer the sweet-pea would make," she said to herself. "And if we could plant robins to sprout and sing out of the winter earth, what a queer lovely world 'twould be!" But as though to defy her dream, a great woodpecker arose as out of nowhere, lumbering into the sky with colours as bright as any flower.

She reached the bed of the valley, crossed a narrow plank over the stream and walked upwards, away from the sea. At the end of the valley a dark arm of grey roofs stretched up the carn to the sky; leaning away from the houses, the sombre opalescence of the church tower. They were as integral a part of the landscape as the moors upon which they stood, carved, as it seemed, from the granite of the sky into which they merged. Further inland were two mountainous slags thrown up from the clay pits.

Between the slags and the town was a black huddling wood which bore the only trees for miles around. Once this wood had been the Vicarage garden; decaying through neglect, the forlorn house still stood in the middle of it. Nobody had lived there for twenty years. They said it was haunted by the ghost of one who had been murdered, but Tansy knew little of a half-dead story. She rarely went into the wood, for trees frightened her, who had spent all her life upon open moors. But she walked now in that direction, for Mrs. Noggs's cottage lay a few yards away from it.

She tried to find a reason for her restless mood. Was it an interest in Mrs Noggs's visitor, she asked? Mrs Noggs had said he was a young man from London—one of those painters. But Tansy never took much interest in strangers and could not pin her restlessness down to him. As for Mrs Noggs, with her squinny little pig's eyes and her cunning smile—she hated her. It could have nothing to do with her. Yet she walked quickly, clutching the basin of cream like a nervous child fearful of dropping it.

She went along by the small stream where her mother had given her her name. The banks were bright with violets and campions. In the distance over the stream, and at the bottom of a sloping field, she saw a dense haze of white blossom. It was cloudy and so like smoke that she half expected it to drift down the valley. Coming nearer to it, she saw it was a bush of thorn. Under the grey sky its thick purity changed the whole sombre tone of the valley and held in its heavy boughs a certain promise of summer. Tansy put her cream down carefully on the bank and, taking off her shoes, waded into the water. It was ice cold, and she jumped back with the shock. The thorn had made her think of summer and warmth; the cold stream had brought back the east wind which still left its mark upon the land in spite of the rain. Overhead the clouds met into a frowning rebuke, as though they would reproach her for ignoring them. Tansy looked at the blossom sadly, knowing that if she were to pick any of it her mother would never allow it to be brought into the house. It was one of those things about which she was obstinate. Yet as Tansy stood there growing cold and miserable, she knew that the thorn was somehow symbolical of the urgent call of this expectant day; that it said something to her which the ponderous skies never dreamt of. Moment by moment it became increasingly necessary to gather the blossom and hold it near to her. So she waded into the stream again, prepared now for the cold water, and reached up her hand to a spray of thorn outstretched over her head. With a sharp tug she snapped it off, gasping as she nearly toppled over into the stream. But it was a lovely piece! She threw it on the bank, then probed about in the hedge for more. The hedge climbed some feet above her, and she paused with her hand stretched into the heart of it, trying to reach a bough. With her left hand she grasped a tuft of grass in order to steady herself. Jabbing her knee into the bank, she made a dart for it. Then the grass gave and she knew she must lose her balance and fall into the stream. But a wonderful and frightening thing happened. Her hand was grasped firmly through the hedge, and she was held, half on the bank, half in the stream.

It was a moment of tension, acute and deeply felt by both Tansy and the man on the other side of the hedge. As she felt the warm grip of his hand she found herself not wishing to be released, for there was something more than reassurance in his helpful grasp.

She saw him vaguely through the hedge. A young man, very tall and with long loose limbs. Then he spoke to her in a rather precise voice.

"Get your balance and I'll let you go. Otherwise you might fall into the stream."

Tansy felt he was mocking her.

"I'm right as rain," she said. "You may let me go, please." He released her hand quickly, and Tansy, getting on to the bank, started to dry her feet with her handkerchief. She could see the man's head above the hedge and followed him with sly interest as he walked along the field and came through a clearing some way up, where there were stones to cross the stream. Then she heard him walking along the path towards her. Presently he stood immediately behind her and she had a strange feeling that she sat at the foot of a great tree with long bending branches. When he spoke, his voice seemed so far away that she wanted to shout her reply.

"See what comes of trying to pick blackthorn!" He laughed easily, then changed his tone as he asked, "Are you hurt?" He sat down by her, flinging a great bunch of thorn on the grass.

"No, I'm not hurt," replied Tansy. Then seeing the thorn she exclaimed, "Did you manage to get all that then? I tell you I had some job even to get one piece." She pointed to her own spray.

He laughed. "You made the mistake of trying to get it from the wrong side," he said. He drew out a large silk handkerchief. "Your handkerchief is hardly large enough to cover your little toe," he said. "I'll dry your feet."

"Oh no, thank you!" said Tansy quickly, a conventional dignity overcoming her interest. And then blushing, as she saw brown eyes looking at her with a strangely grave humour, she added, "Oh, well, you may as well as you've a mind to."

He took her foot and began to chafe warmth into it. It was a berry-brown foot and he held it in his hands as a connoisseur might hold and balance a priceless vase. Tansy was fascinated by his supple fingers as they tentatively smoothed over her cold skin and sent a singing warmth into her blood.

"Feet are beautiful," he said simply, "and drying them makes me feel very Christ-like. You remember He had a Commandment about it?"

"Did He? I—don't know," murmured Tansy, a little bewildered. Was he making fun of the Lord? Tansy was not sure. She had a sudden desire to stroke his hair—long flaxen hair sweeping down to the nape of his neck, and flowing across the centre of his head, one dash of it, darker, more glowing than the rest. She touched it lightly, as one who would pass his finger through a candle flame. He looked up.

"I'm very sensitive there," he said quickly. "You really mustn't do it."

"There was a—wasp——" said Tansy clumsily.

"Wasps in April?" He laughed, and took her other foot. Tansy, half ashamed of her impetuousness, did not speak. She felt very quiet inside, more certain of something in herself. She avoided defining her certainty as taking tangible form in this stranger.

He began to roll a cotton stocking on to her foot, but she withdrew her leg guardedly, instinctively provocative.

"Reckon I can do that, thank you," she said.

"Yes, I reckon you can," he mocked, then laughed again as she pushed her lips into a pout of indignation. He stood up and pointed a long arm to the sea and the restrained sunset.

"You know, it's spring," he said casually. But Tansy felt it was the first lovely truth of her life.

"I've had a feeling all day," she said, "that I've been waiting for something. D'you ever get like that? That's why I wanted the blackthorn. It seemed to—well, I don't hardly know. But it's some lovely isn't it?"

"You'd better have what I picked," he said, "in memory of the rescue."

"No, it's no use my having it," she replied. "Mother won't have the stuff in the house. It's bad luck, she says, and nothing'll make her have it indoors."

"Oh, I know," he cried impatiently. "The crown of thorns or some old nonsense! It's all rubbish! And, anyhow, if Christ's death meant anything to you, wouldn't you like to live with the tree that made a crown for His bloody head?"

"No, I wouldn't," replied Tansy quickly. "But all the same I don't believe it ever was the crown of thorns, and I'd dearly love to take it home."

"Where do you live?" he asked, gathering up the blossom as he spoke.

"To the farm," replied Tansy cautiously, not wishing to tell him any more.

"Are you going there now?" he continued.

Remembering the cream, Tansy suddenly guessed who the stranger was.

"You're at Mrs. Noggs, aren't you?" she ventured. And when he nodded his head in surprised assent she told him she had been going there.

"Then we'll walk together," he said gravely. "You take the cream; I'll take the thorn."

So they walked along, Tansy fearful lest they should pass any-body who might betray what she knew must be kept secret.

"What's your name?" he asked. She told him.

"Tansy——" he mused reflectively. "A good name. I like you, Tansy," he added directly.

"What's your name then?" she asked boldly.

"Roger—Roger Chailey." He added the surname as an after-thought.

"You paint pictures, don't you?" she asked.

"Yes, when I'm inspired," he replied.

"What's that then?" She would not pretend to understand him.

"Oh, when the Lord wills it!" He laughed with his mouth closed. Tansy frowned. He was too free with the Lord's name, she thought.

"What sort of pictures do you paint?" she asked.

"People," he replied carelessly. "Oh—and people's bodies."

"Yes——" She was not quite sure how to take that remark, but she hesitated to pursue it. Instead she asked, "Do you make a lot o' money with your pictures?"

"Very little," he said solemnly. "You see, I am a very good painter."

She wrinkled her nose. "You boast a lot," she said rudely. "If you paint so handsome, why don't you paint an old duchess and make a bit o' money?"

"I don't know any duchesses," he replied. "And I believe, anyhow, that they generally prefer to be photographed."

"What sort of people do you paint then?" she asked.

"Young people," he replied. "People like you."

"Oh——" Tansy drew in her breath, for he looked at her suddenly with a savage, almost resentful smile. They stopped walking, for they were at the end of the valley and near the dark wood. They could see the smoke piercing straight into the sky from Mrs. Noggs's cottage. In the clouds were streaks of russet red.

Chailey stood very large, ominous in the shifting half-light of the silent evening. His clothes were loose and heavy. Tansy saw his face half smothered by the blackthorn; two alert eyes that watched her through the nebulous blossom. His free arm hung very loosely from his shoulder; an arm that could do lots of things, thought Tansy, lots of things. It seemed to be independent of his body. And suddenly he put the thorn down on the ground and moved his arms helplessly towards her.

"Are we still waiting for something?" His lips curled slightly on the words; his nostrils quivered with impatience.

In that moment, high up and far away, yet contentious in its truth, they heard the first dissonant notes of the cuckoo. And after it a small breath of wind shivered joyously in the trees; a lamb blurted into the silence; a thrush found a single lucid note to sleep upon. Out of conclusion the world moved again. Then Tansy knew that the man standing before her stirred her as nobody had ever stirred her. She stood before a great fire interwoven by intangible pictures, leaping spirits, half lovely, half terrible. To touch his hair had been like the candle flame; to touch his body would be like the fire. Her thoughts drove her forward, so that she stood very near him. And when he saw her so near with such bewilderment on her face, he sighed because of her easiness. But roused by the flush in her cheeks, the quick stiffening of her body, he leant forward and touched her lightly upon the breast.

"Tansy," he murmured, "I should like to paint you. Will you let me? Because I believe I see what you really are."

He saw in her misty eyes the blue pool in the oblique rock. She trembled a little. "Oh, no," she whispered. But he began to make arrangements as though it were all settled.

"You can come to the cottage on Thursday," he said. "Mrs. Noggs is going into market then——"

"I couldn't get away," she objected.

"One can always get away," he insisted, taking her hand and pressing it hard.

She drew him into the shade of a tree as a couple passed by. She spoke cautiously.

"You mustn't tell anyone about this. If they knew at home they'd be—— You don't know. They'd never give me no peace." She made an irresolute attempt to drag herself away from him. But he caught her vehemently and had her pressed against him.

She gasped, and simulated an indignation she could not feel, even though she tried. But the alphabet of her environment could not face this attack.

Chailey muttered in her ear. "Tansy, witch Tansy, am I the first to kiss you?" And when he opened her mouth savagely under his, she shivered with delight, even though an inherent sense of purity told her he was a wicked fellow. Then he let her go, and swaying uncertainly with the sudden release, she felt like a leaf that he might have dropped from a tree. She clung to the basin of cream still, as one would cling to a truism in an iconoclastic argument; watched it foolishly as it trickled down in a yellow line to the ground. She was stupefied and could not speak, because the fire of him had burnt her too greatly, yet never enough. He took the cream from her and thrust the thorn into her hand. He was a dark monster in the shadows, the sun branding a red scar across his twisted lips. Tansy could not place herself as anywhere save in the shadow of his long arms—arms that drifted over her like wings.

"Tansy," he said, "you must go back before it gets dark. I'll take the cream. You'd better say I met you near the cottage."

She didn't move.

"Come, Tansy"—he waved his loose arm impatiently and touched her again lightly on the breast. It was a flippant gesture which hurt her strangely—"you must go," he urged. "There's Thursday. And every evening I shall come down the valley if you want me."

"I—can't come again," she whispered. Then in a heavy voice: "Oh, dear Lord, I wish I'd never set eyes on you! You burn me like a fire and it don't do me no good."

He laid a nervous hand on her forehead. His sympathetic fingers sustained an easier rhythm in her troubled mind. He broke off a small piece of thorn with a quick gesture.

"Keep this," he said, "because of this evening, which was lovely. And like this evening the thorn will lose its whiteness, but the shape of it will always remain. Keep it, this lovely twisted little tree."

He left her then, and walked quickly away. Presently she turned towards the sea and, half dreaming, started the walk home. Above the sea she saw a white star lying over the curved horn of the young moon.

And suddenly she was conscious of herself as a living part of this evening beauty, as vital as the moon and the star. Life was a lovely, joyous thing; it was her, and she was life. So she ran, singing crazy pieces of old songs, her limbs quickened by the rich rhythm of life. And running thus, she did not stop till she saw the orange glow of the lights in the farm. Then her footsteps slackened; the zest in her grew ashamed and died.

CHAPTER II

THE front door was open and she saw her father standing there in conversation with a neighbour. The lamp stood by the window in the living room and there was a light also in her parents' bedroom. Tansy thought the opaque surface of the house was like a face with crooked eyes burning to search out her secret. The shadow of the farm overclouded her adventure and ridiculed it as a child's fairy tale. She hesitated, holding the thorn as evidence of what seemed a dream.

She heard whistling and presently saw Joe coming into the yard from a field at the back of the house. Quickly she opened the gate and ran up to him. Joe stopped whistling in surprise when he saw Tansy out of breath and with the thorn held close to her.

"Mother back from town then?" she asked—even with Joe, always her confidant, trying to hide her uneasiness.

"Yes," he said, "and seems she's a bit slight." He was looking at the thorn. "You're daft if you bring that stuff in the house," he added.

"I don't care," said Tansy. "It's some stupid if I can't have a bit of flower up to my room."

"Do as you've a mind to," said Joe. Then curiously, "You been a long time. Where've you been to?"

"I met that artist chap down to Mrs. Noggs," replied Tansy. "He guessed the cream was for them and we got talking a bit about the place. He hasn't ever been here before."

"Oh! Did he give you that stuff?"

"Of course not, Joe. Don't be stupid! I picked it coming back. That's why I'm late."

"What sort o' chap is he?" asked Joe.

Tansy hesitated a second then plunged into a lively description, more true to her real thoughts than she imagined. "A nice man I thought, but a bit queer. Shouldn't want to meet him in the dark!"

She found it easy to deceive Joe, whom she loved more than the other members of her family. But with her mother, who saw more deeply into her nature, she knew it would not be so easy. Joe received her remarks without any suspicion. Had she emphasized a strong dislike of Chailey, he would immediately have tried to discover more. He changed the subject.

"Arthur's in there." He grinned impudently. "Wondering why you wasn't here to go out with him."

Tansy frowned. It was generally understood that she would marry Arthur Progis, a young miner whose parents had died abroad and left him, as a boy, in the care of an old uncle. He had never asked her to marry him. For so many years he had been accepted as one of the Penderils that to consult Tansy upon such a point would have seemed almost an insult to the family. She liked him well enough; admired his rough, stocky body, his rather dull, honest blue eyes. He had always been good enough for her, she had felt; was clearly the type of man the world would choose for her husband. Whether she chose him herself was hardly worth considering. Here was a fine youngster with strong hands, honest eyes and a good heart; a potential father of strapping sons. What more should a girl ask of life?

What more? Tansy already began to feel that she had behaved like a fool and when she went into the house through the back door and stood by the long kitchen table, she knew she was as much part of this place as the garishly coloured picture of the Good Shepherd which hung on the wall. Like herself, it might be removed for an hour or so when the time for spring cleaning came round, but it would always be returned to its rusty nail. She could not imagine it permanently in any other place. In Chailey's room, for example, together with his own pictures. She laughed.

It was unimaginable. But she stopped laughing as she put the thorn on the table. He had told her to keep that one piece, and she knew that however often she might look at the Good Shepherd for confirmation of the reality of life, she would look as often to the blackthorn for evidence of a dream.

She shovelled some coals on the dull glow of the kitchen fire. She could hear Arthur and Andrew speaking in the next room, and beyond that, her father, still talking to the neighbour at the door. Then the front door slammed and she heard Nicolas come into the living-room. Would she have to go in and face them all—the three men who governed the course of her life? Who would all rebuke her if she were to tell them what had happened that evening? Yet she longed to tell somebody; felt already that the secret was a burden to her.

She heard somebody coming towards the kitchen door, and hastily stuffing the thorn into the window seat, she bent over the fire, poking with well-feigned concern at its fortunate reluctance to do anything more than smoke.

Her father came in. She did not turn round. He was whistling and rubbing his hands together rather smugly. To Tansy's surprise he made no comment on her reappearance, but sitting down and taking off his boots, remarked, "Well, I just done a handsome deal, my girl!" He chuckled and shook his head artfully.

"What's that, then?" asked Tansy, glad to seize this chance of obscuring her own affairs.

"Well, I just sold that stony bit of land at Penth Bottoms to old Stone. He offer me thirty pound for it, see? I stuck at thirty-five, and he accepted as reasonable as could be."

"What—old John Stone?"

"Yes. I know his idea, mind you. He was secretive like, and wouldn't out with his mind. He always had a crazy notion about tin being there. Of course it's well known there aren't nothing of the sort. Else why didn't they work it a century ago? They knew what they were about in them days more than what we do, I calculate. And if there'd been anything in that ground they'd have had it out, sure as nuts."

He coughed, as a thick cloud of smoke puffed down the chimney.

"What're you at, child?" he spluttered. "Where's the sense in lighting the slab when it's almost come bedtime?"

Tansy was lost for a reason. "I want to scald some milk," she ventured, and hurrying into the dairy, came back with a great pan of unscalded milk. "How's mother?" she asked, seeing in Emmeline a fresh topic of conversation.

Nicolas spoke cautiously. "A bit queer, Tansy. She've been in buying some sheets and such like, and the walk from the bus tired her out I fancy."

"Sheets?" said Tansy quickly. "What do she want with those?"

"Why—for you and Arthur——"

Tansy wheeled round upon him in amazement. A day before, the remark would have seemed perfectly natural. But this evening, the almost immediate prospect of a home with Arthur was so ludicrous that she wanted to laugh—or cry. She began to say something, to protest or acquiesce, but her mouth was dry, her tongue sticky and hot. Through the small window she saw in a haze of sudden tears the last drifting tatters of burning clouds. On the wall a faint orange reflection of the window sank slowly, until the place was dark. Nicolas sat solemnly staring at her, one half of his face shining in the light of the lamp from the other room. Tansy wanted to slap the stupid, expressionless face that planned and ordered all her actions: that calmly announced an impending marriage in as casual a tone as one who might announce the birth of a new calf. In just such a tone he would no doubt determine the number of children she was to have. He might even call for a boy or girl as required, if that were possible. And he sat there like a piece of untroubled dough . . . if only he would say something that could reasonably rouse her temper! His damning tenderness robbed her of her arms. She could never fight one who loved her so blindly that he could not visualize her doing anything contrary to his wishes. Creating Tansy in his own image he would never even believe in a woman with a will and mentality as strong as his, and entirely antithetical to his.

Tansy was beaten. Suddenly she knew she was beaten. Here were good people—people without a spot on their lives. And she was one of them, like the Good Shepherd on the wall. Her life had been planned in the casting of her body; to deviate from that purpose would be a task beyond her. The cuckoo might go on calling; it didn't matter. People like her were never supposed to hear it.

She sat down at the table, feeling heavy and dead. Andrew and Arthur came into the room. She surveyed them as a detached and curious onlooker recording the habits and manners of a rural community.

"Well, Tansy, I came to take you out," said Arthur, lumbering towards her, his eyes in a possessive stare upon her.

"Did you, Arthur? I'm sorry. We'll go another night." She turned away from him and began to attend to the pan of milk on the fire. She felt herself almost overpowered by the three men in the room; overpowered by their insensitiveness to her woman-hood.

"Yes," said Nicolas jocularly, "the long evenings are coming in and you and Arthur'll enjoy yourselves as you should. Oh, you'll soon be having all you do want, I reckon!"

Tansy shuddered. All she wanted! Her father would almost put her to bed with Arthur. She laid out cups, plates, and knives with a calmness that amused her.

"Is mother coming down?" she asked.

"Mother's stupid," said Andrew. "She wear herself to death carrying parcels from town and then wonders why she feel queer." He sat in the window seat, then jumped up hastily as a piece of the thorn pricked into his thigh.

"Darn the old stuff! What's this?" he held it up for all to see. They laughed. And seeing Andrew holding out her thorn with an elementary air of ridicule, Tansy dimly understood that between their superstitious contempt of the blossom and her own ideal-ized exaltation of it, lay the whole nature of the gulf between them and her. She knew moreover that she would allow nobody to rob her of the one piece that Chailey had told her to keep. She snatched it out of Andrew's hand.

"If you must go sitting on other people's stuff," she said spite-fully, "I hope your bottom may suffer for it!"

"Teasy, aren't you?" jibed Andrew. "Silly gaby of a maid, set-ting store by a bit o' mangy thorn as'll drive mother mad, and you know it. She hate the stuff——"

"Maybe," said Tansy, "but I'm going to keep it for all that."

"Now, Tansy," said Nicolas uncomfortably, for he had seldom seen her in this mood, "don't be stupid! Mother's slight already. Us don't want to upset her over a trifle."

"Then why should you all want to upset me over a trifle?" snapped Tansy. "Can't you see this pretty flower—oh, darn it all! You don't see nothing, any of you."

They all looked at one another with wide open eyes. Arthur tried to restore her temper but only made her worse.

"Leave me be, Arthur. I tell you you're all stupid if you make a fuss over a bit of blackthorn, and I shall tell mother so, too!"

This roused the anger of Andrew, who suddenly tore the thorn out of her hand. The delicate flowers drifted slowly like snow to the ground.

"You don't tell mother nothing of the sort," growled Andrew. "You're a foolish, obstinate maid, and if father won't tell you as much, I will."

But Nicolas was scared. To be crossed by Tansy was something outside his imagination. He mumbled, and began messing about with his pipe. Arthur bit his nails, as though nothing had disturbed the peace. It had thinned out to a quarrel between Andrew and Tansy, and Andrew, savage at being resisted by a woman, knew that his authority was at stake and that he must act accordingly. He seized all the thorn in the window and strode to the back door. Tansy ran after him and caught his arm by the door. He was too strong for her, and struggling silently they stumbled into the yard.

"It's no good my just throwing it away," muttered Andrew, "else you'll have it in again so soon's my back's turned. I know you, midear."

"What you going to do then?" cried Tansy.

"You'll see," said Andrew, shaking her away from him and bringing a box of matches from his pocket.

"You're never going to be such a beast?" cried Tansy.

"Aren't I?" He struck a match. She tore and clung at him furiously. Joe came across the yard, and seeing the swaying shapes of their bodies, ran over to them.

"Eh!" he exclaimed. "What you think you're at there, you

two?" He saw the trampled thorn on the ground and guessed the cause of the fight.

"Joe, you must stop him," panted Tansy. "He's going to burn my blackthorn——"

"Well, it aren't much good to you now, is it?" Joe temporized, fearful of defying Andrew yet sorry for Tansy. She saw then that as long as she struggled with him, Andrew would have his way. So, playing the reserve card of her sex, she began to plead with him.

"Andrew, just let me have one small piece and you may burn the rest. I only want one little piece—please, Andrew."

"That's fair enough, Andrew," said Joe.

"Oh, you hold your gab!" snarled Andrew. "You do always take her side." He suddenly flung the matches down on the ground. "You may do what you've a mind to. But I tell you this—if you bring any of that old stuff into th' house you'll wish you hadn't done it." He swung away savagely.

Joe tried to comfort Tansy.

"Leave it, Tansy," he said gently, "and come in. It's silly for us all to squabble like this."

"It's that Andrew," she maintained childishly, and snivelling a little, she allowed Joe to lead her back.

Her mother was in the kitchen sitting by the fire. Nicolas and Arthur looked at Tansy quickly when she came in; evidently Emmeline was unaware of the storm. Andrew was in the other room, pretending to read a paper, but he came in when Tansy had made tea. Silently he took his place with the others as they sat round the table.

Emmeline was talking about her visit to town.

"Such crowds," she said in her low, rather laboured voice, "I had some job to get on to the bus."

"How're you feeling, mother?" asked Tansy, remembering that Emmeline had been unwell.

"Better, dear. But my head's funny. Nothing to speak about. You're glum to-night," she said to Arthur, who was sitting next to her. "Not like you usually be. You're all glum if it come to that. What's matter?"

Arthur stirred awkwardly and Nicolas spoke for him.

"I reckon he's pining, mother; that's where's to. Pining because he came round to take Tansy out, and she weren't in."

"Oh, he's the makings of a proper husband," said Emmeline. Her eyes stayed in thought. "I bought some pretty bedding to-day," she continued. "There was some brae good stuff going cheap. 'Tis a pity you two can't get fixed up before May month. I always heard 'twas an unlucky month to get wed in."

"We can't rush things like that, mother," objected Nicolas. "There's only a few more days to April."

"What's that matter?" fretted Emmeline. "Six days or six hours, for that matter, is time enough for a maid to get married. And I don't like seeing our Tansy working herself to death in a house what'll never belong to her. The time's come for the maid to work her own house. And you know Nicolas, so well as I, that the cottage at Boscedjack is all ready for them to go into."

She referred to some property of Nicolas's, a mile away on the moor.

"I thought it was falling to pieces," said Tansy.

"Well, I've had the roof done and a lot of other repairs," said Nicolas with some pride. "'Twas going to be a surprise for you, my dear, but now mother's been and out with it."

"I'm sure it's very kind of you, father," said Tansy, with so slight a sneer that nobody detected it. She glanced at Arthur sitting by her side. His knee touched hers; it was a clumsy direct message to her, entirely devoid of any subtlety. She knew exactly how he would treat her when they were married. The thought of it was too dangerous an anodyne—too powerful an attack upon her spirit. It was, after all, an effort to be free. Individuality implied industry of the soul; surrender meant complete mental sloth for the rest of her days. Even love-making would be part of the ordered round; the bearing of a discreet family, another part. She studied her mother's patient face. It was long, narrow and prematurely lined. But it was not an anxious face. The eyes, set deep in the forehead, were like Tansy's, only thinner and firmer, like slanting pieces of slate. Sometimes, when the sun caught them, they would glint with sharp facets of light. Her black hair was drawn stiffly over each side of her head. She gave one an impression of tremendous latent strength; of a potency that time had smothered. Her voice was the echo of that power. There was the undulating moan of waves in it—a lost voice. In some ways she was a terrible woman, thought Tansy; a creature who had been stifled. Yet according to the standards of her kind, she was fulfilled. Pinned to her black dress was an imitation gold brooch, with the word "Mother" worked in it. She loved the brooch and always wore it. Sometimes she would sit silent through a whole evening, upright in a chair, never drooping—her head held high; her eyes a thin line of thought. Labelled for all to see: "Mother." . . . To tell everybody, thought Tansy, that she had done her duty. Yet must there not have been a time when those stiff limbs, those infrangible eyes, quickened to the adventure of life? When all her blood sang through her joyous veins and her lips yearned for the lips of a lover, not for the heavy claim of a possessor?

Tansy did not want to have a gold brooch pinned to her dress like a certificate of merit. She wanted freedom, yet she could not tell of what freedom consisted. She heard them discussing her dispassionately, while the sleeping mutiny of her eyes examined them one by one.

Her mother was singularly loquacious, urging her desire to see Tansy married as soon as possible. Her staunch yellow head swayed from side to side as she spoke.

"Tansy's twenty," she was saying, "and that's an age when a lass ought to get married, I do say. And Arthur's twenty-two. If he's not wedded soon, he won't ever want to be. He'll just get into bad ways."

Arthur wriggled a little under this open scrutiny.

"There's time enough, Mrs. Penderil," he said. "Eh, Tansy?"

"Time enough!" She echoed his words.

Emmeline turned to Joe. She often sought him in these rare moments of obstinacy.

"What does m'knabs think?"

"Oh, Joe don't think nothing," objected Andrew, anxious suddenly to show his interest in Tansy's affairs—to side with her in order to erase the squabble over the thorn. "Joe's too much of a baby to speak his mind on such things." Andrew lit a cigarette, calling for silence with his lighted match. "I see what mother do mean," he continued. "She don't want our Tansy to sweat body

and soul on this farm when she might as well be sweating herself
for Arthur——" He stopped, aware that it had not been a fortunate remark. They were silent. Then, with quiet emphasis, Tansy
spoke to her mother.

"We can't get wedded in April, mother. That's clear, to my
thinking. And when I go, you've got to have somebody else to do
the work here. So we'd better leave it till June. That'll give us all
May to arrange things, and"—she added softly—"to change our
minds if need be."

"Change your minds!" ejaculated Nicolas.

"Yes," said Tansy. "I wonder whether you know that Arthur's
never even asked me to marry him. He don't even kiss me, save
as a duty."

"Well—darn 'em!" Nicolas fell into slightly uneasy laughter.

"Talking about kissing!" exclaimed Andrew, "plenty of time
for that yet, I s'pose."

Emmeline looked at Tansy rather wistfully. Then she looked
at Arthur who grinned, and tried to simulate the swagger of mas-
culinity. Inwardly he was furious with Tansy for making a fool
of him, although everybody but Emmeline thought that Tansy
was the fool. But Emmeline understood. She looked at Tansy's
mouth—at the small breasts rising in agitation. All she said was:
"I know I'm right. You ought to get married to-morrow." She
took a candle and rose slowly. "I'm going to bed. My head's not
what it should be. Good night, Arthur."

She left the room and the supper party broke up. Arthur took
his cap and a muffler.

"I must go," he said. Then, with an effort, "See me to the gate,
Tansy?"

She laughed scornfully and followed him to the front door.
They walked down the path in silence. When they reached the
gate Arthur came out with a torrent of words.

"What d'you want to go and make a fool of me for? D'you
think I haven't got feelings, same as you? Tansy, you want slap-
ping and that you do——"

"It takes a man to slap me!" she mocked, a rising flood of
mingled anger and sensuality in her blood.

"Do it then?" Arthur's tongue tripped over his words. "Come

out here, you!" He caught her by the arm and pulled her a little way along the road, out of the searching lights of the farm. "And I'm no man, I s'pose?" Then he kissed her, pressing his hard mouth upon hers and holding her with all his strength so that she gasped for breath. But he would not free her. And in the darkness Tansy found a man—never Arthur the calf-eyed swain.

She dragged herself free from him, because his direct attack had stirred nothing in her blood; because his lips were like iron upon iron. She ran to the gate and mocked him over the bars.

"You started well, I reckon," she cried, "but if you really do want to marry me, you'd better learn when to stop."

She ran into the house. Arthur bit his cap and went cursing up the lane. But he was very proud of himself. . . .

Tansy found Nicolas sitting alone with his stockinged feet stretched out before the fire. The others had gone to bed. "I'll just wait up for this cream," she said. "You can leave me lock up." But he had waited to speak to her, feeling troubled in his mind. She was hard, he saw—hard as her mother could be when you least expected it. Nevertheless he said, "Tansy, what's the matter this evening?"

"Why, nothing, father——" He was trying to rob her again, she told herself; to rob her with the gentle weapon of his voice.

"Do you love Arthur?" he asked bluntly.

Tansy turned round on him slowly.

"Do mother love you?"

He looked at her with startled eyes. Then slowly, without a word, he lumbered away upstairs. He never forgot those words.

Tansy looked at the simmering cream, her fixed eyes clouding it to shadowy shapes. Then she sat down, brooding with her head on her hands, her elbows jabbed on to the table. She felt a warm muzzle pressed against her thigh. It was Simon, the sheep dog. She patted him affectionately and he came nearer to her, pressing his shaggy head into her lap. She gave him a crust which he surveyed distrustfully and would not consume. The house became quieter. A mouse scrabbled in the wall. Tansy's eyes drooped and she jerked her head back with an effort to keep awake. Then she became all alert, listening carefully for any sounds of talking from above. But she could hear nothing. Softly she went to the back door and opened it. Simon followed her but she drove him back under the table, where he lay with his head on his paws, watching her with a sapient eye. She took a lantern, for the young moon had gone, and went into the yard. By the pig-trough she found the trampled skeleton of her thorn, its pure blossom crushed and spattered with mud. She disentangled the small piece he had given her, a piece little larger than her hand, shaped like a crooked letter Y. Then she crept into the house with it, pausing by the door for the sound of any movement from above. She bolted the door and putting the thorn on the table, sat very still, looking at it with fixed eyes, like a seer who ponders over a crystal.

CHAPTER III

TANSY's bedroom did not reflect her personality. The room followed the regular design of a hundred such in the neighbourhood. A narrow iron bedstead covered by a faded pink and white counterpane lay along by the wall behind the door. There was a shaky chest of drawers; a wash-stand that had once been white; and a creaking old rocking-chair that Tansy had annexed for herself from the sitting-room—a room which was a museum of Penderil history and was never used save on festal occasions. Tansy had an affection for the rocking-chair, remembering how she had curled up in it as a little girl, reading the fairy stories which had first opened her eyes to the lurking iniquity of an apparently guileless world. She still half believed in gnomes and bad duchesses and would not willingly banish their twilight forms from her imagination. In the rocking-chair she had learned to observe strange folk with a more suspicious eye—to be on her guard against the ogre in the prince. Much of the complexity of her nature came to life in those early quixotic moments. Whenever now she had anything profound to consider, any difficult decision to make, she would recede into her old chair, looking out to the sea from her window, and like as not entirely forget the problem which had confronted her in hazy speculations of a more romantic character. From her chair

she could watch the sea reflecting the time of the day. In winter
sometimes it was so desolate a prospect where fields were only a
blacker shadow than the sky, that a man, slouching along, looked
like Caliban with a load of remorse and despair on his uneasy
back; in summer at sunset often so bravely fired by the sweeping
gold of the sun, that a man standing on the edge of the farthest
field, looked like a poised archangel ready to cleave the skies with
shining wings. It was when Tansy sat in her chair seeing demons
and angels under black and fiery skies, that she felt in herself a
love for this country which the men of her family entirely lacked.
She would not include her mother amongst them; she knew that
from her she inherited this perception of the world as a changing
drama rich in colour and design. But the men were different. A
fine summer merely meant a fine harvest. Nothing more. Tansy
sometimes could not tolerate this casual reception of the world's
vital loveliness. She would lose patience with them, and dash out
of the house or up to her chair where in silence she would try to
grasp the ever elusive quality of nature. She did not possess that
wider view which would have accepted her father and brothers
as so strongly a moving part of the drama of nature, that moving
in it—contributing to its perfect design—they were never consciously aware of it. In her deliberate attempts to seize the whole
heart of the beauty she forced herself outside, and consequently
suffered as an appreciative onlooker suffers when faced with a
work of art in the creation of which he had no part. And seeing
her men move about, whistling or silent in the fields, as demons
or angels, she was most grudgingly aware that if they were to be
for ever removed from the scene, the picture would lose its balance. It hurt her, this realization that she who valued it so much
more than they, should nevertheless remain outside it. It hurt
her and drove her into a desire to record her sensitiveness to the
earth; but she could find no means of recording it. This was what
Chailey had seen in Tansy—what any artist would immediately
detect—namely, the spirit of the true artist who suffers because
he cannot offer to man as fair a gift as God offers to him.

At sunrise, Tansy moved in her sleep. Long habit had made it
almost impossible for her to sleep when the sun had risen. She lay
on her back, one hand stretched out of the bed, the other under

the pillow. Her sleep was uneasy, though very deep; her face was drawn into a frown of perplexity.

The last storm clouds of the past two days raced towards the horizon, flushed by the searching colours of the sun in the east. Tansy's eyes opened in surprise. She heard birds singing and the riotous sound of an honest north wind. With joy she jumped out of the bed and ran to the window to look at the sea. It tossed with little chunks of white foam. The aquiline rocks at the end of the valley were half obscured in an incessant spray of spume. She saw a dazzling flock of geese cackling their opprobrious parliament along a field; an old sow crunching laboriously under her window. She laughed. It was a spring morning such as she loved; a morning when she delighted in taking complete control of the farm's domestic affairs, treating them all in the same efficient, somewhat contemptuous manner. She was perfectly conscious of her strength that morning; well aware that she had the power to overcome even Andrew and her father if she could but summon it. The arrogancy of the north wind sped into her blood, and pulling off her nightgown she folded her arms on her breast and surveyed her pliant body in the mirror on the chest of drawers. She smiled and stretched her arms out towards herself. "If a man could see me like this," she murmured. Then she suddenly thought of Chailey, and hastening over to the washstand, began to rub soap vigorously into her face.

When she was dressed she went downstairs and put a kettle of water on an oil-stove. Then she opened the back door and the windows and let the wind scuttle through the house. In a few minutes she had raked out the fire and laid a new one.

Andrew came down and pulled on his boots.

"Morning, Tansy!" His voice was gruff, but Tansy knew from the very fact that he greeted her that he was feeling gracious towards her.

"Handsome weather," she said tentatively.

"Yes, I s'pose," agreed Andrew.

"Joe not up yet?" she asked.

"No. Y'know what a chap he is for bed!"

He went into the dairy and came out with two clean pails.

"I'll get on," he said. "Give Joe a knock when you go up with the tea." He went out with a half-ashamed smile on his dark face. Tansy knew his mood. For no particular reason he had awakened feeling happy, and Andrew resented inconsequential happiness. Therefore he would be miserable all day. Tansy suddenly felt she had found him out.

The kettle sizzled on the stove and, making tea, she poured two cups for Nicolas and Emmeline. She had a sudden impulse to carry a cup up to Joe and talk with him a moment. So she added a third cup to the tray and went upstairs.

Nicolas always took his tea with an air of dignity and slight amusement. He could never quite reconcile himself to the extravagant fact that he, who since the age of fourteen had worked hard from sunrise to sundown with hardly a day's holiday, should now be waited upon in bed by a grown woman who was his own daughter. But as he sat up this morning and took his tea, he looked at Tansy rather sourly.

"How's mother?" asked Tansy, supposing that Emmeline was still asleep. But she rose slowly and with wondering eyes gazed on Tansy.

"Lor' child," she murmured, half to herself, "if dreams are true you ought not to be here!"

"Why ever not?" asked Tansy as she took her the tea. "What did you dream then?"

"Dreamt you was married with the prettiest baby that ever you saw. I'm sorry it aren't true. But perhaps it is true," she added quickly. "Why, I believe you're married all the time and won't tell me nothing about it!"

Nicolas grunted. "You always was a fine dreamer, mother, and you always will be I reckon!"

Tansy frowned, wondering what strange fancy it was that possessed her mother, and leaving the room, went over to the boys' bedroom. Joe lay, a huddled figure, awake under the clothes and resenting the derision of the bright sun. He hated getting up though he was never lazy once he had made that supreme effort. For eighteen years he had loved to feel that in the early morning, in the stupefying embrace of bedclothes, he could defy time. A secret sensualist, he revelled in the warm surrender of his limbs to the caress of sleep. He loved his body—took an ingenuous pride in the comely straightness of his long legs. And Tansy was the only one who knew this in him. She looked at Joe's body, at the compact arch of his thigh under the bedclothes, and she envied the woman who would one day share that body. She sat on the bed and drew the sheets away from his face. He tried to clutch them back.

"It's no good, Joe," she said. "You got to get up. Look! I brought you a cup of tea."

Joe pulled himself up and ruffled his hand through his thick hair. It was reddish-brown, curly and full of light. He was unlike his father and Andrew, more beautiful than Tansy yet lacking her latent vitality. His face full of freckles, his eyes a clearer, more lively blue than Arthur's, his neck tall and a ruddy brown—Tansy looking at him wished that Arthur were more like him. She loved Joe as she saw him sitting up in his untidy bed, smelt the warm moisture of his body and saw his careless clothes thrown anywhere about the room. Had Joe known the full extent of her thoughts he might have run away from her in alarm. But he saw only a pretty girl, his sister, one who was kind to him and whom he loved but certainly never brooded upon.

"Whatever made you bring tea for me?" He gulped it down with a slow smile.

"Why not?" said Tansy. "They do have it. Why not you?" She was still thinking of her mother's dream, and began to talk about Arthur.

"Joe," she said. "How many girls d'you suppose Arthur's been out with?"

Joe liked Arthur and was immediately on his guard.

"He never had a maiden before you, Tansy. Everybody know that. He's a straight chap. Wouldn't see another girl while you was about. And I reckon he set his mind on you, even before he left school. He's always been soft on you. But what d'you want to ask me for?"

"Mother's had a funny dream," she said. "At least, not so funny really. She dreamt we was married. She seem to think we *are* married."

"Well, that's all right, isn't it? You are as near married as can be—at least——" he paused awkwardly. "He's a darn good old chap," he added hastily, "and you're stupid if you doubt him!"

"I don't doubt him," she said. "But, well—isn't he *soft*, Joe? Not so much a man as you or Andrew. Soft and shy, seem to me."

"Don't know about that at all. He got me down proper one day, wrestling. Easy as could be. The only thing he's soft upon is you, my girl!"

"Yes. Well, I wish he weren't soft upon me. I wish he'd see other girls a bit—go wild. I tell you Joe, he treats me like a lamb, and reckon I'd rather be treated like a lion for a change. I wish he'd go wild like you."

"Like me?" Joe chuckled, and got out of bed.

"Yes—you," iterated Tansy. "Oh, don't try to take me in, Joe. Father think you're a good boy who wouldn't look at a maid. But I know you better'n that. And I don't blame you, Joe, neither. When you're young you've got to live I think——"

"Here, what trash've you been reading?" ejaculated Joe.

"Oh don't be mad with me," she cried, laughing. "All I say is, don't go getting yourself into trouble. With that pretty face you're easy enough to trap, Joe, mark my words!"

She left him with a puzzled smile upon his face. She was annoyed because he had defended Arthur, not admitting the lack of virility which she felt in him. She knew Arthur was faithful to her alone; she did not need anybody to reassure her of that.

As she went over to the cow-sheds she thought of her mother's strange preoccupation with her and Arthur. She wondered whether her real attitude towards him would ever have declared itself had she not met Chailey.

Andrew, at the other end of the shed, did not say anything to her. As she milked, she hummed a tune to herself. The sleek fawn cow turned and looked at her with large lackadaisical eyes. She patted its flanks, coveting its benign detachment from human affairs.

"We can leave the cattle outdoors to-night, should think," she said to Andrew.

"Think the weather's set?"

"Enough for that," she said. "Why, summer'll be on us in a day!" She spoke sadly. Summer upon them in a day! For the death of spring lurked in the birth of it. June would come and the fields be full of hay. Above the stone hedges the bluebells were hanging their languid heads, tired under a more indolent sun. Down in the cliffs by the sea the grass was bright with primroses and speedwells. Soon it would all be over and the wind sigh in a different tone upon a different land. She saddened herself with the thought of the transience of nature: the concealing of the sloe in the blackthorn bush. Her mind still full of these autumn thoughts, she finished the milking and went towards the house. The postman passed along the path and Tansy hailed him. "Good morning! Nothing for us?"

"Nothing, midear!"

He passed on, whistling callously. There never was anything, muttered Tansy. Why couldn't somebody write? Yet who was there to write?

Joe was down and her father moving about upstairs.

"Done the milking then?" said Joe.

"Yes," she replied. "You'd best be off and drive the cows down to the far field, else you'll have Andrew mad."

He went out and Tansy, lighting the fire, began to lay the table for breakfast. A little later, when Nicolas had come down and Andrew had finished the milking, they started to eat. Emmeline appeared, smiling a little nervously.

"Well Tansy," she said, and there was the tone of truth in her voice. "It's a real handsome morning."

"Yes, it is, mother. Can you eat two eggs?"

"Nothing for me, please midear. I haven't got no appetite to-day for eggs. Some bread and butter'll do for me."

"What, no appetite, mother? You'd best try an egg," urged Andrew impatiently.

"All right," she said. "Only do it a bit hard, Tansy, there's a dear." She inquired after Joe and was told that he was driving the cattle down. "Well, don't cook his breakfast till he come. I don't like the boy eating cold stuff, and there's nothing nastier than a dish of cold bacon and eggs to my thinking." And when he came in presently, she fussed him in a way that irritated the others.

"You boys better go and get a barrel of water after breakfast," said Nicolas as he crammed a piece of bacon into his mouth and washed it down with tea. They drew their drinking water from a pump in the valley.

"I've got to go to town," said Tansy. "Any of you want me to get anything?"

And an hour or so later, when she had made all the beds, swept out the living room and the kitchen, flung open the stiff window of the fusty sitting-room and washed the breakfast things, Tansy swung into the yard with a large basket on her arm. She had cocked a blue cap on the side of her head and wore a dark blue skirt with a white cotton blouse. The skirt was long and made her look very tall. She felt always more of a woman in this skirt, less of a child. So she walked with an independent assurance along the rough path towards the town that stretched its arms of houses up the clear hills. Westwards, on her right, lay the glittering sea, speckled by a fishing fleet. Eastwards, the sinuous ribbon of the road along the valley. Tansy found herself looking in that direction. The very act of leaving the farm for a few moments had filled her with a surge of nervous excitement. She was thrilled by the searching quickness of the eager morning. The town seemed to be a new and sweeter place as though the sun and the rain and the wind had conspired to wash away the soot and cobwebs of winter. Everybody was busy, laughing and swearing jovially at the daredevil wind. Tansy came out of the grocer's with a heavy basket, walked across the large square and looked for a moment into the medieval plain that had once been the scene of rural mysteries. Two massive oblong pieces of granite stood at one end of it, austere emblems of a calmer, sterner age. Tansy watched some boys playing cricket in the plain with a warm heart, for she loved children. Their ragged clothing could not mar the brightness of their bodies as they ran along the bumpy pitch. Bemused by the scene, Tansy forgot where she was; in the clean sunlight the shouting children were like little figures out of one of her old fairy books. She did not want them ever to grow up; ever to reach the summit of their lovely youth, then decline as the year would decline.

The ugly tower clock behind her struck ten with a clang of materialism; it was followed by the cracked reflective summons of the church bell. A prettier sound, thought Tansy; a quieter, less imperative reminder of the passage of time, even if the old clock slipped back a minute every half-hour. And leaving the plain, she crossed the square, remembering that she had to go to Angwin's, the pork-butcher. She came into the larger market square, where in one corner stood the long, low ark of the church growing into the austere guardian of its tower. The flag was flying; a plain red cross on a white background. She wondered why, then remembered that April 23rd was St. George's Day. She began to think about the saint as she went into Angwin's. She visualized somebody very tall, grave, yet slightly smiling, with arms like folded wings waiting to take a timorous mortal to his argent breast. With eyes that glowed like fire, deep and very large. Hair like the hungry flames of the fire. A voice like a violin in the wind, piercing and compassionate . . .

She heard him speak.

"You look afraid of something——"

The centre of her vision, his lithe frame loomed at her across the blurred image of the shops in the market square. Her whole being was flooded by him; she felt she could neither speak nor move.

"I say you look afraid——"

The sesame to a land of shadows, his strange loose arms fluttered helplessly towards her, then fell to his side as though the action of one small nerve had suddenly robbed them of all their power. Slowly she found her voice, began to realize that she stood outside the butcher's shop, with people moving rapidly about her, carts rattling over the cobbles, and Roger Chailey looking with sensitive humour into her face. She dropped her head and became immediately on her guard, sly and secretive.

"I'm all right, thank you," she said.

"But you looked at me as if I were a ghost!"

"I was—dreaming, I suppose. I was thinking of St. George. It's St. George's Day to-day. The flag on the tower made me think of it."

Chailey looked up quickly. "It's Shakespeare's birthday," he said. "'In delay there lies no plenty'—but I'll tell you the rest of that later. But where *are* you roaming?"

"Why do you speak strange like that?" she asked, irritated by his manner.

"It's a song. You shall hear it all presently. But come—I'll walk along with you. Give me your basket."

"Oh no," said Tansy. "I've finished shopping, thank you. I'm going home."

"Then I'll come with you."

"No—oh, please——" Tansy was bewildered, feeling the eyes of the town upon her, anxious to escape yet longing to be near him. Why was she never free to be herself, she thought? Why must she always avoid the most direct impulses of her heart?

"Let us get away from here anyhow," said Chailey, and he began to walk slowly towards the church. Tansy wanted to seize the moment to run away from him, but she could not. Instead, miserably and with a dry tongue, she followed him. They walked past the church, over a stile and into a steep field falling into the little wood. There was nobody about. Chailey dropped down on the grass, his bright green tie tossing in the wind.

"I never wanted to see you——" began Tansy, but could make no truth of it.

"But why?" There was a contemptuous surprise in his voice.

"You don't understand," she said. "They know your business here before you know it yourself."

"But does it matter?" he asked, with genuine astonishment.

"Of course it matter! They soon talk a girl into trouble."

He beckoned her down on the grass beside him.

"What trouble could I possibly get Tansy into?" he murmured laughingly.

"Oh you don't know," she cried. "They say all sorts of wicked things. I can't ever do what I want to do."

"But Tansy," he said equivocally. "What *do* you want to do?"

She got to her feet suddenly. "I can't stay here like this with you! I just feel—if anybody sees us they'll know it at home. Somebody may have seen us already."

"Come into the wood," he said carelessly, "where nobody can see us, and let's talk it all over rationally, this business of not being seen and so on." He pointed to the black cluster of trees a few yards below them. Tansy shuddered.

"No, I must go now. They'll wonder where I am."

"You'll have to find some excuse next Thursday——"

"I'm never coming. I can't ever come——"

"But you are coming," he said. "And before then you must meet me again somewhere where you're not fearful of being seen. Silly Tansy——" he whispered, touching her hand so gently that she only felt it in her blood. "When are we going to meet?" he insisted.

She heard her audacious voice saying, "Sunday night—after church——"

"Church? When is that?" He laughed slightly. Tansy did not like the sound of it.

"About seven," she said. "I'll come then for—the last time and explain—explain why I can't come again."

"But Tansy——"

"No! Please don't argue with me now," she pleaded.

"I'll be in the wood by the old Vicarage on Sunday about seven," he said.

Nonchalantly he played with her ears.

"What lovely ears you have!" He spoke in a low contemplative voice. "I should like a plaster cast of this one ear and of your foot. They are so small, so perfectly shaped. I almost feel they don't belong to you, Tansy. I believe they are mine. I really cannot believe they are yours at all."

He ceased abruptly. His voice quelled her desire to get away from him. She could not interrupt the low witchery of his voice, as insistent in her ears as a millstream at evening.

"In the wood, then. Don't fail me Tansy. I pass this way but once only——" He mocked her now.

"I—don't like the wood." She hesitated from admitting her fear of the whispered lament in the trees.

"Really? Why?"

"I don't know——"

"It's the secret place, Tansy. The only secret place where I can tell you the rest of the song. And since you say I am to see you for the last time, would you have me tell you the song where others too can hear it?"

"I'll be there——" and suddenly she ran away towards the church tower. Chailey shrugged his shoulders with an amused smile. Taking out a pencil and a sketch book he began reflectively to draw Tansy's ear as well as he could remember it.

CHAPTER IV

EMMELINE was not well. She had struggled through a breakfast disagreeable, even repulsive to her and had spent the morning in an arid round of perfunctory domestic tasks. A thin, insidious pain crept in her breast, a pain too slight to mention, she told herself. And in an effort to conceal it from the others she chattered incessantly in a semi-incoherent manner foreign to her who was usually so quiet. The others ascribed her loquacity to good-humour, although some of her haphazard observations left them confused. During dinner, for example, she suddenly flung out the gratuitous statement that it would be an early harvest and soon time to send for the threshing-machine. Nicolas, hastily looking at the calendar, laughed awkwardly as though he were ashamed of the stupidity of his woman. But Emmeline, cramming a soggy slab of pie-crust into her mouth, again remarked on the imminence of harvest. She hardly knew what she said. Her gorge rose as she swallowed the heavy food with an effort, but she went on talking and they noticed nothing.

Tansy had come in about midday, out of spirits and inclined to be snappy. Emmeline studied her through her thin eyes and was uneasy about her. After dinner she went upstairs. She felt sick, knowing that the food she had eaten rebelled against her. She drank some water, sat down on the bed and gripping the mattress forced back the nausea that arose in her. She got very hot; little sparks of tingling sweat pricked her forehead. But she would not give way. She hated sickness; felt it was a shameful thing. So slowly she recovered her control and coming downstairs found that the house was empty.

There was a knock on the shed door and an old woman, yellow and lean as a scraggy hen, came in for some eggs and butter. It was Rosie Williams, the mother of a young miner stricken with phthisis in a battered cottage in the valley. Rosie's face was a graven presage of despair too heavy to scald her rimy eyes with any tears. Emmeline never saw her without hating herself for her good fortune. She patted her on the arm and brought her into the kitchen.

"Well Rosie? How't a doing?"

Rosie, her withered head shaking ineptly, gave Emmeline a little basket. "Middling. Any eggs hast a? And a bit o' butter please, 'Meline."

Emmeline went into the dairy. "How many?" she called.

"Please?"

"How many?"

"No more'n two please, 'Meline. I can't afford eggs."

Emmeline put six eggs into the basket with a sigh. She did not see any butter. "I don't see no butter," she said. "Tansy makes to-morrow I s'pose. But if you care for a bit of ours to carry you through, you're welcome." She cut a piece from the pound slab on the table. "There midear." Wrapping the butter in grease-proof paper she laid it over the eggs so that Rosie did not notice the number.

"How much?" she asked, furtively jangling twopence in the pocket of her tattered coat.

"I can't tell. Penny each egg's enough. I don't want nothing for a bit o' butter."

"It's kind, some kind you are," murmured Rosie as she gave her twopence to Emmeline. A shadowy smile stirred under her eyes like the last flame of a dying fire. Emmeline brought her into the living room and made her sit down.

"Will you care for a glass of last season's blackberry wine? Warm you up proper," she said.

"That's kind, midear. That's some kind you are."

"Oh go on!" muttered Emmeline. "Where's the kindness to that?"

She poured out the deep rich wine and gave it to Rosie, who sipped it slowly. She saw a picture of a little boy that hung on the wall; a crude photograph of a little boy with a bat and a ball in his hand. Rosie looked at it for a long time. Then she pointed to it and turned to Emmeline.

"Is that there pretty dear your Joe?"

"Yes," said Emmeline.

"A handsome little face," murmured Rosie, "and he's made a fine man I think. A pretty boy."

"I'll show you some more." Emmeline, her heart heavy, brought out a thick black album. They turned over the pages, their heads bent low over the pictures, Rosie's head nodding all the time. Emmeline described the pictures, one by one.

"Pretty little dears," said Rosie. "Some lovely children you've born, 'Meline."

They were silent. A shaft of dusty sunlight came through the window, laying its long arm upon the metallic hair of the two women.

Emmeline's head fell forward.

"And how's Sammy?" she asked.

"Sammy? Not much better, dear. Not much good, I reckon. He wan't do much more. He was a good boy too——" Her voice was sweeter and more distant. Emmeline could not say anything. Rosie got up. "A lovely wine, 'Meline. Thankee. I'd best be going." She went into the kitchen and took her basket. Emmeline patted her arm and the shadowy smile flickered again in her features. Then she turned to the door and went out . . .

Alone again, Emmeline did not know what to do. It was half-past three, a silent and moveless time of the day. She wandered into the sitting-room, fingering little pieces of china that had been wedding presents, never used for fear they should be broken. Her sewing machine and a basket full of cottons and wools, needles and pins—stood on a table near the window. Emmeline decided she would give the machine to Tansy; the girl would have more use for it now. She found some old chintz material that Tansy had bought for curtains and never used as Nicolas had insisted on keeping to white lace. It was a pretty pattern; big red roses against a pale green background. Emmeline thought she would like to make it into a bedspread for Tansy. But she did not want to work in this lifeless room. She thought of the old rocking-chair in Tansy's bedroom, a comfortable chair to work in, and the room brighter, more snug and companionable than any other. So Emmeline panted upstairs with the heavy machine, and coming down for the material, her eyes caught sight of the family album lying where she had left it on the table. She went to put it away in a drawer, but lingering again over its faded pages, could not resist taking it with her.

In Tansy's room she brought the bamboo bedside table over to the window and putting the machine on it, sat down with a sigh of relief. The chair creaked in satisfaction. How wise Tansy had been, thought Emmeline, to insist on keeping it. There was more life in this old chair than in anything else in the house. She swayed herself, gripping the arms affectionately. She felt easier; her pain seemed to become lighter with the movement of the chair.

The sun was warm on her forehead. She looked over the fields to a group of cottages held fast in a nebula of sunlight. Two magpies darted over a hedge; Emmeline was glad she had seen more than one. The cows over in the far field were recumbent upon the grass, their heavy jaws tirelessly moving round and round. Simon, exhausted and full of old dreams, was stretched out on the wall of the little garden. The spring flowers were nearly over. There were a few delicate jonquils, and a mass of trailing periwinkle spattered its pale stars along the wall. The jonquils bending in the wind were like people listening at a door. The sky was cloudless; the sea, silver-blue.

Emmeline saw Nicolas lounging along in the distance, idly chewing a piece of grass. Nicolas, her man, that she had taken for better or worse.... It hadn't been such a bad bargain, she thought. Nicolas was staunch, pure, open and loyal. He would never do a body harm. Emmeline remembered when first she had seen him as a lad, standing in a hayfield, his somewhat gaunt temples glittering with sweat, his hair tousled like the hay, his long supple arms swinging with the great scythe. For twenty-five years she had retained this picture of him clear in her mind. Every detail was clear. She remembered a hole in his sock and a fly that would settle on his nose and make him swear.

She turned over the pages of her album, half reluctant to open the clasp and disclose so much of distant days. But it was sweet to dream of a time when life had been a looking-forward. Now, so often, it was a looking-backward.

... There was a picture of her father, the Wesleyan preacher, solemn with a string of buttons, a black beard and a watch-chain like a Mayor's. Emmeline laughed softly. A good old chap.

... And here, one of her mother, a rotund ruddy countenance with a dress large enough to cover all her family.

... And here, young Nicolas, grave in an unbelievably tall collar which pinched his face and drew out his chin. A shy solemn face. He could not have been more than eighteen. A timid little moustache frowned reluctantly on his lip. Such a youth, for all the world like a piece of china on show! She came to more recent pictures of him; one standing by the thrashing machine in harvest time, gobbling a pasty larger than his face. There were children standing around, prim waxen figures in their big boots and wide sailor hats. And amongst them was Tansy, nearly submerged by a tremendous hat bound in ribbons which hung over her shoulders. Tansy, solemn and demure, but even then, so artful, such a devil if you didn't watch her. And, when discovered in some naughtiness, so full of astonishment, that it was hard to have to punish her. Emmeline remembered her, an urchin of five, industriously smearing little Joe's firm bottom with the blue-bag. She had done his legs and was working upwards.

("Tansy, my gosh, I'll learn you to treat poor baby like that!" And Tansy's bewildered, even impatient answer. "But Mammie, I tell you as Joe *like* it! It's good for him, Mammie. He's learning all about them old ancient B'iton's!")

Emmeline sighed. "Ah dearie me! To think as how the maid's grown up now with a lover of her own, just like me and Nicolas!"

She turned through the book. Her heart throbbed as she looked at a picture of the baby Joe taken in his cradle; nothing but a round head and a long mass of pure white woolly clothes. A lovely baby ...

Her hand stole up to the brooch at her dress, as though for confirmation of her vocation. Yes, she was Mother, she assured herself. Whatever she failed to do, whatever rich flowers she had left ungathered, she had laboured with this lovely child, out of her body had scattered the good seed of man on the face of the earth. Even if now she was very tired and only wanted to sit in the sun, she had used her life rightly. To her it was a wonderful, incomprehensible thing that these three strong children should have been endowed with their life from the womb of a body which now seemed a burden to her.

She looked over the fields again. A lamb was kicking up its joyous legs, impelled by the power of life to a movement it understood not but could not resist. If it thought at all, it might have said, "I must kick—otherwise how shall they know I am really alive?" Nobody told it to stop kicking, thought Emmeline. There were no watchful parents to keep it in check. And like Andrew, Tansy and Joe, out of the top-heavy old ewe this bounding energy had sprung.

"What a queer mystery us women are," reflected Emmeline. Always giving, giving, giving, and then away we go so that others may go on giving. For a brief childhood bounding like the lamb; then a glorious moment of union with our man; then the impending sway of the pendulum in another direction. The gradual slackening of the intense nerves and the alert muscles— and Lord! How alert they had been! The lingering fading of the quick senses; the increasing desire to look back—to turn over a picture album pretending that memory was reality.

Over the sea flew a lean cormorant, a hungry ghost by those impregnable shores. Emmeline saw it dimly through a haze of memories, saw also the gradual darkening of the sky, the faint red glow that began to fire the cottages seawards. Another day was travelling over with the sun. Something more to add to the great storehouse of memory. More hours, minutes and seconds that could never come again. No looking forward, only a looking backward. . . .

But with a sudden jerk into her world the sewing machine reminded her that she had come upstairs but to look forward. "There's a woman I am," she said, "all this time in dreaming and nothing done at all."

The clock struck half-past four. They would soon be having tea. There was no time to finish her task now, and she hated starting a thing and having to leave it. She began again to think of the practical necessities accompanying Tansy's marriage. She thought about a wedding dress. Tansy would hate anything elaborate, she knew that. But the child would want some new clothes. Emmeline rose and pulled open the drawers of the chest in a desire to see what Tansy had. There was very little. The small top drawers were full of handkerchiefs and stockings; then, farther down, a drawer half full of underclothes, plain garments that had been patched a dozen times. It was a shame, thought Emmeline; Tansy ought to have some new things. Arthur couldn't marry a woman in rags. Emmeline came to a drawer crammed with all kinds of oddments. Old letters, school books, photographs.

"Nothing here," said Emmeline to herself, having no desire to pry. As she withdrew her hand from the drawer she pricked it on something sharp and jagged. She wondered what it was, but forgot about it, because the sickness mounted in her again, and for a moment the room rocked about her. Blindly she stumbled back into her chair, waiting breathlessly for the moment to pass.

She felt very thirsty, and hearing somebody moving about below, she called, "Tansy, is that you?"

Tansy's voice came up. "Yes, mother. You there, then?"

"I'm in your room, dear. Feeling a bit funny. Can you bring me up a glass of fresh water, there's a dear."

Tansy came up immediately, surprised and anxious. "What's the matter, mother? Fancy you in here! I thought you were out somewhere."

Emmeline took the water eagerly and drained it down. Tansy placed a hand on her head and knelt by the chair. "You're not well, mother," she said. Suddenly she realized that they had all neglected her. But Emmeline spoke rather stiffly.

"There's nothing wrong with me. I—eat too much dinner and got feeling sick. Pastry don't agree with me and it never did. Don't worry over me. I aren't an invalid."

"But, mother—your head's all hot——"

"I'm all right. I'm all right." She clutched Tansy's hand and held it close on the arm of the chair. "I was thinking of the old days," she said slowly, "and how strange 'tis that time passes away so quick we do never know whether it's yesterday or to-morrow."

Her sad voice held Tansy silent.

"There's a picture of your dad," continued Emmeline, pointing to the album. "A brae good bit of a lad! And now there's your Arthur, the same sort of lad. You like I was then. We're like the flowers, aren't us, going on just the same, come spring, come winter, different flowers but the same way of living and thinking. And I want for you to be happy with your Arthur and to have pretty children like I've had."

"Arthur's good——" murmured Tansy. She wanted to tell her mother so much that she could not begin. Then Emmeline spoke again and the moment was lost.

"I want for you to be married soon, dear. A maid should marry young, not when half the life has gone out of her. So don't delay. For Arthur's as firm as a rock, and you don't find another like him for the asking. Firm as a rock——"

A rock, thought Tansy. And looking at the cliffs cutting the sun's fire, she wondered whether she could lay her head and sleep sweetly on a rock.

"Look," said Emmeline, "I meant to make you a bedspread out of this pretty stuff, and all I done is to make myself miserable looking at old pictures!"

CHAPTER V

"Rend your hearts and not your garments, and turn unto the Lord your God."

There was a crazy thing to tell a chap to do, thought Joe, as he shuffled uncomfortably to a crouching position over his pew. "We have done those things which we ought to have undone . . ." he snapped loudly after the Curate, who, lifting his eyebrows with disapproval, spoke the next phrase of the belaboured Confession with marked deliberation. Joe sniggered, and was dug in the ribs by Andrew, who with chinked hands over his roving eyes pretended to be wrapped in a shattering examination of his delinquencies. But Joe made no such pretence; he knew he came to church only because his parents wished it, and once there he liked to wink at the girls in their pretty frocks. Not that there weren't moments when the service interested him. He liked the Psalms sometimes, particularly when they were about whales and leviathans. But there was nothing to-night, he grumbled, as he found the 119th Psalm, thankful at least that they hadn't to sing all the way through it. Lord, that would be a service, that would, if you had to bellow through—how many verses?—176 he found. Joe wondered whether Parson really did anything as he held up his hand, made a funny sign at them all half-sitting there, and said: *"He pardoneth and absolveth all them that truly repent . . ."* Well, my Gosh, he could put that little bitch Sally Treweake against a hedge, Parson would make the sign at him, and he'd go straight to Heaven. So perhaps there was some use in religion, after all. . . .

"Glory be to the Father and to the Son . . ."

The congregation struggled wearily to its feet with an obstinate sense of duty to the Trinity. The young lady who played the organ jabbed out a four-foot flute, jabbing it in again hastily in the middle of a chord, as it gave out a piercing squeak of protest. The Curate urged the people to praise the Lord. This having been attended to, everybody frenziedly rustled their Prayer Books to Day Twenty-six.

Tansy was in a reverie. She had not even found the Psalms, but held her book upside down at the Table of Kindred and Affinity. Her eyes were upon the long line of the sun as, coming out of a cloud, it sent an orange path through the west window in the belfry and fell on to the blue altar frontal. The two altar candles were meagre points of light in the flood of the sun. Some blood-red tulips on the altar dropped their ponderous heads as though the sun had uncovered some shameful secret in them. Tansy wished they had used the red frontal instead of the blue. She wondered how often they were changed and whether Parson just took it into his head to have the colour he was in the mood for. Then she remembered they always used white for special days like Harvest, Easter and Feast; days also when Parson wore a beautiful cloak embroidered with a picture of Mary and the baby Jesus, held around his neck by a great metal clasp; when hot little boys wore red cassocks, bobbing round by the man who swung that lovely smelling incense at them. Her father always stayed away then; he said incense made him sick, but in reality she knew it was because they were taking after the Pope. Father loathed the Pope; he always spat when his name came up. But Tansy rather liked the stories she had heard about him, even if some were rather wicked. And she certainly liked the incense. . . . Her eyes came back to the Prayer Book, and she saw that a woman may not marry her grandfather. An insane desire to giggle almost overcame her. Then she read right through the catalogue of forbidden fruit. Apparently the only people you could not marry were the people you had known all your life; that seemed strange somehow.

"*Great is the peace that they have who love Thy law . . .*" An old woman behind Tansy spat the words viciously out of her unctuous mouth, so that Tansy, startled to a realization of her surroundings, hurriedly found the Psalms just as they finished.

The Vicar was reading from Isaiah: "*Blessed are ye that sow beside all waters . . .*"

There was consolation in that, thought Emmeline, as she listened to the lesson with her lips pressed tightly together because of the fierce twinge of pain she had felt. She had sown all right, and if she was to be blessed for it, it was no more than her just due. But what of poor souls like Rosie Williams, who had sown to corruption? Emmeline shuddered. She caught Tansy's eye and turned away quickly. There was a hectic flush in her cheeks which Emmeline did not like to see. She wished Arthur were in church with them. She had a sudden feeling that Tansy did not want to sow beside all waters. And the sight of Arthur, standing beside her, would have reassured her. She and Nicolas had sown and would be blessed for it; and Tansy and Arthur must sow, and others after them. But if Tansy were not taken soon Emmeline did not like to think what might happen.

"*For He hath regarded the lowliness of His handmaiden . . .*" Well, if He had—thought Emmeline, the strident tide of the Magnificat beating upon her thoughts—if He had, she couldn't help thinking it was a pity He hadn't regarded the lowliness of Rosie Williams a little more. She bit her lip, vexed with herself. "There's a thing to say about the Lord," she muttered, "when for all I know there may be mansions in Heaven for poor Rosie, and maybe she'll be sent over from old Abram's bosom to parch the tongues of me and such like who fret and grumble down here."

"*Pleasant are Thy courts above . . .*"

The robust waltz bore the people along in defiance of the

snivelling organist, who hastily kicked the swell pedal down and loudly wiped her nose. Her calculations as to the exact position of the pedal G had been entirely upset by Nicolas, who bellowed so rapturously that she could barely hear the choir. Nicolas loved the hymn. He felt in it the surging sway of a thousand souls gathered through dark outer-worlds to the final world above. He sang as in a dream; deep down within him was the rich benison of a confidence he also felt when he ploughed a black field in November. A dim realization that he and all his kind were being carried to ultimation by something powerful and irresistible. The unceasing wheel of life turned and turned in that hymn. Nicolas knew it. He was a living, human force, acknowledging the call of an ancestral Godhead. Driven on like a cloud that is sent sailing over the moon.

A quickening wave of life passed over the church so that the stone walls seemed to tremble and lean upon it.

"And there was war in Heaven . . ."

The Vicar had mounted the pulpit and was speaking about St. George. Tansy quickened to interest. She never understood half of what he said on the rare occasions she forced herself to listen, but to-night there was something intolerant and consuming in the old man's words. His eyes shone with a fierce tenderness; his face was glowing like the face of the Saint himself. The face of the Saint. . . . Tansy clutched on to the pew. The old man pointed to the figure of George in the East window and spoke about the dragon, painting it in vivid colours as the apotheosis of all evil.

". . . George in his shining armour, his noble countenance burning with contempt, beats him down, again and again; drives his untarnished sword into the corrupt hide of the monster. He will conquer—he is bound to conquer, surrounded as he is by the pure fire of the living God. He stands for us, beloved, as the incorruptible messenger of all that is of good report. He is ever valiant, ever impregnable, ever assiduous in his defence of whatsoever things are lovely. And the thing that he destroys, lying twisted and bloody at his feet, surely it is a picture of the Devil that we should do well to keep before us? Milton, in his epic of *Paradise Lost,* portrays the Devil as a being of dignity, a gentleman, one who would rather reign in Hell than serve in

Heaven. We begin to feel sympathy for him as the champion of a lost cause. But you must put aside that dangerous doctrine. You must see the Devil as George and Michael saw him—a disgusting, formless abortion; loathsome, vile—a writhing mass of corruption . . . something before which our gorge rises, like a headless slug crawling over our floor at night, leaving wherever it goes a trail of foul slime. A thing that we stamp upon and utterly destroy . . . utterly destroy. . . . It is the sickness that destroyeth in the noonday as much as it is the pestilence that walketh in darkness . . ."

The Vicar towered above the troubled people and lashed them with the driving whip of his words. The usual whisperers were awed to silence.

Nicolas bobbed his head in assent. This was the stuff to give the whoremongers and fornicators. My Gosh, he would like to bring them in here and make them crawl on their bellies! He looked round suddenly, as though in search of any sinners he could force to their knees. But he only caught the baleful eye of the Churchwarden's wife, who glared at him with such implacable malevolence that he felt uneasy in his new office as flail-bearer to the Lord.

The Vicar gave out an appropriate hymn: *"He who would valiant be 'gainst all disaster . . ."* Bunyan's staunch words were like a shield against Andrew, who threw out his chest and scowled at his neighbours under frowning eyebrows. He held his book rigidly out before him as though it were the terrible book of Seven Seals. Some girls, seeing his handsome, angry face, tittered in their books. Andrew did not notice them. He went on singing throatily, grovelling in a cacophonous bass when they reached a part of the tune too high for him. "Darn the old tune," he growled, and, turning his eyes on the organist, forgot that they were taking the collection. Hot with confusion, he kept the row of people impatient with their pennies as he surreptitiously rubbed his fingers along the edges of the coins in his pocket. But the only smooth-edged coin he could find was a halfpenny, and dignity forbade that as too modest an offering. Embarrassed under the eye of the sidesman, he hastily dropped a bright new silver shilling in the bag. He did not sing any more after that—hating the hymn and

the whole church; hating the dithering old Parson and the emul-
sive Curate; above all, hating God for thus fortuitously relieving
him of the price of twenty cigarettes in exchange for the doubtful privilege of worshipping in His holy temple. Then suddenly
he banished these thoughts as he saw Emmeline's drawn face
contract to a wrinkle of pain. She was ill, he suddenly saw. She
was ill and never told them. That was like her, so quiet in life that
she would probably die and they still imagine that she was somewhere about the house. Andrew loved his mother more than any
of them realized. He never fawned upon her like Joe; never took
advantage of her generous tolerance like Tansy. Neither did he
ever outwardly much consider her. But when he saw the expression of pain pass across her face he wanted to carry her out of the
church, away from all this humbug, and put her to bed.

"Mother," he whispered, as they knelt for the Blessing, "you
look queer. Do you feel bad?"

But all she replied was, "My head's aching. 'Sh. I'm all right."
She was frightened of the pain now. Did not dare tell them for
fear they would call a doctor and he disclose something that
ought not to be there.

The Curate announced the recessional hymn, *"Sun of my soul
Thou Saviour dear . . ."*

With lachrymose faces the people began to snivel the tune.
Having, in the last hymn, marched the Christian opposition upon
goblins and foul fiends, it was convenient to rest now upon the
Saviour's breast. The choir filed lugubriously down the church,
so slowly that the leading choir boy was filled with a reasonable
desire to stick a pin into the old man who carried the cross. One
lady, possessed of a strong mystic sense, crouched before the
cross as it passed her. Her neighbour sniffed with disapprobation.
Then abruptly the singing ended; the choir assembled in the
belfry bowing impatient heads to the vestry prayer; the people
knelt in the final convention of privacy with God. Then a scram-
ble of coatless figures from the belfry, a frantic rush on the part of
those far from the door to get out before the crush, a lurch into
some hardy Handel from the organist—and Evensong was over.

Tansy, at the end of the pew, slipped down the south aisle
before the others could notice her. To her relief she reached the

porch before Nicolas and the others had left the pew. Avoiding any of her friends, she quickly walked towards the old Vicarage. A black formation of cloud, massed in the east, slowly mounted up the sky and threw dark banners towards the sea, where the sun grew heavier in its descent. The wind of yesterday had dropped and it was a humid evening. Tansy, walking in a half-dream, could think of little but the Parson's strange sermon. Most vivid in her mind was a vision of the Parson's devil. Like a slug . . . something that we stamp upon and utterly destroy. Utterly destroy . . . she repeated the words to herself. But it required the valour of George to do that. Surely nobody but George could do that?

She went down the field where yesterday Chailey had lain on the grass, sprawling his long idle limbs among the daisies. She remembered his tie, greener than any of the trees that huddled before her under the ominous cloak of cloud. All her hatred and fear of the little wood came over her again. It would be cold there—she knew it would be cold. And all silent except for the incessant requiem of those enshrouding trees. Nobody but Chailey could have brought her there.

The trees were over her now. She felt at once that softer music in the air which always moves with trees. There were firs and sprawling elms; a cedar with dark green saucers laid out under the sky; an old yew like a moth-eaten coat; a eucalyptus hiding its epicene foliage from the sun. And sticking out like a barb above them all, a ginkgo tree that had lost all its foliage save for a few ashen leaves like bits of blown parchment at the top.

Tansy came nearer to the reticent face of the house. The broken windows gaped at her like the open mouths of dumb people. The scrolled doorway seemed to dare her to enter those musty, echoing rooms. She came on through some rhododendron bushes until she stood in a little clearing some yards away from the house. Then she saw Chailey. He was standing so still against the wall of the house that he was like a carved figure in it. He had not seen her. He stood with his hands behind his back, his head thrown up to the tree-tops.

The powerful notes of a cuckoo lumbering away over her head alarmed her. Chailey followed the bird as it disappeared over the roof, then his eyes lowered and he saw Tansy standing on the grass under the cedar tree. He called and began to walk towards her. Tansy did not move. She was fascinated by his slow, ponderous walk; the way his whole body seemed to hang and swing on shoulders keen as blades. Before she believed he could have covered the distance, he was standing before her, overshadowing her with his long lean body, like a hollow tree trunk. Tansy lifted her eyes unwillingly to his. They quivered with that slightly contemptuous humour which Tansy neither liked nor understood. His throat moved as though he were swallowing, and he looked at her through half-closed eyes.

"I don't like you in those clothes," he said. "Why do you wear them?"

"Because it's Sunday," she murmured.

"Ah, yes, Sunday! The compelling Christian Sabbath! And was church enjoyable?" He did not appear to want her to answer. Instead he made a gesture of impatience. "Can you take off your hat?" he asked. "Hats don't suit you, who have hair like a dark little medieval page. And I want to see if my sketch of your ear comes anywhere near the original."

Tansy obeyed rather sulkily, throwing the hat down on the grass. She wondered why she had been fool enough to come here just to listen to a lot of nonsense about her hair.

He put his hand out suddenly and held her ear between his thumb and forefinger. Tansy jumped back.

"You can look without touching, I reckon!"

She spoke with an acidity which amused him. He laughed softly. "Can I indeed? But, Tansy, why do you stare at me as though you were Little Red Riding Hood and I the wolf? Do you think I want to gobble up little girls in the dark wood?"

"I shouldn't be frightened if you did."

"You're a wise girl, then," he said, misconstruing her meaning. "For wolves never gobble people up. They only bite small pieces off, like this." And he seized her hands, caught her to him, and kissed her ears. She struggled free and glared at him.

"You take too much upon yourself, I think!" she cried fiercely.

"But, Tansy, look!" He took out his sketch book and showed her a large delicate drawing of her ear. "Yes, it is like it," he murmured.

"If I had ears as big as that," said Tansy, "my face would be bigger than the Church clock."

There was a sudden scuttling in the bushes.

"What's that, then?" cried Tansy, laying a hand on the lapel of his coat. He held it under his own.

"A fox," he said, "who came just at the right moment."

She drew her hand away quickly. "Can't you leave me alone at all?" she cried. "Can't you see I came here to tell you——"

"——that you're never going to see me again. Yes, I know, Tansy! The irrevocableness of life is terrible, isn't it? To think that you and I should be facing one another for the last time on earth! That I, who found you like the spirit of the spring, who saw you as nobody else has ever seen you, should meet you now in the dark wood for the last time——"

"Don't," she cried, "oh, don't! Your voice mocks me when you do speak like that."

"Does it?" Then he changed his tone. "Let's walk round this old forgotten garden." He took her hand like a child might.

"I don't like it here," she said.

"Because it is sad?" he asked. "But all lovely things are sad. Like you; like me."

"It's the trees I don't like——"

They were walking towards the gingko tree, standing amidst a copious growth of fleshy tree ferns. Up high above them, blood-red against the dark foliage, a straggling rhododendron spattered its crimson blossoms. The place was luscious and sickly with vegetation, in the twilight like an African jungle.

"I don't like the trees at all," repeated Tansy, glad enough now to feel the protection of his hand.

"You have never lived amongst them, I suppose," said Chailey, "and do not easily make friends of them. But I love them. I envy the woodcutter who lops off their strong limbs and chops them into blocks for firewood."

"But why do you want to cut them down if you love them?" asked Tansy. "Seems silly to my thinking."

"I never said I would cut them down," murmured Chailey, more to himself than to her. They walked along a dank avenue of rhododendron and laurel. Chailey spoke in a fanciful, dreamy voice. "I would shear off the limbs, those beautiful, straight, strong limbs which the wind longs to snap as I do. But cut them down—no! I could never cut the trunk, the secret centre of the body from where sprung the limbs. I could never cut the trunk. There is firewood enough without that. . . ." He soliloquized histrionically. Tansy did not understand him, but she was held by the rise and fall of his charmed voice, like the incantation of a priest before an altar. She no longer felt he was speaking nonsense.

They came to a little pond where water-lilies floated in the choking weed and a locked army of bamboos rattled starkly.

"Do you know what happened here?" said Chailey, breaking off in his discourse upon the trees. Tansy had heard only vague stories of the old Vicarage tragedy.

"I heard tell of a murder," she said. "But I don't want to know nothing about it, I reckon."

"Yes," said Chailey, disregarding her. "A murder. Mrs. Noggs was telling me all about it. The Vicar's young son, a beautiful boy, I'm told, was murdered by a maniac——"

Tansy shuddered, but wanted to hear the story now.

"He got away from an asylum on the moors," continued Chailey, "was hunted for days by the police, but they could never find him. He must have roamed about like a poor starved tiger escaped from a circus." He stopped, his face heavy and full of pain.

"What happened?" whispered Tansy.

"It's a bloody story," said Chailey. "He got to this garden and hid himself one night. Up there somewhere, where they grew bulbs in those days." He pointed to a field thick with weed. "There was a full moon. In spring it was. Perhaps twenty years ago to this very day. The Vicar had a daughter, a girl of sixteen. Nobody quite knows why, but she took it into her head to leave her bed at midnight when the moon was high, and come down into the garden. So she came out, down here to this pond."

Tansy shivered, clutched his arm and looked into his face. Chailey, growing into the story, sank his voice to a sibilant whisper.

"The wretched fellow saw her, Tansy. He did not know what he did. He was hungry. He was like a broken, desperate beast.

They say he came rushing through the narcissi in that field, tearing up the flowers and crying like the man whose devils were legion. The girl's screams brought out her young brother, whose room was nearest to that part of the garden. He must have been a little knight-errant, burning with the fire of righteousness, never giving a thought to his own danger. Nobody knows quite what happened. Their cries awoke their father, who came rushing down a moment later, a gun in his hand, to find the boy lying in his own blood. You see, his throat had been cut. The girl was unharmed, but possessed with the raving laughter of madness. She never got back her———"

"Oh, my God! Don't tell me no more———" breathed Tansy. But immediately she added, "Did they catch the brute who did it?"

"Yes. They caught him that night and shot him. Shot him without compunction, as one would shoot a lion in the jungle. Poor devil! Poor twisted devil!"

"Poor devil?" echoed Tansy. "What about the little boy and the girl? Don't you give a thought for them?"

"Yes, they were unfortunate victims of fate," muttered Chailey. "But, surely, the figure to whom our hearts should go out in compassion is the murderer. What do we know of the circumstances that led to his imprisonment on the moors? The world was ringing with the history of the unfortunate Vicar. But nobody gave a thought to the poor twisted devil who supplied such purple copy for the press."

Tansy made a gesture of disgust. "I should think not!" she exclaimed. "Give a thought to such a creature!"

A heavy drop of rain fell on her head. The cloud had blackened all the sky, save for a line of gold over the horizon. The trees stirred and hissed malignantly.

Tansy drew Chailey away from the pond. "Let's take shelter somewhere," she urged. "There's rain coming."

Chailey was morose and deep in his own thoughts. He did not heed her. Tansy tugged at him impatiently.

"Oh, let's leave here!" she cried. "It's raining and I don't like it here. Are you stupid?" She found herself shouting at him. He came to his senses, smiled at her, and, putting his arm round her waist, ran her along under the dripping rhododendrons to the house. The rain came down heavily as they got to the door.

"My hat!" cried Tansy. "It'll be soaked——"

Chailey dashed out and came back with it. The trees quickened to life. Everywhere leaves rustled, twigs crackled, and the rain hissed. Standing in the doorway, they got splashed by the rain.

"Come into the house," said Chailey. "At least it is warmer there."

"What shall I do?" Tansy whimpered a little, "if it goes on raining like this? Father'll be mad with me."

"You can have my raincoat," said Chailey.

She snapped at him. "And you think they wouldn't ask whose it was? Oh, I don't mind getting wet. It's being here I don't like——"

"There are worse troubles, Tansy. You might be here alone." He was mocking her again.

"I'm not sure I wouldn't rather!" she flung at him, trying in simulated anger to conceal her terror of the long, empty house.

"Here alone?" he whispered, "with the forlorn ghost of the little knight-errant to comfort you? The house is haunted, you know. Let me take you up to a room where the old man used to sit in silent grief, day in, day out, after his son was buried. We can watch the rain over the sea from there and think about that unfortunate old man——"

"No, no—I don't want to go——" she cried.

But, he speaking always in a low compelling voice, she had to go with him, even when she was heavy with dread.

They went up the rotten stairs to a landing yawning with swaying doors, and reached a long room thrown out of the side of the house like a gaunt arm. Here, at one end, were French windows, the glass broken, ivy trailing through to the damp-stained walls. There were some ashes in the rusty fireplace. The moist smell of cobweb, mildew and soot hung about the room. The boards creaked and the rain spat through the holes in the window, dancing in gibberish rhythm on the floor.

"Here he would sit," said Chailey, speaking in a lost voice, "in this long faded room with dusty books all round him. Sit over his fire mourning his little lost son and his crazy daughter."

As he spoke he slowly drew her into his powerful arms till she was enfolded by him and could smell the burning bracken of his coat. His forlorn voice drowsed her so that she closed her eyes.

"—Day in, day out—till he died and went with the little knight to glory over the poor twisted devil who had ruined his life."

"Don't talk about him," she whispered. "Please don't."

Then he lifted her head from his coat and tilted it back where it lay inert under his arm. Her lips were moist; her eyes a labour of unwilling desire. She saw his face bent near hers. With his right hand he smoothed her cheeks, played with her ear. She was consumed by the basilisk spark in his eyes, the perilous smile at the corners of his mouth. Her limbs were weak, her body breathless. He pressed down upon her, opening his mouth upon hers until he learnt the savour of her tongue. There was a rushing surge of her blood towards him; she felt him stiffen against her belly; felt his nervous fingers searching for the aching centre of her being. He kissed her throat and her breasts, forced her further back against his arm and fondled her like a dog. There was but one channel for the racing peril of her blood. She forgot where they stood, forgot the dismal story he had told her, forgot her home and her family. Only knew that she was alone with a man whom all her body craved.

Then he spoke: "You will come on Thursday?" His words were a certain knell in her ears. Even then she temporized.

"I—can't. Oh, why do you kiss me like that? Why do you hold me so that I never want to let you go?"

"It will be lovely on Thursday," he said, smoothing her hair back from her temples and tracing a design on her forehead with his finger. He gripped her round the waist till she cried for pain. "If you don't promise me you'll come, I shall keep you here till you do. Tansy, my lovely, promise me; because it's so easy to back out of life. Too easy for you and me."

But she was looking at something on the floor. A long silver line was traced along the boards. Black and baleful, she saw it slither towards her foot. She screamed and tore herself free.

"Kill it!" she cried. "Kill it!" Distracted by a dread she could not name, she wanted to stamp upon it but could not do so. She felt sick at the thought of it.

But Chailey chuckled and bending down picked it up. He let it writhe along his hand. His smile twisted his mouth. He edged his fingers along the slug's viscous body; soothingly he paused with his fingers arched.

"Kill it?" he said. "Kill a harmless slug? A lovely creature of good luck? Who would be brute enough to kill a slug?" He laughed wildly.

Tansy ran to the door and got downstairs. The fœtid smell of the house stank in her nostrils. She felt assaulted by an obscene force; a fungus of malignant power coiled itself round her heart.

She heard Chailey running down the stairs after her. As she got to the door, gasping to feel the utter purity of the sweet rain, to see the brilliant new green of the washed trees—he caught her and held her pressed back against the wall.

She saw there was slime on his hands.

"Leave me go!" she cried. "Leave me go, I tell you!" But she could not get free.

He laughed in her face.

"Not until you promise, little Graymalkin, lovely Gray-malkin—not until you promise! I shall keep you here till then."

She gave her word desperately, never meaning it, only mad now to get away from him and the wood.

"Oh, yes; I'll come. I promise you faithful. Only leave me go now. Leave me go——"

Then suddenly he let her free. Out of his grasp she ran through the trees, never stopping till she had left the wood and was on her way to the Penth valley.

CHAPTER VI

OUTSIDE the church that evening, Andrew gripped his mother's arm and spoke to her with harsh commiseration.

"You're going home and straight to bed."

Emmeline blinked.

Nicolas looked at Andrew, astonished. "What?" he said. "Is mother slight again, then?"

"Yes, she is. She is slight and won't say nothing about it."

Joe gazed at them in consternation. "We'd best get you to bed and have a doctor," he said weakly, even indifferently.

"I aren't going to have dealings with no doctor," muttered Emmeline.

Nicolas was looking for Tansy. "Where's Tansy?" he asked.

Emmeline replied vaguely: "Maybe gone off to see old Mrs. Hichens. She like to go sometimes of a Sunday."

"Well, he's coming to rain," said Nicolas. "I hope she won't be long."

Gloomily they walked home. Nicolas noticed the clear black slabs of the Scillies and felt the patter of rain in his bones. A flock of gulls flew calamitously inland—the screeching chorus of Nicolas' thoughts.

They got home just before the rain came down. In spite of Emmeline's whimpering assertions that she was not really ill, Andrew insisted on her going to bed. He ministered to her flamboyantly, getting her a hot bottle, putting more blankets on the bed, and offering her all kinds of food which Emmeline could not bear to think of.

"I won't have nothing, thankee, Andrew. Nothing at all. I'm better with an empty stomach."

Finally he coerced her into having a cup of tea. She sipped it while he watched her anxiously.

"How's that?" he said, sitting on the bed and placing his heavy hand on her arm. Emmeline said it was fine, and thought she might sleep.

"How're you feeling?" he asked.

"Better now. But I can't eat nothing. I got a pain——"

The words slipped out before she knew it. Had the pain been troubling her at that moment she would not have spoken about it.

"Where?" asked Andrew.

She bit her lip irritably and drew herself under the clothes.

"Over my breast," she said.

Andrew got savage. "How've you been so stupid," he muttered, "as to keep this to yourself all the time?"

"Oh, go on! It's nothing."

"I'll have a doctor to you in the morning."

"You wan't do nothing of the sort," cried Emmeline. "I hate th' old doctor who'll only fiddle about with me, give me some stinking medicine that aren't no good to no one, tell me to keep to bed and like as not charge thirty shilling for thumping me on the chest with his old tubes. I wan't have no doctor to me, not till I'm gasping, I wan't. I can get well without that sort of crowd hanging around."

"Some stupid," muttered Andrew. "Some stupid you are!"

But Emmeline was thoroughly angry with Andrew for uncovering what she had so closely concealed.

"My good Lord—anybody'd think I was a corpse, way you do go on. I tell you, if you do want me to be a corpse fetch th' old doctor, for he'll make me one."

"Well, if you won't have him, I tell you what I'll do," threatened Andrew. "I'll get Aunt Janet to come over, that I will. Reckon she know more about you than what we do."

"Oh, do as you've a mind," said Emmeline wearily, only wanting to be alone. "I don't care if Janet do come."

Janet was a widowed sister of Emmeline's.

"I'll write to her, then," said Andrew. He went to the door. "If you want for anything, mother, you've only got to call."

She did not reply and Andrew went down, conscious that in trying to help his mother he had done little more than irritate her. But he would get Aunt Janet over; he was determined on that. She would be able to take control of Emmeline, if nobody else could.

Tansy came in about half-past eight, hot and panting. Nicolas sighed as he saw her hat and frock were dripping with rain. She took her shoes off and held them before the fire. All the time she talked, rapidly and extravagantly, about the fickleness of the April weather.

"Mother's ill," said Andrew with a dark hint of triumph like an uncompromising angel. "I've put her to bed."

"Oh!" Tansy looked at them all quickly, then back again to Andrew's tight mouth.

"Is she really bad then?"

"Worse than she say she is," opined Andrew.

Tansy left her hat and shoes by the fire and went upstairs.

"Don't disturb her if she's sleeping," called Andrew after her. "'Twas trouble enough to get her to bed."

Tansy opened Emmeline's door softly. In the twilight she could faintly distinguish her grey head over the bedclothes.

"Is that you, Tansy?" she asked.

"Yes, mother; it's me——"

"Come here, child, and shut the door."

Tansy went in, hardly able to believe that this quiet figure in bed was her mother. She knelt down by the bedside, smoothed her forehead and could find no words to say. In all her time she had never known her mother take to her bed; it was impossible to imagine Emmeline giving way to a sickness.

Tansy mumbled sympathy, but Emmeline put the matter aside petulantly. "Andrew's asking your Aunt Janet for to come here," she remarked.

"Aunt Janet?"

"Yes. Andrew reckons he's some proper man!" She chuckled cynically. "Glad to have me ill, I s'pose, so's he can show off a bit, like. Wanted me to have the doctor. Me have a doctor! But go along, child—go along. 'Tisn't right as I should keep you from Arthur. He'll be wondering where you're to."

Tansy frowned. "But Arthur's at the mine, mother. How should he want me?"

"Dearie me now—is he? There's a thing!" Emmeline's face was flushed and her breathing heavy.

"Mother, don't talk so," said Tansy. "It only excite you. How're you feeling now? Your head's hot——"

"How shouldn't it be, with a bottle to my feet and about sixteen blankets on the bed? That Andrew thinks he put an iceberg to bed, if you ask me! Never mind. He's a good boy I s'pose, even if he's a bit solemn. Now you get along, child. Arthur'll be mad——"

"But, mother, Arthur isn't here. Why do you keep speaking of him?"

"Here!" she exclaimed indignantly. "Should think not, indeed! What cause have a chap to be with his woman's parents? He's down at his own home waiting for his supper, I'll be bound——"

There was a movement at the door and Nicolas came in. He

stood tentatively at the foot of the bed, biting his finger-nails. Tansy looked at him with a bewildered face.

"Who's that then? Who's that?" asked Emmeline. "If it's that Andrew, I don't want him here."

"It's me, mother," mumbled Nicolas.

"Oh, you," she said. "You. You come in some soft, I thought you was the Lord Himself." She put her hand out and touched Tansy's frock. "Why, child," she exclaimed, "you're as wet as a duck! Where've you been to?"

Tansy looked away. "Just for a walk," she said.

Emmeline looked at her closely. "Well, go and change your clothes," she said, "else there'll be another brought to bed. Go along now. Don't argue!"

But Tansy did not want to argue. She left the room, changed her frock and went downstairs to get supper. Andrew was in the living-room, bent assiduously over a pad of writing paper.

"Well, what do you make of mother?" he asked.

Tansy hesitated. "She's—queer," she said. "She's—got something on her mind, I think."

"Yes, she have," agreed Andrew.

"You writing to Aunt Janet then?" asked Tansy.

"Yes, I am. She won't see the doctor, and I don't like the looks of her at all."

"What d'you reckon's the matter with her?"

"She've got a pain in her breast—that's matter enough. She didn't mean to let on about it. I saw her go all white and screw up her lips in church. Now mother don't take on like that unless she's mighty bad. She've been bad this long time and wouldn't complain. That's where's to. And it's time us thought of her a bit, and less of ourselves."

Andrew so obviously wished to exclude himself from his last remark that Tansy, stung by the implied reproach, flared up at him.

"Well, your particular way of thinking of her don't do her much good," she sneered. "My Lord! Bottles and blankets! The poor soul's sweating to death up there. And she say if she sees you up there agin, it'll be the end of her. So turn that over in your mind!"

She went into the kitchen in a rage, knowing that Andrew

was right, that in revealing Emmeline as a sick woman he had pierced them all in a weak spot. She was furious with herself for remaining blind to her mother's condition, and vented her rage upon Andrew. And she had hit Andrew, who went pale, snapped his lips together and resumed his letter-writing. He knew Tansy had spoken the truth. Whatever he tried to do for his mother she would only resent it. Emmeline would never love him, unable ever to believe that he loved her. All his life he had concealed his deep love for her. Scorning to express something that should be understood, he had concealed his love so deep within him that now she would never find it.

Nicolas came down in a perplexed mood. He went to Tansy who was laying supper in the kitchen.

"Tansy," he said, "I don't like it."

"What?" she said. "Mother?"

"Yes, mother. She's wandering in her mind. It's wisht, to my thinking. I can't make her out at all, but she seems to think as how you and Arthur are wedded. She keeps telling me to send you on home as though you don't belong here any more. I said to her, not understanding, see? 'They aren't wedded yet, mother.' And she says, 'It oughtn't to be.' I say to her, 'Don't take on so— come midsummer they'll be wedded.'"

He looked at Tansy with imploring eyes. None of the old imperiousness remained in him. Then he said:

"Tansy, she do fret about you. I can't help but think the sooner you're——"

"Oh, father—I know! I *know*! I can't talk about it now. Arthur'll be here on Wednesday. Maybe mother'll be easier when she sees him. And I daresay Aunt Janet'll do her a heap of good——"

"Aunt Janet be darned," growled Nicolas.

"I'm with you there," said Tansy. "But maybe Andrew's right all the same."

And to a certain extent he was, for that redoubtable lady, Mrs. Janet Trudgeon, arriving with a flop like the landing of a great fish on the following evening, brought a more cheerful spirit into the house. The moment she came, the house seemed to shrink to half its normal size. The widow of a well-to-do grocer in Penzance, a respected Rechabite, laid to rest with many esoteric tokens of esteem, Mrs. Trudgeon was as ample of tongue as of stomach. Nobody knew the reason for her prodigious obesity since Emmeline's people had all been tall and lean. Janet, from a little girl, had blown her way through life. Perhaps that was why Emmeline had always been so ruminative and introspective. To finish a sentence was difficult with Janet in the room; to finish one of Janet's sentences, almost impossible. Nobody knew where they began and few had heard them end. Janet was the antithesis of Emmeline in feature and physique. Her eyes were black, her hair black—everything about her black, except her dress and her face, which were scarlet. She wore the most astonishingly bizarre clothes; dresses that showed far more of her massive legs than one wished to see, and ill-concealed her bountiful bosom. She had lately taken to rouging her lips and cheeks, applying the cosmetic with the same extravagant excess as she might apply a coat of paint to her front door. She continually shocked Nicolas with her broad jests. When she got really bawdy, he concealed himself behind the unremitting temple of the Parish Magazine, and tried very hard not to chuckle.

To strangers, Janet was always referred to as a "trained nurse", though where that training had been accomplished, it was hard to discover. The truth was that she had once practised a little mid-wifery in the days when children were born more haphazardly. From this tin-trumpet of obstetrics she effectively flourished a sennet of therapeutics.

Yet nobody ever took Aunt Janet for a woman of doubtful reputation. She was generous, indiscriminate in her love of the human race, a most ingenuous and delightful snob, and utterly aware of her eccentricities. Since living in Penzance she had formed the habit of referring to her people as "country folk"—a term which infuriated Nicolas beyond anything else. She had once been to London with her husband on a fortnightly excursion, and was so carelessly full of accounts of the London season, that the innocent listener often found himself believing that she had been presented at Court, instead of being one of the thousands debutante-gazers in the Mall, as, of course, she had been. She floundered so irrelevantly in conversation, that no purpose was gained in attending to her. Sometimes, also, she assumed a recondite air that had been known to impress those who were unaware of her inherent simplicity.

When she arrived on Monday evening, it was pouring with rain. In two minutes the lower rooms of the house were littered with her personal effects. She tottered amiably to a chair, leaving a trail of water behind her wherever she went. The Penderils wandered round the room, picking up dripping garments.

"Oh, my dears"—she heaved up and down, dabbing at her nose with an enormous powder-puff—"what a night! Trafalgar Square isn't in it, if you ask——"

She gaffled at the cheeks and Nicolas spat in the fire. Nobody had the least idea what was intended by the reference to Trafalgar Square. Least of all had Janet herself.

"—*And* the buses," she continued, in an agonized diapason of complaint, "never saw *anything* like it. I've brought some ointment——" she announced gratuitously.

"Ointment?" rumbled Andrew.

"—Always useful." She held up a podgy ring-laden finger, then dug it into her nose and worked there avariciously. "A basket of stuff there for Emmeline." She pointed to a basket magnificently. "Jellies and a few nutmegs. For egg-custards, you know. I know just how difficult nutmegs are in the——" She was about to say "country", but stopped as she saw Nicolas's ominous eyes fixed upon her. So she said "custards" instead. It did not really matter. She liked the random sentence she had thus composed, and repeated it significantly. "I know how difficult nutmegs are in the custards——" It was superbly stated. Everybody immediately realized that all their difficulties in life had been entirely due to the presence or absence of nutmegs in the custards.

Tansy tried to speak, but could not get there.

"—And a poultice," breathed Janet. "She'll need a poultice, poor, silly woman. She's probably got an œdema——" This was delivered in a somewhat sinister and very loud aside to Tansy.

"A what?" ejaculated Andrew.

"Never you mind. But it's very nasty at her age. Dangerous. But never fear. I've looked it all up. It may be cataract and you're not to worry about giving me a bed. I know how scarce beds are in the country——" She waggled her hands at Nicolas and went on rapidly. "—I've taken a bed at the Commercial, and shall just stay on till Emmeline is better. And you can leave the housekeeping to me, Tansy. Time for you to have a rest. And how's that boy of yours keeping? Tickle you up much, do he? Time you were tickled up proper because—— Joe, my boy, if you will keep playing about with your fly-buttons like that, I shall see what's wrong for myself. Anybody'd think you was—— But as I was saying, what Emmeline wants is——"

"You'll be seeing of her in a minute?" burst Andrew.

"—Yes, there's one in my bag," she continued dreamily, entering now upon the realms of inconsequential theorizing. "I should say three times a day, *before* meals. Have to go careful, of course, otherwise——" She winked her eyes and clicked her tongue against her gums with dreadful portentousness. "—The point is—— Won't have a doctor, you say? I don't wonder. I *don't* wonder. Of course, if she was in London now, somewhere near Harley Street. Nobody never dies there you know, it's that full of doctors—and you'll hardly believe it, but it's God's truth——"

Nicolas groaned and left the room.

"You'd better come up to mother," said Andrew, who was beginning to wonder whether he had done the right thing in sending for Aunt Janet. She arose at the invitation, threw her hat down on the floor and said she was ready to visit the invalid. Andrew took her up and came down again immediately. For perhaps a quarter of an hour they heard nothing but a continual volley of remarks from Janet. Then she came down, not in the least subdued by her sick sister. Nicolas was back in the living-room again.

"Well, old pigeon-face," she hailed him, "cheer up! She ain't going to die if Janet knows anything about it."

The sobriquet did not encourage Nicolas to receive the information with any show of credulity. All he said was:

"Indeed, ma'am?"

"No, indeed—yes, indeed!" she mocked. "But you better not sleep with her to-night. She wants peace, otherwise—mind you, I'm not saying it—but she *might* go off—up—like this"—she accompanied this stupendous prophecy with a series of gyrating levitations with her hands—"and it'd be your fault!" she added.

"Thankee, ma'am," said Nicolas sourly. "I'm sure I'm glad for to know."

Janet turned upon Tansy suddenly.

"What d'you mean by it, then?" she demanded abstrusely.

"Mean by it?" echoed Tansy, entirely mystified by Janet's reproaching finger.

"Yes," she continued, "getting married without so much as telling your old aunt. Or perhaps you had to? I daresay——"

The others looked at each other stupidly.

"Did mother tell you that?" asked Nicolas.

"Well, do you think I read it on the bedclothes? Ain't it true then? Come on—tell your old aunt. Don't be afraid. Worse things in London, I could tell you. One day in Regent Street—never saw *anything* to beat it myself. Don't believe in it, of course. But then——"

"That's proof enough," pronounced Nicolas, disregarding Janet's excursion to the metropolis. "Mother's wandering in her mind. It's gone to her brain."

"What did she say to you, Aunt Janet?" asked Tansy uneasily.

"Nothing much. Quiet like as usual. She said it was time the girl went home. Arthur'd be waiting for her, though what he'd be waiting for at this time of the evening is beyond me. I said, 'What, they married, then? This is news to me.' And she nodded, then got excited and said about a baby, so don't go blaming me if I thought you'd been having some nonsense before the Parson had made it all square, so to speak. Mind *you,* I'm not one to worry about such things myself. Girls will be girls, and I always found that boys *will* be boys, and bring 'em together they behave pretty much the same as rabbits or earwigs for that matter—but, my good Lord——"

"Hold your gab!" shouted Nicolas. "You'd soon talk the King off his throne."

"Well, I very near did," she said suavely, "when I was in London. I could tell you——"

"Listen, Aunt Janet." Andrew shook her so roughly that her breasts flopped up and down like blancmanges. "Did mother really tell you as our Tansy was wedded to Arthur?"

"I'm saying so, ain't I?" she gasped.

"Then mother's saying things she don't know of," said Andrew. "I call it serious. She's out of her mind. That's what it's come to."

Aunt Janet was plainly disturbed. But in a moment she recovered.

"It's all part of the illness," she observed sapiently. "They think forward, so to speak. A little nursing, light diet—she'll come right. She've plainly got it into her head that you two are married. You very nearly are, I s'pose?" she suddenly demanded of Tansy.

"I don't—— What do you mean?" Tansy was flustered.

"Oh, darn the girl!" snapped Janet. "Have you been to bed with him then, if I must speak plain?"

Then Nicolas brought out his thunder while Joe giggled in a corner.

"You great shameless woman," he bellowed. "The sooner you're——"

"—Gone the better!" added Janet. She took her hat and forcing it down on her head, went to the door, gathering up her cloak, gloves and umbrella on the way. The rain slanted ruthlessly along the light from the house.

Pulling on her gloves, Janet delivered the ultimate outrage upon Nicolas.

"You country folk"—and here with deadly truculence, she paused—"you country folk speak as though you don't know why you take the cow to the bull."

And opening her umbrella into their faces, she rolled into the rain.

Joe suddenly felt very sorry for her and walked with her to the gate.

"Shall I put you up to the town?" he asked. "This rain's awful!"

"My Lord!" she cried. "Think a drop of rain hurts Janet Trudgeon, my handsome! But harkee"—she changed her tone—"it'll be a good thing for Emmeline when Tansy *do* get married. For it's a prey on her mind, though I can't tell for why. But if you want to see Emmeline well again, you just do what you can to get Tansy married right away. It'll mean a lot to Emmeline. Sure of it."

She dug Joe in the ribs rudely.

"You're a pretty lad," she said. "I reckon Tansy'd be married to-morrow if it was you. That Arthur—he's too slow. I know. In London they do things different——"

"Listen, Aunt," said Joe. "Be serious for a minute. Do you think mother's real bad?"

For an instant Janet's bucolic countenance clouded. Then she chuckled hugely.

"Not near so bad as she will be if you all hang round her with mopy faces! See you early in the morning," she cried, as she lumbered away into the darkness.

But as her valiant rotundity staggered against the driving rain, she sighed and murmured: "Poor Emily! Poor, dear Emily! Such a pretty maid she was too——"

CHAPTER VII

TANSY's criticism of Arthur, coupled with Aunt Janet's assertion that he was a slow youth, had made an impression on Joe's mind. Consequently, when Arthur came round to the farm on Wednesday afternoon, Joe took him out into the yard and began to give him some romantic advice as to the proper treatment of young women in love.

"You want to save her life or something," ventured Joe hazily. "Do things that other chaps don't do. You've got it in you, anyone knows. Swim to the Prison Rocks. That'd tickle her fancy no end."

"I don't mind," said Arthur a little sourly, for him, "that she's often in danger of losing her life."

"Well, you've got this afternoon," said Joe impatiently. "Make the most of it. Darn well make her go out with you, for one thing. And when you gone out, do something new."

Emmeline was in the living-room with Janet and Tansy, sitting over the fire, and surrounded by the decorative dishes with which Janet attempted to coax her appetite. The whirlwind ministrations of Janet had encouraged her to come downstairs, and Janet had not resisted this, although even her empiric eye saw that Emmeline was far from well. She ate very little, and lived in constant dread that Janet would get the doctor.

When she heard that Arthur was in the yard, she called him in eagerly. "Now, you're to take Tansy out," she said. "She could do with a good breath of air."

"Well," Arthur dashed into a great decision, "I was thinking we might go down to the pool. The weather's warm enough for a swim and Joe's got a costume he can lend me."

They were momentarily silenced.

"Catch your death——" muttered Emmeline.

"Go if you like," remarked Tansy airily. "Only you don't catch me in that old pool this time of year."

"Well, anyhow, you'll come with me?" mumbled Arthur, who was already regretting his decision.

"Oh yes, I'll come all right."

She would not give him any credit for this departure from convention, though inwardly she wondered what had happened to him. Arthur was the only good swimmer amongst them all; the others rarely went down to the sea except on hot days in the height of summer.

Aunt Janet loudly applauded Arthur.

"You throw her in," she cried, "throw her in with all her clothes on, then you'll have to undress her to get her dry again. Oh my, what a lark! Go on—go on you two, and don't come back till dark, otherwise you'll drive me to reading the Bible in bed, an awful thought——"

She pushed them out of the back yard, screaming all the time. "And you smack her bottom, Arthur, if she sulks! That's what they do in London. Time was—but I suppose I daren't tell you that, otherwise you'll be saying I've a coarse mind and that Nicolas will turn me out——" she was still howling at them and waving her arms about as they lost sight of the house and began to dip down into the valley. They walked along the bed of the valley towards the sea, a way that Tansy had not been for a long time. The soft spring day drowsed her, so that she was unable to do more than respond listlessly to Arthur's remarks. Glad as she was to leave the farm, she was totally unmoved by Arthur's presence. For a looming shadow at the back of her mind, the figure of Roger Chailey, silently commanded her being. She would pretend that he had no existence for her, would deliberately concentrate upon something else, but inevitably he would return so that looking at the stiff green fronds of the young bracken, the bright flames of the gorse, the last few celandines falling in whiteness under her feet, she saw in all these the half-humorous, half-grave face of Chailey. Her mother's sudden illness had prevented her from trying to see him since Sunday. And to-morrow was Thursday . . . to-morrow was Thursday . . .

The three words hammered in her brain. To-morrow was Thursday . . . and she was walking down the valley with Arthur Progis. . . .

His voice sounded from another life altogether; a monotonous bugle summoning her from a land of shadows.

They were near the sea. Curved in the horseshoe cove, the receding tide left the rock-strewn shore almost devoid of water. The stream grew less definite in its straight course and fell by several gullies into the sea. Arthur and Tansy walked over a ridge of slag thrown up years ago in mining operations. Immediately before them was a jagged fortress of granite, pressing into the sky like a man with a hooked nose. Their path led them round the rock. Tansy was fascinated by the quivering feldspar glowing in the black rock.

"See," she suddenly said to Arthur. "This black rock's full of colour when you look close at it."

But he was ahead of her, eager to reach the pool, and did not hear her voice. Tansy hurried on, feeling now that it would be lovely to sit on the rocks while Arthur swam, and watch the waves break in fountains of veined colour. She rounded the dark wall and stood against Arthur looking at the sea.

In the cove where the calm sea was shallow, the rhythmic sway of it shifted green arabesques in the rocks below. Further out, it was blue, broken sometimes by riding crests of foam. The cove lay in the long rounded arm of the Penth Peninsula, a point that tapered its direction finally northwards, and stretched along the sea like a dragon with a scaly back. About a mile beyond the peninsula, rose the hazy mounds of the Prison rocks. Northwards, the scowling brow of the coast fell more savagely upon the sea. The house at Boscedjack lay above those cliffs, and further on, Retallack Mine, where Arthur worked.

The hillside on which they stood was soft with warm tufts of thrift, still in bud. Tansy lay on the grass, and begged Arthur to stay a moment. He sat down beside her.

Half unconsciously she began to compare him with Chailey. Arthur was much shorter, his head firmer and more solid, his limbs thicker. There was no glow in his eyes, no tension in his hands, no quivering intuition in his nostrils. She could never feel afraid of Arthur. But he had something which Chailey did not possess. Looking at his moveless figure on the grass, Tansy felt that he rested there as an animal would rest; more by instinct than by choice. She felt that he was part of the uncompromising harmony of the land as her father and brothers were in their fields. When you saw him on this hillside, it was like coming upon another rock. But Chailey would have been decorative; his attitude would have considered the shape of a daisy. From Arthur emanated so strong a sense of his fellowship with the earth, that had he expressed his delight in it, his posture might seem ridiculous. And seeing him thus, Tansy knew that of all men, these were the closest to those made in God's image. That over them flowed the slow fire of life, not the devouring fire of living, which man has made of life. Tansy saw clearly what Arthur could give her. Yet he lacked something for her which Chailey alone seemed able to give; the power to make her realize her own solitary identity in a world where no two creatures were the same.

She laid her hand along his knee suddenly. His muscles were relaxed; his blood untroubled by the message of her hand. Only he turned and smiled slowly, his blue eyes hazy like woodsmoke in autumn. Then he put his arm round her waist. She pressed his hand under her breast, waiting for the subtle spark of affinity to waken in him.

"Well, Tansy," he said gently, "you're some quiet. Happy are you?"

"I'm happy enough, Arthur, I reckon. I was thinking of you just now."

"Thinking of me?" He seemed almost alarmed.

"Yes. I wondered—what made you come out bathing to-day? 'Tisn't like you at all."

He did not tell her of Joe's advice. "Do you mind?" he asked a little anxiously.

"Mind? Why should I? I'm glad. But it isn't like you, that's where it is."

"Oh, well," he said vaguely, "there's a lot you don't know about me yet."

"Arthur," she said earnestly, "isn't it a handsome day?"

"All right, you," he agreed carelessly.

"See that seal!" She pointed to the bobbing cork of a seal's head in the sea. "It's pretty—the way they let the waves beat them about."

Arthur looked at the seal.

"Yes, I s'pose," he said.

Tansy sighed.

"Come on," said Arthur. "Let's get down to the pool before the tide gets over it."

They got up and scrambled down some steep smooth rocks until they reached the shore. They saw the pool deeply imprisoned in the rocks, clear as a witch ball. When the tide was low, as now, it left the pool clear and motionless, a circular mirror in the sloping slabs of granite. But with the tide high, it was impossible even to tell its position. To-day they could see clearly down its eighteen feet of water to the weed and stones at the bottom. Arthur threw a stone in and watched the endless voyage of its ripples. Then he began to search for a place where he could undress.

Tansy sat in a curved rock and laid back to the sun. She saw Arthur moving away from her.

"Where are you going now then?" she called.

"Over behind that rock," he answered, "where I can put my costume up."

Tansy was irritated by the convention.

"I don't see why you should have to move a mile away for that," she said. "Why can't you undress here?"

Arthur went red. "Darnee," he muttered, "'twouldn't be proper at all!"

"Proper," she laughed scornfully. "I wish we had Aunt Janet here. She'd tell you whether 'twere proper or no!"

"She told me to smack your bottom, if you was saucy," grinned Arthur.

"Well, you won't be able to do that if you go half a mile away to take off your old clothes." She began to wheedle him, and then, feeling very wicked, her imagination led her further to unheard-of impropriety. "And I tell you more," she exclaimed, "if you do love me as much as seem to think, you'll dive into that pool stark naked!"

"My gosh!" cried Arthur, frightened and outraged. "What next will you want? S'pose somebody was looking from up top? You know as well as I there's always some sneaking scoundrel prying about with a glass."

"I don't care," she retorted. "No more do you, really. You're frightened," she added with a little sneer.

"I'm not frightened——"

"Yes. Frightened—because you haven't stood up naked before a woman since your mother scrubbed you as a baby in your bath."

"'Tisn't proper, that's all I do say——" he hedged nervously. Tansy turned her back on him.

"I don't care about that," she said. "I won't look at you for five minutes. If you want to prove you're a man, you'll strip off your clothes and dive naked as you was born into that pool."

Joe's words were ringing in Arthur's unhappy mind. "Do something new." He looked at Tansy's sulking back and the shining sleekness of her black hair. Suppose he were to lose her? He could not visualize life without her any more than he could visualize life in another land. He looked hastily up the hillside, but saw nobody there. Then he made up his mind and with a beating heart, tore off his clothes, shivering as he felt the breeze on his naked skin. Tansy heard him, but did not turn round. She could not believe he had given way. Then she heard him run down the rocks behind her. Turning her head swiftly, she was in time to see a flashing whiteness strike the glassy surface of the pool. Down, down his body went, green, sinuous and deathly, his limbs flickering like the supple fins of a great fish. She stood up to see if he would touch the bottom. He did so, found a stone, then released himself and surged towards the surface. His spluttering head bobbed up, his hand threw out the stone and he shouted to her.

"How's that?"

"Fine!" She clapped her hands. "I never thought you'd do it!"

Arthur was proud and began to exhibit his strokes. In the water his body was a swift purity. Tansy could not believe in the clothed shape she had seen on the hillside. He seized a shelving rock and drew himself out cautiously. Mounting the rocks, he stood for a moment, keen with the breeze singing through his wet body, a new zest for life in his soul. Standing on the edge of the ocean, he was unaware of his beauty, entirely unconscious of himself. The golden gleam of the sun fired him, so that he looked like one who had swum in a pool of gold dust. Tansy was thrilled by him. She had never seen a man's body before. The strong clean arch of his straddled legs, the firm curve of his buttocks, the glistening valley of his back, the stiff column of his neck, the head thrown back in supplication to the sky—all this was Arthur, her lover, and she had never known. She had never seen the man, her lover. All she had seen, a masculine obtuseness in thick clothes. She had a sudden temptation to throw his clothes into the sea.

Arthur moved away, disappearing from her sight.

"Where you going to?" she called.

"Over the other side," he cried back. Tansy took off her shoes and stockings and followed him to a place where the open sea flowed up a little fissure in the coast, and echoed like a gun in the heart of the hollow hillside. The channel was perhaps a couple of hundred yards across—an easy swim for Arthur. Over the other side was a part of the coast impossible to reach from the cliffs.

Tansy saw Arthur standing on a low rock half in the sea. Then he dived rather clumsily and began to swim across. She got to the point where he had dived, and followed his body as it got smaller and smaller. She did not like him to swim across there, so small and helpless a shape in a sea that had suddenly become black. Tansy looked up the dark entrance to the cave, where the sea, thwarted of further invasion, thundered its anger like a beast. She shuddered, and turned again towards Arthur. He had landed on the other side. She saw his small white body scrambling over the rocks. He waved to her valiantly, and she waved back. Then he dived in and started to swim back. The sea was strong, bearing him upon its restless bosom with an utter contempt for his courage. But he came on slowly, until with a sigh of relief Tansy saw him just below her, tossing about like a piece of wreck-wood.

He tried to land, but the sweep of an unbroken wave carried his hand away from the rock and dragged him out again. He waited calmly until the sea had quietened. Then again he tried, with the same result.

Tansy was alarmed. "Here, take my hand," she cried. She suddenly thought how easy it would be to push him back and back until he was exhausted and lost in the rising sea. She shook the thought away, and crouching down on the rock, held out her hand. The rock was slippery with weed and she found it hard to keep her balance. A wave hurled Arthur forward, and he grabbed the rock with all his strength, jabbing his knee sharply against a pointed edge. Tansy caught hold of his wrist and dragged him up. In a second he was out, and staggering against her, would have overbalanced her had she not caught him round the waist.

For a moment of tense relief they stood thus. Then Tansy knew he was naked and exhausted in her arms. The spear of manhood she had marvelled at a moment ago, was pressed close against her. Then she kissed him full on the lips and pressed her body down to him.

But Arthur, stricken with shame, pushed her aside, and bending down, wiped the blood off his knee with his fingers.

Tansy cried. "Poor Arthur! I reckon you won't ever want to swim over there again. Here, let me bandage it."

She folded her handkerchief into a bandage. But Arthur retreated from her like a frightened animal. He did not want her near him then. He could not bear to have her soft compliant body so dangerously near to his. For in his hips there was a strange, lovely aching, and his loins were heavy, a burden to him. His heart thumped, because he wanted Tansy but was terribly afraid of her womanhood. "Do something new . . ." Well, he had done it. He could go no further.

And while he turned all this over in his mind, he felt Tansy's soft hand steal along his knee. He jumped away and began to run across to his clothes.

"Reckon I'd better get dressed," he muttered. Tansy was kneeling on the rock, the bloody handkerchief still in her hand. There presently, Arthur found her, gazing stupidly at her feet. He did not know what to say. His clothes made the last few lovely moments something idle and shameful. Then he remembered that without her he might never have left the sea alive.

"I never thanked you, midear——" he began haltingly.

"You needn't thank me." Her words were like ice.

"I—thought as how it'd be nice to walk to Boscedjack and look at our little house," he ventured rashly.

She turned round on him slowly. Her body felt drained yet not empty. She tried to tell herself that what she saw standing before her was the same naked spear of manhood who had sundered the glass of the pool. But it was a vision she had seen, something too lovely to believe in, like the vision of the Saint. A thing that died the moment life throbbed in it.

All she said—"It's too far to walk now, Arthur. Reckon we'd better get along home. I could do with some tea."

So they walked sadly up the valley towards the farm, embarrassed by the heavy silence between them.

As they started to mount the little path out of the valley, Tansy saw in the distance a tall figure standing by the stream-side. She caught Arthur's arm and pointed up the valley in that direction.

"Oh look Arthur—how beautiful the sun strikes in the stream!"

But shading his eyes, he turned towards the tremulous evening sea.

"That's a prettier view," he said.

CHAPTER VIII

CHAILEY ran his fingers through his hair, crumpled up the sketch he had just drawn and threw it on the fire. He rose from his chair and looked out of the window. The land was silent in a white mist; the black arm of the little wood only a shapeless smudge on the hills. Chailey looked up and down the road impatiently, but saw nobody. He went back to his chair, idly examining a portfolio of rough drawings. One he selected and studied carefully. It was a charcoal study of a youth's leg from the thigh to the ankle. Looking closely at it, he chuckled and held it away at arm's length. Then he added a quick stroke with his pencil, which decreased the thickness of the thigh and attenuated the shape of the whole limb. He was pleased with this, and still laughing, he kissed it suddenly.

He took some more pictures from the portfolio. Most were rough anatomical studies. Amongst them he found a large photograph of the Donatello David which he pinned on the wall over the fire. There was a life-size head of a young girl with curiously narrow eyes and a flat forehead. This also he seemed to like. A picture of a female torso which he studied carefully, he placed back in the portfolio.

The clock struck four. He went again to the window but saw nobody. He paced up and down the small room in a feverish impatience.

The room was a musty cottage bedroom packed with ugly furniture. By the window Chailey had set an easel with a large sheet of drawing paper pinned to a frame. Over the bed in the corner hung a Sunday School version of the words 'Seek ye the Lord'. The corners of the frame projected into four crosses; the words were heavily embellished with pink Protestant twirls, and nestling securely in the L of the 'Lord' was a grossly sententious robin. Chailey wrenched the frame from the wall in sudden anger and stowed it away in a cupboard. On the wall now was a dark mark where the paper had not faded. Chailey did not like that, and looking for something else to put in its place, he found a reproduction of Michael Angelo's 'Creation of Man'. He pinned it there, fondly caressing the massive limbs of the sprawling Adam. He wondered why he had borne with the text for so many days. He wanted to destroy it, but had a strange fear of doing so. The pretty commandment contained a truth. Seek perfection. And had he not always sought it?

He thought again of Tansy and went to the window. As far as he could see the road was empty. The mist surged slowly up to the window and clouded the glass. It was very close. He opened the window, but the mist drove eagerly into the room. He closed the window, but finding the room unbearably hot, took off his clothes and put on pyjamas and a black silk dressing-gown. The cool clothes refreshed him. He stirred the smoky fire to life, and stretched his legs easily as the flames spluttered out.

There was a scratching at the door and he rose to admit a little black cat. Chailey loved cats.

"Graymalkin," he murmured, "come and be caressed."

The cat purred amiably and arched her back. Chailey suddenly swooped down upon her and lifted her in the air by one of her front paws. With his other hand he traced a lingering line down the knobbles of her spine, inclining his head to the cat's, and whispering in her ear. She cried in pain and he swung her over the flames. For a second his eyes fell till they seemed to meet in a concentrated blaze of energy pressed down over his long nose. The flames cackled and singed the cat's fur. Chailey's fiery hair fell over his eyes. He was blind, because in his head a firmament of colour toiled in a dazzling attempt at design. But the design would never make itself clear . . .

He took the cat and caught her in an extravagance of affection to his breast. But she was frightened and tried to struggle away, biting and clawing at him. He would not let her go. "You who I love so, Graymalkin," he murmured, "to think the lovely fire nearly ate you up!" And as he soothed her with his voice and with his hands, she became easier, began again to purr and dug her claws happily into his shoulder.

The front door bell rang and he dropped the cat and ran downstairs. Tansy stood in the doorway, her clothes shimmering like gossamer in the clinging mist. He drew her in, closed the door with a bang and kissed her.

"Why are you so late?" His voice was a harsh complaint. Before she could answer he led her quickly upstairs and closed the door. He took off her hat and wet coat and made her sit by the fire. Kneeling at her feet he took off her shoes.

"You are too late," he said. "Where have you been?" He held her foot as he had held it a few days ago by the stream. Tansy observed the room in a half-dream. She was out of breath through running, and could not clearly realize her surroundings. The fire penetrated to her body. The chair was deep and easy, and she was conscious of his fingers smoothing over and over her foot. These things were like wine in her senses, so that she found it hard to speak.

Chailey leant over the chair, when she did not answer him,

and looked into her eyes, so that she saw deep down into the mobile depths of his pupils and felt in her own eyes the blue pool quicken to life as if disturbed by a little gust of wind. She gasped into speech.

"I—had to go to Penzance. It was the only excuse I could make to get out. Why did I have to come?"

He laughed. "You could have stayed away had you wished," he said. "You could easily have broken your word."

He took off her stockings, his hand grasping her leg very firmly. Her head reasoned with her heart, and she wanted to protest, but the warm motion of his hand stole her resistance away. Into that caressing of her white leg by the fire he concentrated all the charmed power of which he was capable, so that through his fingers his mind came in old conquest to her mind and the lovely certainty of her womanhood flowed richly through her veins. She lay back in the chair in a stupor, bemused by his touch, the singing stillness of his voice and the considered approval of the purring cat.

"Tansy, before the light goes I must make a quick drawing of you." He spoke with quiet finality, and rising, walked over to the window. "I don't suppose I shall see you again after to-day."

She did not reply. Gazing into the fire she saw a creeping flame hiss and curl under the coals.

"I must draw you at once," continued Chailey. "Will you take your clothes off, and stand with your back towards me, by the fire?"

She started to life.

"I couldn't do that," she said.

"But why——?"

"I—couldn't——" was all she could say.

"You're afraid of the wolf," he taunted. Suddenly she remembered yesterday with Arthur.

"I couldn't do it for anybody but you," she said.

"Of course not," replied Chailey impatiently. "Hurry. The light is going."

She undressed and stood before the fire.

"Why do you want my back to you?" she asked.

"I can remember your face," he said. "It is your back that I do not know."

He began to draw rapidly. Tansy neither moved nor spoke. Now that she was with Chailey in his place of shadows, she thought of Arthur, naked and glorious in the sunlight. Arthur. . . . She could have cried. For this room was hateful to her—her whole being hateful to her. She did not regret coming here, for it was done and nothing could alter it. She did not love Chailey then. But most vitally was she aware of him. And in the darkening room, while she balanced these two men in her mind, Chailey suddenly threw down his pencil, came over to her and dropped his hands like two cords over her breasts. He kissed the back of her neck and put his tongue on the stubbly hairs. She could do nothing but catch his hands and press them into her breasts, because from his fingers little ripples of dim sensuous ecstasy ran down her body, and the ripples grew to waves so that she was devoured and lost in a creeping sea of desire. Then he caught her back in his arms, swayed her over till her back arched over his elbow and her head swung in a loose surrender below his half-open mouth. She rested her body entirely on his arm, her feet on tip-toe, her arms hanging limp down beside her. She saw his head come closer, his mouth open wider, his eyes grow into a pin-point of light.

Then suddenly she was horribly afraid, and breaking away from him, hid her face in her hands. He made no attempt to recapture her; only laughed mockingly and went over to look at his picture.

"I have finished," he said. "That is—all I can do. I shall never have finished. But it will remind me."

She recovered her control, wondering why she had been frightened, and began to put on her clothes. Chailey threw her his dressing-gown.

"Take this," he said. "You'll be cooler and I'm too hot already."

She put on the gown and revelled in the smoothness of it against her skin. Then she looked at his sketch. It was a delicate suggestion of her body.

"I don't think it's much of a picture at all," she said.

"It doesn't matter what you think. You didn't come here to be painted."

"What did I come for, then?"

"Oh come—Tansy! Don't provoke me with idle questions. Would you like some tea?"

"Shouldn't care."

"I'll get the things. We can boil the kettle here on the fire."

He walked to the door. Tansy stopped him, speaking anxiously. "There's nobody in the house——" she stammered.

"Nobody." He smiled at her. "We are—alone and unobserved for at least the next two hours."

"I can't stay long. Y'see—mother's ill——"

He came over and took her hands in his.

"Tansy," he said, and his voice was honey-sweet, "whenever we are together you weary me by talking of leaving. Please do not say any more about it. Time is what you make it. We have two hours together in this queer warm room, which is a sanctuary from the misty world outside. Two hours! And you would put an invalid mother between us!"

He laughed carelessly, and she had to smile. She played with the buttons of his jacket, suddenly realizing that he was not properly dressed. She touched his chest lightly. He was warm and red in the firelight, his body so near to her, so supple and smooth under the silk clothes that she wanted to run her hands along him and find the secret of his desire. She smelt his faint sweat and the cool purity of his clothes. But he would only smile at her.

"Why aren't you dressed proper to receive a lady?" she asked.

"Surely," he replied, "surely this is the only way to receive a lady when one is about to—oblige a lady?"

He laughed again and went out of the room. Tansy stood with a puzzled expression on her face, then she looked again at his drawing of her. It was like any other girl, she thought. How shouldn't it be when her face was turned away? She looked at the other pictures about the room. The Donatello and the Michael Angelo. She was revolted by the bulging muscles of man in God's image, but thrilled by the poised valour of David. The pictures did not shock her as they would have shocked her father or brothers. Vaguely she was aware that this was art, that they treated such things very seriously, not in the sniggering way Joe might treat them. She sat down before the fire and noticing the portfolio behind the chair, she took it up and began to look at the pictures. But she closed it quickly, not liking something she had seen. Yet the desire to open it again was very strong in her, and while she was fighting it in her mind, she did not realize that Chailey had come in and was standing behind her chair.

Suddenly he snatched the portfolio out of her hand and spoke furiously to her.

"Why do you poke your foolish head into something not meant for you?"

He put the portfolio away in the cupboard, and stood over her, his face white with anger.

"I—I'm sorry——" she stammered. But the hazy memory of what she had seen preyed on her mind. "I—saw something——" she halted through her words; "something I didn't like——"

"There are many things you would neither like nor understand," he stormed at her. "In such cases you should avoid them."

Tansy got back her courage, because when he was angry he was also, she thought, slightly ridiculous.

"Well," she said. "You shouldn't leave your pictures where people can find them if you don't want them looked at. Don't go talking to me like a schoolgirl. I'm not."

"My God, you're not!" he cried. "You're certainly not!"

"Then don't treat me like one," she retorted.

"Have I done so?" he asked her. And then he sighed. "Tansy—Tansy—you make things so easy for me——"

He went to the door and came back with a tray of tea-things.

"What d'you mean?" she grumbled. "You're always speaking riddles to me, and I'm tired of it."

He pushed the kettle down on the fire and sat on the floor. "You're not a schoolgirl," he said. "You should be able to interpret riddles."

The firelight played on his hair and flickered in his face. Tansy did not try to parry words with him any more. The kettle began to sing, the mist pressed closer outside, and the fire sent their two shadows, a dark prophecy up the wall. Chailey looked at her gravely.

"You are lovely in the firelight," he said. "I am glad to have seen you in the firelight. Why are you so elusive and shadowy a beauty? The fire makes of you a chameleon, never the same for two minutes. When I look at one loveliness I am missing the next. There's nothing I can keep——"

"You can remember——" she said.

"Yes, but memory's an artful trickster. I shall perhaps remember you when you are solemn and still, forget you when you are angry and full of movement."

"I should've thought you'd want to forget that."

"No, because it's another you—a just as perfect Tansy. I shall never bear all this in my mind. I shall have only the vaguest picture of your lovely body in my mind. That is why I drew you as I saw you, with your back to me. I could not draw your eyes, Tansy. They keep something back from me . . . there is a barrier somewhere. Something that looks out of you and is—half afraid. Tansy, why are you afraid?"

"Sometimes," she said in a low voice, "you're like two persons."

"Am I?" He smiled and poured some water into the teapot.

"Yes," she continued. "I—hate you sometimes. But—y'see, I have to come. I've got to come. I reckon you've got hold of me somewhere. It's like a sickness. I came back with Arthur last evening. He'd been swimming. And I saw you standing in the distance by the stream. It was like as if the whole valley was you and nothing else. I can't—speak it in words. But I knew I'd have to come."

He poured out some tea as he spoke to her.

"Who is Arthur?" he asked.

"I'm going to marry him——"

"Ah," Chailey sighed. She did not detect a note of relief in his tone.

"I been to Penzance to-day," she said, "ordering things for the house when we're married——" She stopped, her heart beating heavily. "I don't love him!" she cried. "Can't ever love him proper——"

"You do love him," he said in a level voice. "You were made for him. When you look at me, I know that."

"But I don't—I don't! It's you all the time. When he touch me, I think of how you touch me. When he kiss me, I want to scream. Yesterday, coming back with him and seeing you standing there alone, I could have cried to think 'twas Arthur by me and not you."

"I was waiting for you," he said quietly.

"I knew you were. And I couldn't come. It was awful."

"But nevertheless," Chailey drove the words at her, "you're frightened of me." His eyes were narrow and predaceous. Tansy drew away from him half-instinctively.

"Sometimes—I think you are a devil——" she muttered.

"Often I know you are," laughed Chailey. "A cunning little bitch of a devil! Oh, yes, you know you are too. Here, have some tea. It'll go cold."

She drank the tea lifelessly. He took his cup and swung up and down the room in a restless mood. At the window he paused and looked out. "How mournful the trees are," he said, "like phantoms in this driving mist. Why do we burn coal?" He came over and kicked the fire, then picked up the cat, stroking it languidly. "Graymalkin, why do we burn coal—so unexciting and dead a substance? Isn't this a heavenly creature?" He held the cat over Tansy. "She loves fire, you know." A troubled shadow passed over his face. He opened the door and put the cat outside.

"Why do you do that?" asked Tansy.

"Because fire is bad for her," he replied mournfully. "I wish we had some wood logs here, something that would burn fiercely instead of this mutinous black coal. I wish we had a log to crackle and splutter its rage at us. Logs are like limbs. So much more beautiful than the trees. And limbs so much lovelier than the entire body. The human form is too much." He went on speaking rapidly with half-closed eyes. "The human form is too much as an entity. It comprises too much beauty. I am a lover of detail. A landscape presses on your vision, doesn't it? You are incapable of comprehending all it has to show you. But the flower in the landscape, the branch on the tree, the leaf on the branch—these are small beauties which we can grasp and take away if need be. The human form is like that. When I look at you, you are too great a beauty for me to hold. I miss the detail in the entity. But your ear, your foot, your yielding mouth—these things——"

He broke off and put his hands to his eyes as though to escape an ugly picture.

"No, no," he moaned like a child, "I—can't——"

He sat down on the bed and drummed his hands on his forehead. Tansy, bewildered, came over to him and placed a hand on his head. "You make yourself miserable," she whispered. "I don't understand half of what you do say, but I know you make yourself miserable."

His mood changed and he drew her down on the bed, encircling her waist with his arm.

"Why do we waste these lovely precious minutes?" he said, "when so soon it'll all be gone and there'll be nothing but memory to come and mock at us."

He kissed her impatiently and drew her close to him. She stole her arm through the jacket to his bare chest; the tips of her fingers paused on his skin. Under those small cushions he felt his flesh tingle, so that he knew he could not now resist her, even if he tried.

"We have got to go to the end," he said.

And even then the small struggling voice of her soul said, "No. Leave it—where 'tis——"

But the words faltered unconvincingly from her lips, and he did not attempt to argue with her. Silently, swiftly, he laid her down on the bed. A great ribbon of flame sent a shuddering light up to the ceiling. Chailey bent over Tansy's recumbent figure and laid his hands along her shoulders. She did not speak, for she knew now that this moment was the annihilation of all time. The engine of her body was driven to its purpose by a pilot who would not listen to the directions of her mind. She was in a dark low world of energy, as reasonless as the moving sea. The libidinous eyes of Chailey consumed her; his hands found every soft harbour in her compliant body. What was a spoken shame became for her an unspoken glory. And driven on past her shame she became a fury of appetency. A desperate bloody warfare possessed her, so that the centre of her being throbbed with an agony which drove her to forage blindly for what he yielded to her.

The firelight distorted the shapes of their striving figures until they were like a coiled malignant energy. Their massive heads on the wall welded deep together, pressing down and down, merging into one towering cloud of gibbous blackness as the flame hissed in the fire. They had lost knowledge of themselves—were vitally charged with the implacable purpose of life. They strove with something older than themselves, something as undying as the granite of the coasts. And until it was fulfilled—until the cumulative spark of their bodies could generate to breaking point—they could not speak, could not think. That moment came, and with it the lambent tongue of the flame in the dying fire flickered out and left a sinking redness in the grate. The room grew darker and the mist pressed against the window like the foreboding breath of a dumb ghost.

So, without any tenderness, driven only by the relentless urge of the body, did Tansy become a woman in the land of shadows. And lying back on the bed, a white immolation in the darkness, her mind flickered in wild sagas of fantasy. While the clock ticked the seconds away and the fire sank to a fevered eye, she lay there in silence.

Chailey rose and moved over to the wardrobe. She saw him take some clothes and was aware that he was dressing. Still she lay silent, augmenting the vision which mounted up her mind into a tangible shape. She heard Chailey's voice.

"Tansy—I'm sorry——" He stretched his arms out and dropped them to his side.

"You're not sorry," she said. "Why do you say so? You got me here for that."

"You wanted it, too," he reminded her.

"Yes, I reckon I did," she muttered. "Women are born fools."

The vision burst clear before her. She saw the lustrous metallic figure of the winged Saint, his sad eyes a rebuke to her. She felt herself rising as one out of a deep, corrupt water—rising and gasping for breath, yet knowing she would never stand on firm land. Something would always drag her down. And the graven Saint would not raise a finger to succour her. She stretched out a hand to touch him, and felt his breast. Then she cried and sprang up.

Chailey stood before her, calm and oracular.

"Why do you have a face like a saint?" she cried at him. "Oh, my God! How do you deceive me a second time? Oh, why did

I ever come here——" she moaned in distress. Chailey tried to comfort her, but the touch of his hand sickened her now. With a sudden impulse she ran over to the easel by the window. Before Chailey could stop her she had torn the drawing to pieces. He caught her wrists furiously; held her thus as the drawing fluttered in pieces to the ground.

"You had me," she shouted, "you shan't have the mock of me you made——"

She struggled and bit his hands, and with the sudden pain he released her. She dragged on her clothes carelessly, took her coat and wrapped it round her. He stopped her by the door, his anger gone, for he was overcome with sadness that they should part in this manner.

"Tansy—Tansy! Oh, my dear—this is our last time. I go away on Saturday, you see——"

Even then the words were like a judgment upon her. She shook her head stupidly. "Away——" she echoed.

He began to reason with her.

"What I have done, Tansy—what we have done—we couldn't help. Life used us. Don't you see it as something lovely, inevitable, without which we might as well never have met? You had courage; you weren't niggardly. Are you going to be niggardly now?"

"Oh, I can't—I can't!" Tears broke through her eyes. "You've done things—said things as I'll never forget. It isn't your having me, it isn't that. I asked for it. You wouldn't have been a man if you'd behaved different. No, it isn't that. It's just—you—you—I can't tell, can't explain proper. Something—no, you better leave me go now. When you look at me like that it break my heart. You'd better go, go quick away from here and never come back. I've had your body and I'll never have anyone else the same. But you'd better go——"

"Tansy—why do these things happen?" She softened towards him and stroked his hair, knowing that it was for the last time.

"You've been so beautiful to me," she whispered, "so bright and burning like an angel. I'm glad you're going away soon and we won't ever meet again. It's better like that. I could never be with you for always. But when you weep like a baby and speak soft to me, it's hard to leave you."

"Why did you destroy the picture—the only thing I had to remind me of you?"

She opened the door. The passage and stairs were dark and very cold. She shivered. "I can't tell you that," she said. "But I wish you might never draw again."

They walked slowly downstairs to the door. In the mist they stood silently looking at each other, afraid to hear their voices. The invading desolation of the mist and the heavy countryside filled Tansy with despair. She saw a young sparrow with a broken wing moving painfully along the grass.

"Look!" she said. "Poor thing!"

Chailey's eyes misted with a tenderness she had rarely seen in him. He picked up the bird most gently and, with the subtle medicine of his fingers, caressed the vainly fluttering body.

"Where's the nest?" he asked. But they could not find it.

"What shall you do with it?" she said. He folded it carefully in his handkerchief.

"I think I can put it right," he said quietly. "I used to love mending birds' wings when I was a boy. Not many people know how to do it."

She touched his arm.

"I'm glad," she whispered, "glad to see you for the last time just like this. You're different now."

And for a moment she looked at him, engraving for ever on her mind the picture of his careless body, his loose arms, his grave face. Then she turned and went away. She did not once look back, although Chailey stood there for many minutes till she was lost to his sight.

She walked quickly along the valley in the clammy evening, meeting nobody on her way. Her body was spent, yet new and springing to life. She turned up the hill towards the farm, and, seeing lights, knew it was her home. Like an impelled figure in a mime she drew nearer the farm. The lights dazzled her. She wondered why they were so powerful. It was not yet dark, although the mist made it difficult to see far ahead. The glaring lights blazed into the mist.

Then she knew they were the lights of a car. With immediate apperception she knew it was the doctor's car.

CHAPTER IX

SHE found Joe in the kitchen. His face was white; his eyes staring out of him. Upstairs she heard low voices.

"The doctor, Joe——" She hesitated, dreading his words.

"Mother's awful bad," he muttered, "awful bad. Crying out something dreadful. Made me fair sick to hear it, I can tell you."

Tansy bit her lip and sat down on the bench beside Joe. She spoke in subdued agitation.

"Tell me, Joe. What happened, then?"

"She got took with a pain and began to groan up there. Aunt Janet wasn't with her, but she went up quick and come down white as a sheet. Never seen the like in her before. 'Go for a doctor, quick,' she says. And Andrew gets his bicycle and tears up to town like mad. Then she get worse, see—start to cry out some awful. Poor soul too——"

"Have you seen her?" asked Tansy.

"No. Aunt Janet wouldn't have me up there. My gosh, it's been some awful sitting here doing nothing!"

"How long's the doctor been?"

"About half an hour. I don't know what he done to her. Tansy, d'you think she's going to——"

Tansy interrupted him. "No, I don't."

Through her blurred eyes she saw her mother's long grey face distorted with the triumph of pain. And another face, the cold face of the Saint, spread like a cloud over the fair sun of the spring. There was no more sun. It was a judgment. It was a judgment. This graven Saint, who could have guarded her chastity, had sent a devil to deliver judgment upon her. The devil would cling, would drag her down, down, back into those dark waters. All her life this devil, the shame, would stay. A week ago had been the pure spring, but now the mists drove their sorrows upon the sea like a team of hopeless old horses. Yet she must always love her lover because he had sent her body upon a new course, had charged her with a new and terrible energy which she had never possessed before. Because his life had moved with hers he could never depart from her. The shape of this—yes, he had said that—would always remain. And her mother, with eyes of knowledge, would look at her and go up the hill to the graveyard. That solemn loveliness, her quiet mother, suffering to death. . . .

Tansy cried aloud. "Oh, she can't die! She can't!" Then her adaptable mind began to twist this matter into a more sympathetic logic. She had done nothing after all, she told herself; no more than a thousand others might do. It was the man's fault. It always was. He had driven her on. Now that he was going and she would never see him again, she could turn to Arthur and build, slowly and industriously, a certain sanctuary for her fugitive soul. In quietness she could go forward, killing the shame in resignation to the life that was really hers. Quietness would come. The lovely earth would mould itself closer around her, giving her greater depth and strength. Keeping a watch upon her soul she would reach a day when, as an old woman, a mother like her mother, she could look back to this madness, seeing it in retrospect as nothing more than a childish extravagance expunged by the slow toil of time. Suddenly she knew she was a woman. She had done with all that nonsense of girlhood now. She was back with the Good Shepherd on the wall. This house, these fields and moors, the unyielding stones of the seashores—these were a heritage passed secure into her soul at birth. And she must rest now upon a rock.

She began to talk with a lightness that amazed Joe, who having most capably donned the threadbare garments of woe, was outraged that anybody should attempt to tear them off him.

"She's going to be all right," said Tansy. "Something tells me that."

"You wouldn't say that if you'd heard her crying out." Joe shook his head mournfully, rocking his body in old grief.

They heard the others come down, and Tansy went into the living-room. First came the little rubicund doctor with Aunt Janet. Then Nicolas, who looked dazed. Then Andrew, black as a sage of lamentation. Tansy ran up to the doctor.

"What is it?" she blurted out to him. "Is she——"

"Don't worry." He held up a fubsy hand. "You must all keep quite calm. She wants absolute rest and quietness."

"But this pain," insisted Tansy. "What do it mean at all?"

The doctor hesitated. Then, "A small tumour," he said quickly, avoiding Tansy's eyes. "Her heart is a little uncertain, you see. And her mind seems to wander a little. That's to be expected, of course. I've given her something to encourage sleep and ease the pain. You mustn't worry."

"You think she'll be all right?"

"Oh, yes. Oh, dear me, yes! No reason for alarm yet awhile. But, of course, she is very ill. You see——" He wandered into pathological avenues where Tansy did not follow him. Then he went to the door, followed by Aunt Janet and Nicolas, who walked like a forlorn dog in an unpleasant foreign country. At the car they all three stopped and looked at one another. Janet plunged straight at the doctor.

"Tell us the real truth," she demanded savagely.

The doctor fretted and played with his watch-chain.

"Most unfortunate," he muttered. "All these years of suffering and never a doctor——"

"She never told us, doctor." Nicolas shuffled on his feet, uneasy at the implication. "She were always a quiet one was mother—not given to complaining——"

Janet interrupted impatiently: "Is she going to die or not? You've seen that breast of hers. If you can't make up your mind on that, you're more of a chemist than a doctor. Out with what you know!"

Janet was tormented by the memory of a black corroded breast that Emmeline in anguish had revealed to her. For years she had hidden this rotting menace, would never let Nicolas see the mark of her corruption. Janet saw that grey face shuddering in loneliness over her black breast, and her eyes were full of tears. But she would have the truth from the doctor.

"A cancer of the breast," he said harshly. "She can't last long."

"Ah!" Janet sighed with something near to relief. "You won't operate on her then?"

"No; I daren't," he replied. "You see, it's attacking her heart.

She may linger for some months. I can't say with any certainty. I can only tell you she is a dying woman——"

"Doctor," mumbled Nicolas, "aren't there nothing? I thought as how there'd be something you chaps could do for her."

"We're up against something too big here. But I'll willingly get other advice if you wish it. A doctor never knows for certain. The body is beyond us in the long run. But I fear another would bear me out."

"Is she going to suffer much?" asked Janet.

"I'll do what I can for that. She'll have to be tended night and day. If she pulls through this crisis she might hang on for longer than we think. You never know. She's got something on her mind, you know. If you could find out what it is, it would be a good thing."

Nicolas walked up and down by the stone hedge, muttering to himself and biting his nails.

"I can't tell the children," he moaned. "I daren't tell the children." He came up to the car, his anxious eyes blinking in the headlights.

"Doctor," he pleaded, "can't us pretend that she's going to live? If the children know they'll be that sad so's she'll never hear them laugh no more. I reckon she do get worse when folks are quiet and the house wisht. If the children behave natural, 'twill make things easier for her."

"Yes, you're right," replied the doctor. "But she mustn't be disturbed. As long as she sleeps let her sleep."

He shook Nicolas by the hand. "Come, cheer up," he said. "While there's life, you know——" He shook hands with Janet, and with a petulant sigh drove away.

Janet clapped Nicolas on the back. "My gosh!" she cried. "What's the good you suggesting the children behave natural when you're going about yourself with a face worse than a thunderstorm? Pull yourself together, else we'll all be sobbing on each other's shoulders!"

"Why, that's right, Janet—that's right," he said. "I don't believe—she aren't going to die at all, you!"

He laughed idiotically. Janet stared at him, then hugged him suddenly to her great breast.

"Poor Nicolas," she whispered. "Poor old chap!"

And slowly they walked back into the house.

The two boys were sitting morosely by the fire. Tansy stood looking at the picture of the Good Shepherd, inconsequently wondering what she would do if somebody, dressed like this, knocked at her door in the dead of night.

They all three turned inquiring eyes upon Janet as she came in, and sensing the ominous cloud that hung over the house threatening to shadow them in its darkness, she began to chastise them into movement. She realized that if the children were to remain in ignorance of Emmeline's hopeless condition, she and Nicolas must continually keep a guard upon themselves. So she began to chide the family, kindling their tempers, and thus stirring them to more normal activity.

"What's the sense in all standing around like a lot of crows on a roof?" she demanded. "Tansy, you get us some supper."

"I can't eat," said Andrew with woeful arrogance.

"Oh, can't you?" snapped Janet. "You'll eat well enough when she's dead and buried, I suppose? Have a feast here for her funeral——"

They protested, and Tansy got very angry.

"How can you go on like that?" she cried.

"You ought to be ashamed," growled Andrew. Joe snuffled, and Nicolas looked into the fire.

Janet turned on them all savagely.

"Ashamed! Yes; I should think so. But it's darn well true, and you know it. So long as she's sick you'll drive her body to the grave with your long fiddle-faces. Then when she's gone you'll sing hymns of joy to the Good Lord for taking her, and eat pasties on the strength of it. Oh, I do know how you country folk love a funeral and a bit of black crape"—she looked warningly at Nicolas, gratified to see that even he was moved to his old indignation at the scathing reference to rural manners. "I know how you love to wail and have streamers on your hats if they hadn't gone out of fashion. Plumes on the horses if you was London folk—up there they do do things different. If they want a wail they engage a proper choir to do it for them——"

To her intense relief, for the astonishing flight of her imagination was beginning to flag, Andrew interrupted her with a cry of rage.

"You're too bad," he shouted, his eyes thick with anger. "I call you too bad——" He could not say any more. His furious voice echoed to silence in the house.

Janet, almost unnerved by their white, strained faces, pressed her real feelings down, and went on at them.

"Yes, I am too bad, no doubt," she snarled at Andrew. "But this much I know. I don't shout the roof off when there's a sick woman in the house. And now I'm going up to see to her. Tansy, if you don't have some supper on the table time I come down, you'll not hear the end of my tongue for a week. I'm hungry, if nobody else is." But as she went upstairs, she wondered how she would force herself to eat.

Tansy got supper then and they began to move about, all doing useless little tasks, all getting in one another's way and saying "Sorry," but moving, living and being. The cloud over the house began to break up. When Janet came down, she laughed to see the loaf, the butter and the tea on the table.

"That's a better sight," she said. "Come on, sit down. Give me a cup of tea—darnee, child! I said tea, not pea! Tip the pot back and give me a cup as I can't see my face through. I've got something to say, but I'm darned if I'll say it till I've got my belly full, for I'm rawnish as an old shag on a whale's back!"

She crammed bread and butter in her mouth, forcing it down upon a broken belch. Joe laughed, then remembering, drowned it in his cup. Grief was being organized. But they were all keen to hear what Janet had to say, and even Nicolas half believed that she concealed good news.

Not until she had finished eating and had wiped her hands down her dress, did she lean forward over the table, and deliver herself of the following oracular statement. "Emmeline won't get to Heaven this side of Christmas. No." She licked her lips, cocking her head on one side like a showman with a freak in a booth.

"You mean she's going to get well?" said Tansy.

"Yes, I do mean that."

"But the doctor," said Andrew irritably. "He didn't seem——Then her mind all funny, wandering like——"

"Doctors are born Jeremiads," retorted Janet defiantly. "And this one, more so than most. Mind you, Emmeline's ill, there's no sense in getting away from that. The doctor spoke careful, not wishing to raise your spirits too much, and that's fact. But outside just now—you'll never believe me, think I'm all gab. Nicolas, you tell them. They'll listen to you more than to me, though Lord knows why!"

Nicolas gaped fearfully, then dashed into lies.

"Oh, yes! Janet's right. Proper cheerful he was. Wondered why we was making such a fuss. 'She ill?' he said, seeming scornful. 'Ill? I've seen invalids beside which she was a——'"

He could not find a word. Janet hurriedly carried on before he should ruin it in extravagance of optimism.

—"'besides which she was a big bass drum.' His very words!" she recounted magnificently. "'I've seen invalids beside which she was a big bass drum.' Though what he meant by that," she conditioned the remark quickly, "I don't know as I can rightly say. His way of saying she was going to get well in no time, I suppose. Big bass drum——" She forgot the situation and began to play with pleasing phrases in her old irrelevant manner. They were held by her powerful voice. "Anyhow, be that as it may. He went on to say that if we were all moping round the house she'd sure as nuts start moping round the bed, and that won't ever do. Business as usual, as my poor Herbert stuck up over the shop when the roof fell in on everything but the mustard. That's just where it's to! And that's why I spoke rough to you, feeling happy inside and mad to see you all looking like corpses when there's no need for it."

The door opened and Arthur came in.

"Just back from the mine," he panted, "and hearing how Mrs. Penderil was took bad, thought I'd cycle over to know how she fared."

He guessed from their faces that she could not be seriously ill.

"That's kind of you, Arthur," said Tansy. "Mother's been some bad."

"She's better now, then?"

"A sight better," nodded Janet.

"So Aunt say," observed Andrew incredulously. He would not believe it. From the moment he had seen her in church that day, he had had a conviction that she would not live long; that she would never smile on him again, and that he would for ever have to his credit the fact that he had been the one to put her to bed. It was not a selfish thought. It was simply that Andrew had an inherent sense of drama and would not be deprived of this inevitable curtain.

"So Aunt say," he repeated, and lighting a cigarette blew out the smoke with the air of an obstinate god implacable before the sacrifice of a calf.

"And so Aunt mean!" snapped Janet. "Sit down and have some supper, Arthur. I've told them all we've got to cheer up Emmeline and not go about with long faces. So if I see you looking glum I shall pull your trousers down and behave difficult!"

It was her last valiant effort. She sat back as they began to talk spontaneously. Slowly the conversation spread over the supper table as the old habit of forgetting Emmeline's existence took control of them. Even Nicolas, deep in an account of old John Stone, who had that day handed him over forty pounds for his ground, might momentarily have forgotten what lay upstairs. They did not heed Janet as she rose and left the room. Away from the idle babble, she felt a weaker and older woman. Standing by Emmeline's sleeping form, she thought she might almost be dead for all they really cared about her. A human being going . . . less than a flower beaten by a gale. It's only when she screams in pain, she muttered bitterly, that they know she's alive at all. She put her hand to Emmeline's lips and felt the faint moisture of her waning life. Janet decided she would sleep on the sofa at the foot of the bed. It was yet early, but she longed for a sleep as deep as her sister's. She found blankets, some cushions, and arranged them on the sofa. She put the table with the low lamp upon it by the sofa, then taking off her skirt and blouse, huddled up in massive discomfort under the blankets. But sleep would not come. She heard the sounds of a day ending. The rattle of the gate, which meant that Arthur had gone. The laboured tolling of the clock in the kitchen. The sliding of the bolt in the back door.

Somebody opened the door cautiously. It was Nicolas. She called him over to her softly.

"I'm not asleep, Nicky."

He chided her for lying on the hard sofa. "We can make up a bed for you downstairs, and I can sleep here."

"No, no. You'd much better leave me. I'm more able—in case of any trouble."

He stood silently by Emmeline's bed.

"You go on," urged Janet. "Go on, old Nicky, and have one of the boys' beds. They can manage together. I'll keep my eye on her, don't you worry."

Still he did not move.

"It don't seem right, do it?" he muttered. "Her there like that and us trying for to laugh down below. You made me forget her myself for awhile."

"Yes, I know," she said. "It's a way we both have, Emmeline and me, of making folks forget us."

He looked at her queerly.

"Go along," she said. "God bless you, old chap—though whether His blessing's worth having I'm darned if I know."

He went out slowly and closed the door. Janet was left with sleep as an enemy. When dawn came, still white with mist, and the first birds began to sing joyously outside, Janet got up gladly and stretched her aching body. She was prepared for a day of wearisome deception. When she met the others, she behaved much as she had the night before; stemmed the dangerous current of their thoughts with the heavy dam of her conversation.

Emmeline remained asleep. In the forenoon the doctor came, stood by her bedside and clicked his tongue as one who would say: "I thought as much." He went away assuring the children that she was no worse than he had expected.

Then, about mid-day, Emmeline slowly opened her eyes like a child seeing the world for the first time and finding it very strange. She roved her eyes round the room till she found Janet. She did not know her. She struggled with a word. "Black——" she whispered. "Black——" and seemed to be able to say no more.

Nicolas and the others came to see her, but she only looked at them all with mournful, wondering eyes. Random sentences came from her lips. Once she asked if the men had come yet. Again she thought Joe was Arthur and implored him to take care of Tansy. She seemed to want food, but ate little when the first taste of anything entered her mouth. She seemed to suffer no more pain.

In this way, the day wore on like a year, the humid mist killing the sense of time, so that Janet never knew when afternoon ended and evening began. Then as the room got darker and the clock struck seven, the mist slowly thinned out over the sea and the pure lines of the sun appeared. With no perceptible movement the sky cast off its white shroud and the faded bedroom merged into the dim warmth of the sun. It was then, as the sun turned through mist into the sea, that Emmeline murmured the word "Tansy".

Janet went to her. "Tansy?"

"Yes. Tansy." The two sisters looked at one another. There was a sudden gleam of recognition in Emmeline's eyes.

"Is it you then, Janet?"

"Yes, dear, it's me. Sister Janet. Silly sister Janet."

"I want Tansy."

"Yes, dear," said Janet. And calling Tansy upstairs, she left them alone, in a happier mood, going to rest a moment in Tansy's bedroom.

It was some minutes before Emmeline could say anything to Tansy, who knelt by her side, smoothing the moist hair away from her forehead. Then slowly Emmeline struggled into coherent sentences.

"I had a very bad turn, child. Terrible bad. I thought I was near done."

"Yes, mother," whispered Tansy, "but you aren't. You're feeling better now, aren't you? The doctor say you're not to worry at all, only keep quiet and you'll get well again."

"Tansy——" Emmeline seemed frightened of something.

"What, mother?"

"They're not going to take me away, are they? Not to any old hospital? I'd rather die—I'd sooner die in my own place."

"No, mother, you're to stay here. The doctor says you'll be all right. Only you're not to fret and worry."

"Yes——" She paused and moved her dry lips without speaking. Her eyes were like pitted stones in her head.

"Go down to the barrel," she said, "there's a dear, and see if you can get me a piece of ice. I'm some dry and famished for thirst. I wish I was by the sea."

Tansy could not say anything. Emmeline forgot her request and looked deep into Tansy's face. She clutched her hand.

"Tansy, you're the spit of me," she murmured. "Tell me, my dear, are you happy as you belong to be with your Arthur in your handsome little home?"

Emmeline clung to her and looked into her eyes.

"We're not married yet. Y'see, mother——" Tansy was overcome by the perplexed sorrow in her mother's face. "It's all settled," she hurried on, "but we'd best wait till you're well enough, I reckon."

She went on talking rapidly about the wedding, conscious that her mother was easier. "I went into town yesterday," she continued, "to look at some stair-carpet and such like. And there's a pretty suite of bedroom furniture going in Robinson's cheap as can be. I reckon we shall be well away."

"I don't want you to put the wedding off," said Emmeline. "It isn't right at all. I thought you was married all along. You'd best get it over soon, then I'll be happy, child, to know as you're happy. Not until. I wish they had a piece of ice down there. Ah, dearie me! And thrashing coming on so soon. Hast-a written about the machines yet?"

Tansy smiled sadly. "Yes, mother, we'll be having the men in soon." (And, after all, how near autumn was to spring.)

"Then you must come round and help for guldies," murmured Emmeline. "I'll be down then. Give me time. I'll be well soon enough, if the Lord spare me." Her eyes closed. "I don't want the light. Why is it so dark? Is it late, then?"

"After seven, mother."

"Ah, well, the long, dark evenings soon come, I fancy, quicker'n what they used to do. Where's Nicolas to?"

"He's downstairs, mother, I think."

"And Joe," she asked, "is he down there too?"

"Yes, mother."

"Ah!" she sighed more easily. "I don't like for him to go gadding about with his bits of fancies. He's a good lad, I do think, only easily swayed by them as aren't. Like you, child."

"Like me, mother?"

"Yes, like you I said. That's why I want you married before the wrong sort sway you." Tansy's mouth fell open and she closed her eyes.

"Does he rain, you?" asked Emmeline, turning her head towards the window.

"It's been damping," replied Tansy, "but clearing away now."

"Looking more to me——" Emmeline gave a great sigh and closed her eyes again.

Tansy heard a movement and looked to the door, surprised to see Janet standing in the passage, a silent, listening figure. She bent over her mother and kissed her on the forehead. "I'll leave you now, mother. Fancy you'll sleep." Emmeline did not reply and Tansy went outside, softly whispering to Janet in the passage: "I think she's going to sleep now."

They went into Tansy's room and Janet suddenly took Tansy by the shoulders and looked straight in her face. "It'll make the world of difference to poor Emmeline," she said firmly, "when you and Arthur are married. It's just on Emmeline's mind all the time. She's worrying to death about you——"

Tansy was angry and pushed her away. "As though I don't know as well as anybody," she muttered.

"It's no good getting mad with me," continued Janet. "Though you're pretty when you're cross, and God bless Arthur, I say, for he's a lucky one if ever was. But the sooner you're married the better for her. Don't put it off because she's ill. It may mean a lot."

"The way you speak," cried Tansy, "anybody'd think I wasn't ever going to marry Arthur at all. I tell you we'll get married just so soon as we can get the banns out and the house furnished. Week after next maybe. Don't take on at me about it."

"I'm glad," said Janet. "For Emmeline's right. You belong to be with your man before you get all withered up inside."

(Withered up . . . but she was like a rock inside—a rock for the rock of Arthur.)

Janet gazed out of the window where now the sky hung in tattered shreds of puce clouds. The sun, behind a cloud, flung dusty arms like a great windmill upon the sky. The sea was deep blue, so clear, that a boat moving near the peninsula looked as though it were floating in a still lake at the end of the valley. There was no wind. The last sighing eddies of the mist had been sent inland and were drifting over the moors. The scattered panoply of the sky was like Janet, full of crazy colour chucked together with no attempt at design. And as she looked out on it her heart was heavy. A thrush on the garden wall threw out his head with divine arrogance to summon an audience for his song. The fluid notes were the lucid complement to the quiet evening. And in that pitiless purity, defiant with the defiance of old truth, Janet heard the ending of her own songs, the beginning of another's.

"That darn bird," she muttered, "sing and sing year in and year out, making us all feel a hundred years older every time we hear him."

"It's a different bird each year," said Tansy.

"Yes, maybe, but it sing the same darn old song of love. It'll still be singing it when you and I are put to our graves. It don't care a tuppeny cuss about us, I fancy. It just goes on singing like— like a machine with a penny placed in the slot—just like that. It don't know about Emmeline and the sort of things that worry us to death. I reckon when its mother hatched it out, she said, 'Sing, drat you, and go on singing till you're dead, for that's all you're here for.'

"And the first of May to-morrow," she continued mournfully. "Time was when I should have gone to bed light-hearted knowing May-day was coming and ready to blow my May-horn like any old kid with a mad heart. But I don't care now. I don't care a darn."

"Oh, Aunt Janet, Aunt Janet," cried Tansy, "don't talk so, you who belong to be making us all laugh."

She put an arm round her shoulder and they stood with their faces pressed together, looking out of the window. The sun dropped from the cloud and in a rufous sheen revealed the youth of one, the age of the other. A great slow tear rolled down Janet's nose and, caught in the sun, sparkled like a little witch-ball. She did not try to wipe it away and another chased it to destruction.

Tansy kissed her cheek. The new certainty inside her, the strange quietness of her spirit refused to encompass despair. She heard the song of the thrush as the prophecy of summer, not as the epilogue to spring.

"Aunt Janet," she said. "That thrush know more about things than you or I do. You don't listen to it right."

"Maybe," snivelled Janet, "I don't know——"

"We'd better go and have supper," said Tansy. Janet heaved a sigh out of her bosom and smiled through her wet eyes.

"Tansy," she said, "you done me a heap of good. I thought you were a child, and I find you a grown woman with more than a woman's sense and understanding. Thankee, my dear. Don't you go telling them I was silly like that. Don't want them to—they think of me as a sort of film star or fancy woman with a lot of saucy gab, and 'twouldn't do to break the picture. But just seeing you near me—young and handsome and ready for your man, made me cry. Wasn't so much Emmeline as just seeing you there starting, and me just beginning to end, and wondering whether I've ever grabbed enough of life at all. With eyes like yours, my pretty, I shouldn't blame you for whatever you did. I couldn't blame you if you was a trolled-up whore, always provided you enjoyed yourself. No sense in fornication unless you enjoy it, that's what I say about everything as they call a sin. And once you know it's wrong you don't enjoy it no more, however much you try to pretend you do. You've got to keep it fresh, like when you started. But when you're sick of it and still go on—that's wickedness, that is. Then you're a fool——"

Tansy smiled. "Come on downstairs," she said. "They'll be wondering. And you mustn't be sad because I'm starting and you're not. I'll be an old woman before that thrush stops singing."

They went out and on the way quietly looked into Emmeline's room. The generous sun flung his last colour over her head. Tansy and Janet stayed there looking at her for a moment.

"Poor soul," whispered Janet. "How tired she must be."

CHAPTER X

Towards the end of May, on a day of bright sunshine, Tansy was married to Arthur Progis. During the three weeks of hurried preparation for the wedding, Emmeline lay upstairs in her bed, her body weakening, her mind growing stronger. With a defiant tenacity she clung to a life that no longer interested her. She talked increasingly, at first vaguely and with little reasoning, but later with understanding and even humour. The presaging vulture of blackness over her breast spread very slowly. She had moments of fierce pain, which by a supreme effort she contrived to conceal from all save Janet and occasionally Nicolas. Emmeline knew she would not live; had no desire to live, except to see Tansy married. The lively ramble of her mind sometimes made Janet think she might gain strength and recover. But the shattered temple of her body, the heavy swaying head, the eyes that day by day grew deeper like pools wherein the water was running dry—these things were too obvious a warning to be disregarded. In a few weeks Emmeline had become an old woman. Little remained alive in her save the mutinous spark of her mind; this she knew would burn to the last.

Meanwhile the house at Boscedjack was furnished and all preparations were made for the wedding. Tansy wanted to be married without any show, but Emmeline would not hear of that. She insisted on inviting a few carefully chosen guests. So they sent word to Nicolas' married brother, who had a farm at Trewarra, ten miles away. Emmeline's nephew, a dashing sailorman, was on leave at Plymouth, and he was asked. Then Emmeline had a strange whimsey and wanted to invite a lonely old woman called Jessie Vean, whom she had not seen for many years. Few ever saw Jessie nowadays, for she rarely went abroad from her air-tight retreat on the moors beyond Retallack, and if she did, she swathed herself with so many shawls and bodices that she could only breathe with difficulty. But Emmeline

remembered Jessie as a fine, mysterious young woman who had
told her and Janet many wisht stories when they were children,
and sung them sad wild songs that nobody else had ever heard
of. And she wanted Jessie to bring her a little ghost of those days.
So against the wishes of the men, who all disliked her caustic
tongue and her sinister eye, she was invited to the wedding.

The day dawned with a merry wind to keep the sunshine clear.
In the forenoon the house was busy with movement. Before ten,
the baker came with a large basket of coloured cakes and a dozen
hot loaves. Then the grocer came and stayed chatting by the door,
though nobody paid any attention to him. Joe rode to the town
on his bicycle and came back with three bottles of fine old Ruby
Port in a straw basket. Andrew had to take the barrel down to the
valley to get water. The usual customers called for milk and were
all a little teasy because they had not been asked to the wedding,
and considered it indecent that Tansy should be wedded, as they
said, almost over her mother's open grave. The men disturbed
the week-day peace of their fine clothes, and Tansy polished
boots till they geeked at her in dark corners. Janet ran up and
downstairs between Emmeline and an alarming heliotrope frock
she had hitherto concealed. John Stone wandered in with sapient
observations upon the price of tin; he was determined to get to
the wedding and the feast after, though nobody had asked him.
Nicolas moved everything that Tansy had put in its place, then
began a dilatory argument with Janet as to who should be left
to mind Emmeline while they were at the church. Janet said
she would stay; Nicolas swore that he would. Finally they left it
undecided. And while the house hummed with all this industry,
Emmeline smiled upstairs and made strange happy noises. It
pleased her to think that from a sick-bed she had set them all in
motion on this lovely summer day. And moreover, she looked
forward to seeing her sleek young nephew and Jessie with her
breath of dead days. A car was engaged to fetch her and would
come on to the farm with another, and take them all to church.
Emmeline had proposed this, for she knew that nothing would
induce Jessie to leave her cottage unless she were fetched.

At one o'clock, Nicolas' brother, Robert, smouldered up
to the farm in a staunch wreckage of an ancient car which he

had driven with the utmost care at five miles an hour. Janie, his tittering wife, tumbled out as grandly as she could and gave a triumphant glare to Nicolas, who greeted them effusively.

"How's the woman?" asked Robert perfunctorily. He had never cared for Emmeline.

"Getting on grand," replied Nicolas, wondering whether he had spoken the truth, because that morning Emmeline had seemed so bright.

Janie was poking about in the living-room, prodding the presents with her umbrella.

"My," she giggled as Tansy came in, "who'd-a thought as you'd ever get married? Now!"

Tansy hated Janie and made no pretence about it.

"I suppose there were a good many who wondered that you ever got married!" She walked coolly out of the room.

Janie glowered at her. "Little cat," she muttered, "just like her mother!"

A moment later Emmeline's nephew, Leonard Disher, roared up on his motor-bicycle. Brushing himself down, he strode up the path, sleek as a panther in his blue uniform. Leonard was unmarried, thirty-five years old, handsome and mad. He had run away to sea as a boy and had spent the rest of his life running into scrapes from which he always emerged with a wounded and slightly contemptuous air. He loved his two aunts, Janet and Emmeline, and they loved him.

Janet gave him a resounding kiss.

"Well, Jan, same as ever, I see." He grinned amiably. "Only about two stone further on!"

"Go on," she laughed. "You're none too lean yourself. Been feeding on the fatted calf, I suppose."

"Talk about fatted calf," he said, "you seem to have killed it here to-day all right. Emmeline can't be so very bad if she can stand this racket."

"You'll see her," said Janet, leading him into the house. Leonard greeted the others boisterously, then went upstairs with Janet. Emmeline had heard his loud voice and sat up in the bed, a heavy shawl round her shoulders. As they got to the door Janet whispered, "She's changed, Leonard, you'll see. Not the woman——" And for a second, as he stood at the foot of her bed, the expansive smile died on his lips, and his brow creased into anger. But he kissed her and smiled in her eyes. Janet went over to the window.

"Pretty," he said, leaning over her, his charming eyes reminding Emmeline that she had once been a girl. "Pretty——"

"Go on," she tittered, tapping him feebly on the chest. "Sit down and talk to me, you. Where've you been? What capers have you been up to? And what's so pretty that you can't take your stupid eyes off me?"

He sat down on the bed. "Your hair," he said, "that's pretty. And it's pretty to see you. And damme, you too, Janet. Come here, you old mountain, and let's look at you too!"

Janet sat on the other side of the bed and Leonard took each of their hands in his. One so small that he could hardly feel it; the other, fat and dewy, squeezing him affectionately. He looked at them both. "Damme!" he exclaimed, half laughing, yet somehow wanting to cry, "you're two good women! And that's more than I've ever said about any other female except one, and you know who that was."

"Sister Annie," said Emmeline in a low voice.

"Yes," echoed Leonard, "mother——"

Their sudden silence was broken by the sound of hollow tapping on the stairs, of uncertain hobbling footsteps. Emmeline stirred with excitement.

"That's Jessie, that is," she said, and a little dash of colour fired her cheeks. The door opened, and old Jessie Vean, a lean black figure, stood there as though she had really been there for ever, invisible, now suddenly become visible.

"I hate stairs," (and her cracked pipe of a voice was like a hollow minstrelsy from a windy hill.) "Hate them like poison I do. Never go upstairs at home, I don't."

Then she came on, pressing her head before her body, and trundling her stick in the middle of her passage as though she moved upon castors and depended upon the stick as a brake. Wheezing through her shawls, like old violin strings plucked to break, she came and stood by Emmeline.

"Well, Jessie——" began Emmeline. But she was unable to say

more because Jessie's glinting coals of eyes flickered upon too much that had died in the old picture album.

Jessie stood looking at Emmeline without a smile. Then, "You're not the woman you usually be." She turned upon Janet. "No more are you. No more are any of us. Growing old. And I do hate stairs, you. But if there's one thing I do hate more 'tis they steaming puffing great motor-cars. Inventions of the devil, so they are. And who's this? What's he a-doing of here?"

She poked her stick in Leonard's chest, who grinned at her. He very faintly remembered Jessie years ago, but his mother Annie had never tolerated her in their house, saying she was a witch.

"You don't remember me then?" he said. "But I remember you. I remember you singing songs which nobody ever heard before or since."

"I know you," she said sourly. "You're Annie's baby. You're that Leonard what ran away a-whoring."

"Oh, go on!" he said, a little crossly.

"Jessie," said Emmeline, "aren't you glad for to see me and Janet again?"

"Yes, I'm glad," she replied, with no change in her phlegmatic countenance. "I'm glad sure enough. It's nice to come in for a bit of curzing. But no weddun——" she exclaimed bitterly, "no weddun for me. I aren't a-going to go to no weddun! Don't believe in such trash!"

"Same as ever was," said Janet with a sniff. "Didn't approve of your own parents being married, I suppose."

"I never had no parents to speak of," complained Jessie. "I don't know that they went to no weddun at all. How should I be going to a weddun? I come here to see Emmeline and if they make me go to a weddun, I'll leave 'em know. Is it the boy that's getting married, you?"

"Don't be stupid," said Janet. "You know it's Tansy."

"Don't know nothing," she returned. "I 'as a letter. Couldn't read it proper without my glass, and I broke my glass in wrath one day reading one of these here newspapers what do tell about things up to London town."

"—a handsome place," observed Janet sententiously. "A pretty place. Some happenings there——"

"I got fair sick of looking at pictures of women with no backs to 'em," continued Jessie. "I broke my glass, since when I've only been able to read my Bible. That's a proper book with big print, that is. No women with no backs there."

"How're you keeping then?" asked Janet. "You're looking well, though how you keep together with all those safety-pins, beats me."

"They keep the draught out," retorted Jessie. "My Good Lord a-gracious me! If I was to go about naked like you folk, I'd drop down dead in a minute!"

Suddenly, from under her shawls she produced a little bunch of anemones. "I brought a bit of flower for you, Emmeline. A bit of flower cheer a body up, I fancy. 'Tisn't much, but there 'tis. When they open they'll be bain pretty things." She dropped them in a tumbler of water. Emmeline looked at them gratefully.

"That's kind, Jessie."

In the next room Tansy was looking at herself in the mirror, half-angry, knowing she never looked attractive in fine clothes. And the silk dove-gray dress gave her a pallor which made her think she was ill.

The room was stripped of all that belonged to her. She thought it was sad to treat it so churlishly after so many years of its friendship. The old rocking-chair had gone; Tansy had put it downstairs in the new house. The bed with its clean sheets primly reminded her that she might never sleep alone again. The sanctuary of sweet lonely sheets was ended now. And to celebrate the fact that henceforth she would share her bed with a man, they all dressed up and went to church where Parson made it legal. She sighed. An impulse made her open the suitcase in which she had packed the last of her clothes and trifles. There she found the little tree of thorn, and suddenly frightened of taking it into the new house she wanted to destroy it. Standing by the window, she almost threw it out, the lovely twisted tree with the undying shape. But a sparrow twittered at her as though to plead for one who had been good to a brother sparrow. So she put it back in the case, knowing that if she threw it away she would mourn in years to come because she had nothing tangible to remind her of a lovely and terrible adventure.

She went downstairs, carrying a bunch of white Maypinks, and everybody smiled and said she looked pretty. The cars were waiting and Tansy walked quickly down the path. Nicolas, Joe and Leonard Disher went in the one car with her. Janet had insisted upon staying with Emmeline. In the other car were Andrew, the Bob Penderils, and John Stone, who had twined himself so obstinately into their company that they had to invite him.

Tansy looked up at her mother's window as they drove away; Jessie Vean stood there, her saturnine countenance entirely unmoved. Janet stood in the doorway, dabbing her eyes a little obsequiously with her handkerchief.

So Tansy went to her wedding, neither excited nor sullen, grave nor gay, but quiet, with a faint sparkle of amusement in her eyes. Leonard, watching her in the car, wondered whether she really loved the chap; whether she was ever capable of loving anybody wholeheartedly.

Arthur was waiting at the church with his uncle, a wizened fellow with a lachrymose moustache. Arthur wore a new brown suit and a red carnation in his buttonhole. He smiled shyly at Tansy as she walked up the church on Nicolas's stiff arm. Nobody knew much about the Sacrament of Matrimony. Nicolas was dragged here and there by the Parson, who treated him like a stupid schoolboy. Andrew sulked perceptibly, because he had hoped to give Tansy away, and could not bear to see Nicolas doing it all wrong. Janie snivelled all the time, and John Stone, who had not been to church since his brother had sung a solo in a harvest anthem years ago, ejaculated "Amen" whenever he considered it was appropriate, then immediately relapsed into a cataleptic condition. Nobody else spoke a word. Joe, as best man, grinned broadly except when the Parson looked at him, then he blushed. Arthur delivered the ring so promptly that the Parson, who had a bad memory, lost his place in the book. Then he made them kneel down rather impatiently, and said a prayer over them. Tansy's thoughts wandered, until her hand was seized by the Parson, who put it in Arthur's right hand and said: "Those whom God hath joined, let no man put asunder." Joined—echoed Tansy in her mind. Well, that was straight enough! But joined by

God? What about those who were joined sure enough, but not by God?

She felt Arthur's hot hand pressing her and she squeezed him back hurriedly to show him she had not taken her vows lightly. The Parson gave them a special blessing, and then he and the sexton rumbled through a Psalm together, the sexton yapping every other verse after the Parson like a judge delivering a string of sentences.

They signed the register, and the Parson asked them some kind questions as to their future life and Arthur's work. Tansy, remembering that this was the same impassioned preacher who had told them to stamp on the devil, only smiled at him shyly and did not speak. Then they marched down the church to a bombardment of confetti. Nicolas was exchanging jests with friends and relatives, apologizing for not asking them to the farm. "Emmeline, y'see. Her condition hardly justify us having a crowd." And they all nodded their heads sapiently. "Oh, 'es, 'es. Poor soul. Pity, too!" Nicolas gave away a lot of cigars and, getting into the car, they drove away again. So that was that, thought Tansy pensively, as she felt Arthur's affectionate arm pressed against her. She had driven up here a free woman; now God had joined her and no man might put her asunder. She was a little concerned because this stupendous fact had made not the least difference to her. She felt as she had at her Confirmation, when she had expected that the touch of the Bishop's gaunt hand would immediately produce an entire transformation in her mental reaction to the physical world. But she had remained the same, even if avowedly pious intentions had, for a short while, made life rather a wary road to tread. And she felt exactly the same now. Yet she was Mrs. Progis of Boscedjack Common, not Tansy Penderil of Penth Farm. She and all hers were Arthur's; she did not belong to herself any longer. Why did she feel just the same? It was all wrong—all wrong.

Old Harry Progis, sitting opposite her, wiped his moustache with a distinct air of authority, and touched Tansy on the knee. "You're looking brane pretty, Tansy. I wish Arthur's mother and dad could have seen you."

A few minutes later Tansy stood by Emmeline's bedside.

"We're married, mother," she said. And she realized that she spoke as though she had just finished some tedious household task, solely to please her mother. She might have said in the same tone, "It's done, mother. The slab's so bright as a new pin."

Emmeline kissed her and held her arms so tightly that her long nails pressed into her skin.

"It's the happiest day I've had this long time. Bless you, Tansy! Your eyes are that bright. I reckon Arthur won't be happy till he's alone with you——"

Alone with her . . . alone. . . . The words were terrible.

Then Jessie Vean, who had been sitting in the window-seat, beckoned her over. "I hate a weddun," she snarled impotently, "but seeing as you go the way of them all, I brought something for you." She probed into a large black bag and found a drab little gold brooch elaborately worked into a word. She gave it to Tansy. "Here's a pretty trinket," she said, "and don't go a-treating of it rough, for 'tis old and none of your cheap muck like they do wear on they films I hear tell of. It belonged to my mother, see? And I never lived up to it. But you'll live up to it, I do think." She cocked her bobbing head suddenly on one side, and winked slowly at Tansy. "You'll live up to it," she repeated.

Tansy took the brooch and saw through a mist of little tears the old golden word "Mother". She put her hand to her bosom; a strange lightness in her head, a lucid aeriness of her body, momentarily overcame her. Then she kissed Jessie, whose little eyes crackled with jets of secret mirth.

"You're kind," she murmured. "See, mother"—she showed the brooch to Emmeline, who looked equivocally at Jessie and nodded her head without a word.

After that, the day went very quickly. When Tansy got downstairs they all sat down for the feast. There was a large ham and pasties made by Janet; jellies that quivered like an autumn sky; an apple-pie and a massive bowl of crusty cream. A strangely ominous-looking cake which Janet had spent hours upon and which, for some reason, everybody tried to avoid. And plates of rich cakes in weird architecture, studded with angelica, cherries, hundreds-and-thousands, and little silver pills. As the afternoon drew on to evening, tongues became freer, the air grew thick with the smoke of invulnerable cigars and Nicolas produced one of his bottles of Ruby Port. He held it up to the sunshine, proud of its opulent glow.

"That's right, dad," cried Joe. "Bring out the wine, you! Let's make Aunt Janet here drunk!"

"Drunk," roared Janet, "drunk my bottom!"

Leonard slapped his knees. "She's a beaut, she is!"

John Stone put his hands up to his ears, anxiety in his rimy eyes. "Eh? Eh? What's that, then? What she say?"

"Drunk my bottom!" howled Janet. "Time was when I had my magnum opus of champagne every night like any lord. Have it on ice, you do. Seventeen-and-six a bottle," she added darkly. "Herbert used to say he'd just as soon drink Tarragona, but mind you, that man never had a taste for a glass of good wine in his natural——"

"I'm brae fond of that sherry myself," observed Janie with insipid sapience. "We had it up to Plymouth at Bessie Trehair's funeral. A pretty wine. But then they do you well there——" She glanced round the table significantly. Janet was about to retort, but Leonard broke in.

"What's all this damn nonsense about funerals?" he cried. "When here we are at Tansy's wedding?"

He took his glass and stood up.

"Listen. I give a toast——"

Mr. Progis nudged Janet. "Speak pretty, don't he? Give a toast! That's proper, that is!"

"Ah," returned Janet. "He know a thing or two, that boy. Some man he is. I could tell you——"

"I give Tansy," continued Leonard. "And long may she live!"

"Hear, hear!" snuffled John Stone, and then, turning hoarsely to Nicolas, "What's that the chap say, you?"

But Nicolas was proposing a toast of his own.

"I give," he began, and then anxiously to Mr. Progis, "how do he say it? I give——" He sat down abruptly.

"Ah, you can't do it proper," chuckled Mr. Progis.

"The best thing you can give, Nicky," cried Janet, "is another glass all round. There's about enough in these little glasses to cover a fly's——"

"All right, all right!" muttered Nicolas hoarsely, fearing obscenity from Janet, whose eye was exceedingly dangerous. He took the bottle and filled up their glasses. Tansy was very quiet but smiling happily. Arthur nudged her.

"Shan't be sorry to get away from all this," he whispered. "Though they're kind, mind you."

Joe overheard him. "Better time coming, Arthur?"

Andrew broadened to a patronising smile. Standing up, he took his glass and solemnly proposed Arthur's health. He was very proud of this, and sitting down again chewed his cigar portentously as though Arthur's health was bound to be perfect from henceforth.

"Well now, Tansy," he said, "how don't you give us a——"

"—Toast," muttered John Stone, by now understanding the reason for all this organized tippling. "Darnee!" he said, "this toasting do prime a body up proper!" He looked at his glass and took the bottle abstractedly.

"No, a speech," continued Andrew.

"Proper," agreed Joe. "Speech, Tansy!"

"What'll m'knabs say now, eh?" Mr. Progis sat back in his chair, stretched his legs and waited upon Tansy.

"Yes—speech—speech!" They all clattered on the table.

Tansy got up more quickly than was expected. There was a perplexed expression upon her face.

"You're all very kind," she began, "and I'm sure I'm grateful. And all those pretty presents in there, too!" Her eyes filled with tears. "But there's somebody as we've all forgotten——"

Nicolas suddenly looked down at his plate.

"I"—Tansy struggled with words. "I—give a toast, too. I give Mother——"

Janie coughed. There was a deadly silence. Leonard broke it almost fiercely. "I reckon we have forgot," he said. "May she"— he paused suddenly—"have what she deserve!"

They drank the toast self-consciously. And while their glasses were yet to their lips, something very old and sad rippled dissonantly above their silence. From high up in the house, like the loosening of a symphony of little cracked pipes, they heard the song of Jessie Vean as she sang to Emmeline her small ghost of olden days. And nobody could bear to speak when they heard it; could only stand stupidly and listen.

> "My love, he is both tall and fair
> A pretty man to see;
> He went away across the moor
> And never came back to me."

The voice ceased abruptly, the last cadence of the song wailing through the walls of the house. In a dream Tansy moved out of the room and went upstairs. Jessie began another verse.

> "He went away across the moor
> In spring when swallows fly
> And primroses grow on the banks,
> And lambs to their mothers cry."

Tansy slipped down by the window of her naked bedroom, She could hear the low murmur of Emmeline's voice next door. Then Jessie finished her song.

> "He went away across the moor
> And never came back to me;
> My love who was so tall and fair,
> A pretty man to see."

The voice shivered to silence. Like the lover who went across the moor, the song could never end, but only grow so distant that it could not be heard. And then, when the ear had lost even the last flickerings of sound and the house was like a cave swept by the invasion of silence—Tansy wept. As the dull globe of the sun turned her youth down to its ending, she wept. For she knew that she had given something which she could never recover, and that he to whom she had given it, would never come back.

Book Two

THE SHAPE OF THE THORN

CHAPTER I

THE boy had caught a snake and was trying to assure his sister that it was a harmless one. But Alice withdrew against the hedge, nervously clasping her hands together.

"I tell you it hasn't got a sting, you silly maid!"

The boy held the snake by the neck, delighting in the sheen of its brown body against the sun.

"I don't care," said Alice. "I hate the slimy old thing! Don't you bring it near me."

"I'm going to take it home." The boy grinned wickedly. "Maybe I can teach it to do things. Like jackdaws," he added vaguely.

"You'll never do no such thing," argued Alice. "Mother'll leave you know if you do!"

"Oh, hold your gab!" he retorted rudely, making a sudden dart at her with the writhing snake. She screamed, pushed him away and ran along the valley. The boy laughed contemptuously and watched her as she grew smaller and smaller along the path, until she turned up the hill towards Boscedjack and went beyond his sight.

Alone now, the boy was a little afraid of his capture. Sitting down by the stream, still holding the snake by the neck, he studied its head cautiously. Needle-points of malevolence, its little narrow eyes pierced him with painful hatred. The boy half wanted to fling it away into the stream, but he knew Alice would only deride him as a coward if he arrived home without it. Besides that, he wanted to take it to school to-morrow and let it out in the class room. Such a scare would amply repay him, he reasoned, for the beating he would probably get. Yes—he would certainly have to keep it. He looked around for something in which to wrap it, for he did not care to carry it all the way home, gripping it thus round the neck. But he could find nothing and his handkerchief was too small. So he struggled out of his shirt—a bright yellow shirt, open at the neck—and holding the snake down, smothered it till he had made a bag from which it could not escape. Then quickly he started to walk home.

He wore only sand-shoes and an old pair of blue trousers, cut down to make shorts. The fierce sun pressed the sweat through his careless brown chest. His black hair fell over his eyes and he swept it away with a quick movement of his head. His eyes were liquid, brown as old oak and deep in his head; the dream-pools of an imagist. His cheek-bones pressed cleanly out of his russet-brown face. The stride of his limber legs revealed the buoyancy of a confident will; his powerful arms swung easily from sharp shoulders. He was, for a boy of fifteen, tall and of good balance.

As he ascended the hill to Boscedjack, the sudden smell of the sea made his nostrils quiver keenly, like a dog on a rabbit's track. The house at the top of the hill was solitary and prosaic against the sky; a plain granite house with windows where they should be and a blue door plumb in the middle. A strong wall enclosed the house and garden, and decorating the two sides of the iron gate, surmounting the wall, was a triad of smooth oval stones— big, medium and small, looking like loaves of bread.

Tansy Progis stood leaning against the open door, her arms folded dogmatically upon her breast, a slow sardonic smile moving her lips. She looked at David under half-closed eyes. He hesitated for a moment, then came up the path, whistling casually.

"If you think you're going to bring that snake in the house," remarked Tansy quietly, "you're mistaken, that's all."

"Oh! Alice told you, I suppose?" David sneered.

"Yes, she did," admitted Tansy somewhat unwillingly, for she hated tale-bearers almost as much as she hated snakes. "And I tell you this, my son: only a coward frightens little girls!"

"Only a coward's frightened of a snake what can't do no harm!" retorted David savagely. He fell down on the grass, lying on his stomach and digging his toes into the soil while he moodily peered at the snake through a chink in his shirt. Tansy scowled at him.

"That may be," she said, a little weakened. "But I'm not going to argue. All I say is, so long as you keep it, outside you stay!" And duty compelling her, she added as an afterthought: "It's bad enough to go round half naked without bringing a dirty snake into the house!"

David turned his head round suddenly and smiled on her a smile of great charm, secretively sanguine, and embarrassing to Tansy, who found herself compelled to meet it.

"Oh, go on, mother!" he said softly. "You know you don't care a darn about me taking my shirt off! It's hot enough to take off my pants, ask me! You know you're only mad because that Alice came gabbing to you."

"Nothing of the sort!" snapped Tansy, abruptly turning into the house, because his long indolent body on the grass, too easily sapped her authority. She sat down and drank some tea at a gulp. Alice, her usually bland face puckered into an unholy smile of victory, commended Tansy's attitude.

"That's right, mother," she said smugly. "You make him stay out till he's got rid of the nasty old snake."

Tansy glared at her. "It's nothing to do with you," she said unreasonably. "You go on with your tea and be quiet."

Alice began to burble a complaint, but ceased as she caught Tansy's sharp eyes. Tansy was furious with Alice for telling tales; furious with David for doing all the wicked things in a charming way; furious with herself for weakening under his smile. So often had she given way to his blandishments. If she did not harden herself, she thought, he would win again.

She saw him through the window, his chin resting morosely on his hands, his toes dug into the grass. Then she noticed that the yellow shirt lay stretched out beside him. She went to the door.

"What you done with it, then?" she asked.

"I let it go," came the sullen answer.

"Why?" asked Tansy irrationally. He would not admit that he had let the snake free purely to please her.

"No use keeping it," he muttered.

Tansy went over to him. "Come in and have your tea," she said.

"When Alice has finished." He did not look at her.

"Don't be stupid," she remonstrated—but she, too, detested Alice at that moment. The tender blue pool in her grey eyes which in the past fifteen years had almost dried to emptiness, slowly filled again. She touched David's glistening back, learnt the subtle undulation of the smooth nerves, ran her fingers idly and affectionately up the ridge of his strong spine. The boy threw back his head, opened his mouth with his tongue on his lower lip, and laughed deep in his throat, a chuckle of satisfaction.

Tansy could not believe that this lissom branch of boyhood would so soon grow to the grave tree of manhood. His youth, his soft half-conscious knowledge of himself, excited her as youth had always excited her. She remembered a scene years ago when she had sat on the bed of her young brother Joe. She felt she was still a girl of twenty, not a dull cast of herself as she had been fifteen years ago. A score of muddled images rushed through her mind as David smiled below her, his half-ashamed brown eyes warm with love for her. She saw herself standing by her mother's bedside, holding the baby David so as Emmeline might touch him very feebly. She could not speak; could only reach out a rotten arm to David's globular head. She saw old Jessie Vean fumble in her bag for the gold brooch that Tansy had shewn to Arthur when David was born. She saw a fiery old man bent earnestly over a pulpit; saw a valley white with the smoke of thorn; saw a melancholy wood and a solemn house, cadaverous like an old blind face; saw a sad figure standing with a wounded sparrow in his hand; saw the argent wings, the burnished bosom of her grave Saint standing so far above. And all these pictures crowded together suddenly till they merged into one indolent form and she saw Roger Chailey's son lying on his back on the grass. . . .

Her eyes were a grey intolerance again. She took David's shirt from the grass.

"Find another shirt," she said coldly, "and come in to tea." She went in.

Hurt by her manner, David flung into the house and went upstairs to his bedroom. It was a room littered with rubbish of all kinds. Tansy had long ago given up trying to keep it in order. David's bed was invisible under a mound of clothes, stamp-albums, snap-shots, toffee tins, pieces of wire flex, the various parts of a wireless set, magazines and the bowels of an old clock. There was a chest of drawers covered with torn books, papers and a case of butterflies which David had caught years ago and never looked at now. Pinned to the walls were pictures of film actors and athletes which he had cut out of newspapers, and one or two grotesque pictures of sea and sunset which he had tried to paint. He had had a dozen hobbies, none of which ever occupied him more than a few weeks. He had collected all manner of strange pets, from a jackdaw to a shrew.

In his younger days there had been something of David's in every corner of the house, but lately Tansy had made a rule that he should keep his possessions to his bedroom, where she did not much attempt to interfere with him. And David loved the room, very much as Tansy had loved her old room at the farm. Like her, he would often come up to it and sit in moody silence looking out across the moors to the forsaken stacks of the Retallack Mine, where his father had worked before the disaster which had killed thirty men in a falling man-engine and silenced the place forever. That was only a month or so after David's birth, and for years now Arthur had been out of work, drawing dole-money or sometimes picking up odd jobs of gardening.

David would sit and watch the scattered decadence of the stricken mine, sometimes, under the moon, imagining it to be inhabited by the tormented shapes of those thirty men. His father rarely spoke about the disaster; if he did so, it was only to drop some bloody hint which David longed to follow up.

He felt he wanted to know more about the mine, even though it frightened him to think of it for long. Sometimes he ventured to the place. Alone he would go, moping about in fearful silence, climbing ladders rotten and rank with neglect; from a shaky platform looking down miles below to the swirling dirtiness of the copper-coloured sea. He found tunnels; catacombs where arsenic glittered like knives in the clammy walls. He walked over the boards that covered in the desolate place which had rung to the screams of men falling under a falling world. Then David would shout and hear his voice for miles around.

However bright the sun shone, the ominous crags of the cliffs on that coast always seemed black; the sea always a seething contumely where cormorants preyed above darting fishes. David was frightened when he went there, yet fascinated by the mutiny of dead machinery—the inaudible voices of a thousand miners swaying the silence with their staunch Wesleyan hymns. Then suddenly it would become too much for him, break his boy's heart and send him scuttling home like a chased hare.

When he got back and they asked him where he had been, he never told them; they did not like the mine and never walked that way, but always towards the more friendly softness of the south, where the town clustered under the sky and the curved arm of Penth fell along the sea. But northwards was an adventure—David knew that in his heart.

The lovers in the long summer evenings always walked south along the coast; the trippers with their peeling pink faces, went the same way; Sunday school outings and church treats followed suit, making for the warm valleys that cut those cordial shores. But northwards—where no birds sang, no flowers grew and no lovers kissed. David carried imagination further, wondering whether he would ever venture right beyond the mine to the purple crags of carns far from the smoke of any cottage chimney.

Looking over the mine now, he was invaded by a sudden memory. He was driving with his mother in the butcher's cart some seven miles beyond Retallack to see an old woman, a queer frightening creature called Jessie Vean, who lived all alone in a crabbed cottage on the moor. He might have been four years old. He remembered the road twisting back upon its course and getting narrower as they went on. Then, it seemed to young David, they ascended up a mountain, so high that they were driving along in the clouds with nothing but the sea miles below them. And on their right stretched the endless moor, the chucking-ground of a million lichen-red boulders; a gaunt sun-empurpled place, where the few lonely flowers might have been petrified shapes of an old summer; where ravens sat like carved gods, so black that they caught all the colours of the sun in their sleek bodies. A place of hidden eyries and buried bones—static and atavistic.

David, sitting now by his window, shivered, though the sun was warm on his bare skin—shivered as he drew this old picture out of his brain. And enjoying the memory he invited more of it; began to construct the remorseless monotone of that country

beyond Retallack. In the rufous mine David saw the little crabbed
house of Jessie Vean—the little crabbed shape of her body—
heard the little crabbed crack of her fugitive voice. He had been
afraid of her, for she glared at him with eyes so deep and small
that you did not expect them to exist, only knew that you felt
them. He remembered his mother shewing her a gold brooch,
one that she still often wore. And all the time he had clung to his
mother's hand, wanting to get out and home again.

The house was sealed up like an envelope, even though it was
warm autumn weather. There were sacks jammed in the bottom
of the door and rubber tubing in the crack of the window. A fire
in the slab and everything in its proper place. A tabby-cat, very
large and resentful, glowered at them from the top of a cupboard
where he sat—a mound of malevolence. They had drunk cups of
chocolate-brown tea and eaten thick chunks of saffron cake, dry
as biscuit. Then the butcher's cart had taken them back again.

David remembered the warmth of the autumn sun bringing
out strange half-colours on the moor and the lumbering ogres
of fluffy clouds puffing about in the sky. He could not remember
the drive back; perhaps he had fallen asleep. But the rest of it was
overwhelmingly vivid, a fantasia that he longed to grasp. And
he decided that some day he must go over those moors and see
Jessie Vean again if she were still alive.

He was so far away in thoughts that he never heard Tansy
calling him from below. She called again and he did not answer.
Getting impatient she ran up and burst into his room.

"I've called you twice to come down to tea," she cried angrily.
"Are you deaf, then?"

He swung round. He was smiling but not for her. She saw
a world of ecstasy in his dark face; a light in his eyes that had
nothing to do with her. And he swung his arms out as though he
would banish her from his secret world. The gesture made her
furious.

"I'm not coming down to tea," he said emphatically. "I don't
want it, so leave me alone."

"Leave you alone," she stormed at him. "Yes, I should think
so! So's you may sit up here and sulk——"

"I'm not sulking!" he protested. "Don't be unfair, mother. You know I'm not. I let the darn snake go because you got mad. Then you suddenly go and get all teasy for no reason. It's you who're sulking, not me."

She knew he was right. She could only employ her hackneyed authority as a parent.

"Don't answer me! I'm your mother and I'll have you do as you're told. You're too big for your boots, that's where 'tis. There's nobody can keep you in check."

He silenced her with his emollient voice.

"Oh, don't take on so, mother! Give us a kiss and be sensible."

"Go on!" she snapped. "You can't come over me with your soft ways. You think you can——"

Then she stopped, ashamed of the fact that she chastised him for no substantial reason. Yet there was this thought—that she had to keep a guard upon him. Seeing him there before her, calm, reasonable and most beautiful, she resented the torment that he could be to her unless she treated him casually. She could not bear the smiling face that was a rebuke to her hysterical behaviour. And when he spoke, she was afraid of the old music in his voice.

"Mother," he said, "have you ever seen that old woman again since we went years ago? I mean that old Jessie Vean? I was thinking about her."

"No; I never seen her," she replied shortly, wondering what had started the thought in his mind.

"Is she still alive, then?"

"I haven't heard tell she's dead yet. How're you asking about her?"

"I thought of her across those moors." He pointed out. "I want to go there again."

Tansy laughed contemptuously. "You'll never go all that way! Besides, she never comes out of her door, and like as not wouldn't let you in. I hear she've gone mad, and no wonder!"

"I like mad folk," he said, and laughed. "Reckon I'll get over there if I have to walk. And other places," he added with a vague arrogance.

"What d'you mean?"

"Oh, nothing." He threw the subject aside with a careless shrug. Tansy simulated indifference.

"Put a shirt up to your back else you want to catch cold," she said. "And I warn you there won't be no tea save you come down at once."

She left the room. David found a khaki shirt, put it on and followed her down. He found Tansy alone, pouring out tea for him. She had sent Alice out to feed the fowls.

"When do the holidays start?" asked Tansy, making conversation.

"Monday coming," he replied.

"Lord save us! And how long? Five weeks, I suppose—and what'll you do with yourself all then?"

"Lots to do," he mumbled between bread and jam. "I wish I had a bicycle," he added meditatively.

"Yes, I suppose," she said. "And a motor-car and an aeroplane and anything else you care to play around with for a week!" She grinned good-humouredly.

"Tommy Jones got one," he muttered. "Billie Simmons got one; so has that mean little stink, Connie Tresize! Gosh! You can get about on a bicycle."

"So you can on two legs," she retorted. "Particularly when they happen to be young ones."

"Oh, darn that!" He smiled at her. "Can't you get me one cheap, somewhere? They're going awful cheap now, I hear."

"My son"—she changed her bantering manner—"if we could buy you this and buy you that, you don't suppose you'd want for anything, do you? But when you're hard put to it to find food, where are you going to find such things as bicycles? Don't go fretting over what you can't have. 'Twill do you no good at all."

He sighed.

"All right—I wish I could have done with school and get a job."

"You'll have done with school soon enough," she said. "And what d'you reckon you're going to do then? The mines aren't working. There's a hundred lads if there's one, all on the dole same as your father. They might find a place for you to the farm. Uncle Joe'd do what he could. You'd best go up and help harvest time of an evening, and shew them you're not afraid of work."

Alice came in, pouting when she saw David's broad smile. "I've fed the fowls, mother," she chanted. "What should you like me to do next?"

The child's marionette integrity maddened Tansy.

"Oh, do as you've a mind to," she cried.

David finished his tea and went to the door. Alice giggled as he pushed her aside like a piece of furniture.

"You're some mad," she tittered.

He did not answer, but spoke to Tansy.

"The tide's leaving the pool. Reckon I'll go and have a bathe."

"You're not to swim out in the open sea," she cautioned.

"All right," he said. "I'm safe enough in the pool. You won't fret, will you?"

"Not if you promise to keep to the pool." (For she believed he would keep his word.)

"Why don't you come, too?" he urged impulsively. "Do you good to get out, evening like this, and father won't be back till dusk."

For Arthur spent the summer evenings working in a rich man's garden.

Tansy suddenly decided she would like to go. She seldom went to the pool nowadays, and Arthur had long ago lost interest in such things as swimming.

"Alice," she said, "if I leave you to mind the house for half an hour, can you keep out of mischief?"

Alice leapt to the opportunity. Left alone she would be able to rummage through the marvellous secrets of David's bedroom.

So David took a costume and a towel and they walked along above the valley towards the sea. At the end of the path they came to an abrupt chasm where, far below, the little eye of the pool gleamed in the rocks. One or two swimmers were standing by the edge; some girls on the grassy slopes above.

"Darn it!" muttered David. "They old maidens make me fair sick!"

He pointed northwards to the right of the pool where the little black channel cut into the heart of the cliffs. It was the place where Arthur had swum.

"Let's go there," said David. "I can swim there. Mother, let's go there. I don't want to swim in the pool with they old maidens geeking at us all the time."

She did not want to go there. Yet she was tempted to the place where she had found and lost the man Arthur. She dreaded seeing David in the slow, black water, yet she wanted him to prove his courage. So they scrambled over the loose scrabbly stones until they stood hot and panting by the rock that had resisted Arthur.

David tore off his shirt and kicked aside his shoes. Then he hesitated, suddenly self-conscious and wondering why he felt so shy before his mother. He said:

"Mother, I needn't wear a costume here, need I?"

It was a reversal of another scene in this place. Tansy found it hard to believe this was her son. She killed the conventional woman who had married Arthur, smiled at David and said: "Go on, my son. There's nobody here. Why shouldn't you?"

She yearned to tell him how she had made Arthur swim naked, but she feared to talk much of the past. She feared David nowadays every time he questioned her about her early life. Every time she saw a new question in his eyes.

"Go on, my son," she urged. "Only do be sure the sea aren't too strong for you."

But the water was very calm in the channel and David stood on the little rock, ready to dive in.

She was heavy with love for him as he stood there. She grudged him to the women who so soon would fight for his body. This, her lovely son, the fruit of her love ... she did not want to think he was her son. Thinking of his approaching manhood, she was very sad. And tears coming into her eyes she saw him through a faint mistral, the arrogant poise of his body tinged by the showering powder of the amber sun.

He dived cleanly. She watched him swimming smoothly with slow strokes. On the other side he waved to her and vanished behind the rocks. She was anxious for him and wished he would come back. Until she saw him dive in again she could not rest. He came over with ease, reached his hands up to the rock and drew himself out on his buttocks.

"That's more sensible than Arthur," thought Tansy, "who would get out on his knees and cut himself."

David rested on the rock, his legs in the water.

"You're a good swimmer, David," said Tansy. "I'm proud. I do like a man to swim."

"I like swimming," he said. "It's when I'm swimming I feel right somehow. When do you feel most like yourself, mother?"

"I don't know," she cried. She had dropped her mask of conventional motherhood and spoke to him as a loved companion. "I think——" she searched for words, "when I'm not doing anything at all, but just thinking, idle like. Then I'm myself."

"You're yourself now, mother, aren't you?"

He suddenly laid his hand on hers.

"Yes, I am." She spoke with conviction. Then she sighed. "You're growing up, David. A mother don't like to see her son growing up and the years slipping by. Soon you'll be gone off with a maid and no more thought of me."

"No, I won't be doing no such thing," he said. "I do love you, mother. You're the only maiden—I ever want to love, I reckon." He pressed her hand and flushed very red. Then he suddenly jumped into the sea and began kicking up his legs wildly, splashing her as she stood there.

"I want a bicycle," he cried wickedly. "Going to give me a bicycle, are you?"

"Bicycle be darned!" she laughed. "I've told you we haven't got no money for such things."

"That's all b——!" he cried, then checked himself. "Sorry—I forgot 'twas you. But Uncle Joe and Grandad can find money enough if you get round them. I tell you what——" he dived down and stayed so long under water that she got alarmed and called him. Spluttering, his head popped out of the water.

"I'll stay here," he ultimated, "till you promise me you'll ask Grandad to buy me a bicycle!"

"Then you'll stay there all the winter, and freeze till you're naught but an iceberg!"

He floated off on to the rock again and lay back upon it lazily.

"All right," he said. "See if I don't ask him myself. I know how to get round the old chap!"

Tansy laughed. She was sitting just behind him, running her fingers through his glossy hair. David shivered.

"I like you doing that," he said. "It makes me queer-like inside."

Tansy was aware of that and half-amusedly she rubbed her knuckles into his scalp.

"Oh, don't," he said. "I can't bear it. I shall go all soft——"

Tansy was thrilled by his sprawling body, wet and ruddy in the sun. She wanted to slide her hands along down his chest where the young dark hairs were smoothed out by the sea. Almost unconsciously her hand stole to his ribs. He shivered, but did not speak. An unspeakable delight overcame him; a torment of unrealized appetency. Pubescence hammered in his forehead so that he was sick and heavy. In spite of the water glistening on his body he felt hot and clammy. There was a singing fantasy in his head, a trembling of his heart. Little drops of sweat burst out of his arm-pits, trickling down his side like icy globules.

He was overcome with shame and burst into speech.

"Mother, don't do that—don't do it. I can't—you don't know how strange I do feel——"

Tansy wanted to laugh. This, her son, telling her he felt 'strange'! Again the old story. Again the wheel of life. Yes, he was man enough for any woman. She was not sorry to have proved it. He would rouse somebody some day as his father had roused her. Would pass on the fire of his passionate body to another. Would pass on. . . .

She checked her feelings, afraid of something she could not name. What would he pass on? She was full of vague fears. Amorphous spectres of mischief crowded in her mind besieging her with impish gestures. She was submerged momentarily by a torrent of fears that had always been dammed up in her—had never really escaped from her. Again she saw herself struggling in the murky pool, gasping to reach the cold hand of her beloved Saint, yet pulled down, always pulled down by something she could not apprehend. Her mind drove her back again to a fire-twisted room, room of shadows and foreboding mists, the room of her uncovering, her glory and her shame. From that moment—no, there was Arthur, her placid (oh God, how placid!) husband at home; Alice, the stodgy babe she had stoically born. And there was David . . . there was David . . . shaking himself free of her hand and standing with his back to her, his body trembling slightly, his strong nervous hands pressed down his sides. David . . .

A little cloud of spindrift floated over her and dispersed. She got up from the rock and looked towards the sea. The sun had caught them in a blood-red glow, making them creatures of fluid fire. David's nakedness, a God forged in a smeltery. A thin long line of black cloud covered the horizon, the lid of night upon the sun. Through it, the sun's slow wheel turned, dipped and disappeared. A flock of gulls went whistling home. The smoke of a collier rounding Penth stabbed up into the green sky like a black drill.

Time had slipped by them. Tansy had forgotten Arthur in her wandering thoughts. She turned hastily to go.

"It's near half after nine," she exclaimed, "by the sun setting. Your father'll be mad wanting his supper. I'll get along, David, and not wait for you. Only don't stay too long."

He didn't reply. Did not even turn round.

She spoke again and went near to him. Then she saw there were tears in his eyes.

"Why what's the matter, son?" she cried. "What's taken you so sudden?"

He was a boy again, frail, depending upon her for support. Rarely had she seen him like this. Her heart melted towards him as she put her hands on his shoulders.

"I—don't know——" he stammered. "I—had a sudden feeling—it's silly I tell you——"

"Go on," she said quietly. "It don't matter how silly it is if 'tis troubling you."

"——that you didn't really want me——" he blurted out. "That you hadn't ever really wanted me. It's silly, isn't it? Just came over me like—like a cloud, when you was touching me just now."

"Of course it's silly, David." She spoke in a calm, level voice. "How shouldn't I want you when you're my own son?"

But there was uneasiness in her mind, and he knew it.

CHAPTER II

ARTHUR was in a bad temper.

"A fellow come in tired," he complained sourly, "expecting to find his supper waiting. And he don't even find the table laid."

"I'm very sorry, Arthur," said Tansy quietly. "I forgot the time."

"Where've you been to, then?" he asked.

"To the pool with David."

"Ah." Arthur mumbled disagreeably. "And little Alice can shift for herself, I suppose? A pretty thing if any beggarman or such like came to the door!"

Alice twiddled her fingers complacently in a corner of the room. She hoped there was going to be a scene. But Tansy would not quarrel. She invariably met his fractiousness with dignity—resembling her mother, in that she could never be bothered to argue with one for whose opinion on most things she had no regard. She fought fiercely with those she loved fiercely. So she did not answer Arthur but went into the kitchen and began to fry some mackerel.

"What's that your fitting for me?" he called, attempting as he always did, to fire her temper. For nearly fifteen years he had tried to extract the venom which he knew lay under her tongue, but always he had to retreat before the impassive rebuke of grey eyes. She might snarl at Alice, clout David—and he would commend her for that—but upon him she always turned a cool smile. She never complained, never reproached him for being unemployed, shabby and irritable.

"What's that your fitting?" And the damnable soft answer came from the kitchen.

"Some nice mackerel I got from down rocks."

Arthur loved mackerel. It was difficult to find fault with her here. However, he said, "Well, I hope they're fresh, that's all. I hear of somebody died eating mackerel the other day."

She answered him very brightly.

"Did you then? I suppose they were caught over to Newlyn. You never can tell when it's been lying in that stinking market. But this was caught this afternoon."

"Sometimes," he said in utter gloom, "they're bad for you if you eat them too fresh." But his voice trailed off. He felt conscious of going a little too far. He turned his attention to Alice, who still prayed fervently for the scene. He spoke kindly to her, knowing that he could annoy Tansy thus, however silent she might be about it. For Alice was Arthur's darling.

"Busy to-day, my handsome?"

Alice smirked. "Yes, father. I got a prize for good behaviour and attendance."

"That's right," he said agreeably, shaking his head. "David got no prize, I suppose?"

"No. David didn't get no prize."

"That's right." He nodded his head again, even more agreeably.

Tansy, apparently unmoved by this conversation, came in with the fish.

"Here's your supper, Arthur. Don't leave it get cold."

She hummed and went back into the kitchen, leaving Arthur to make the usual loud noises over his food. Arthur always consumed his food defiantly, as though to suggest he was doing a wicked thing and didn't care.

"Where's that lad to?" he asked presently.

And Tansy answered, "Oh, he's all right, don't fear. It's hardly dark yet and a pretty moon rising."

"Anybody down to the pool?"

"A few. But David and me went over to the other side. He swam over and back proper, just like you did years ago." She wanted to say "better", but knew it would be unwise.

"Ah." Arthur paused and looked at her face quickly in the dim light of the lamp. It was a sad face. He could not tell whether she were thinking of him.

When he had finished eating he took the newspaper and read the more purple news aloud to her. This was so regular a part of the daily ritual that little less than sudden death could have prevented it. Tansy sometimes imagined him reading to her empty chair when she was dead. She never listened; only sat with her hands on her lap, perhaps darning some clothes, responding with "Yes," "No," or "Really," as intelligently as was consistent with a wandering mind.

Shortly before ten, Alice dutifully went to bed. David had not yet come in, and Tansy was beginning to feel a little anxious.

"That Princess Margaret's a little teaser if you ask me." Arthur jabbed an artfully nebulous picture of the Royal child under her nose. "Like our Alice, I'm thinking," he mused reflectively.

"Same nose," murmured Tansy, looking at a picture of a well-seasoned bride leaving St. Margaret's in a shower of rain. Arthur went on reading.

"Seems there's a crisis coming," he resumed pontifically. "It's looking we're going off the gold standard." He spoke as though he were personally responsible.

"What's that mean?" asked Tansy obediently. Arthur liked to explain something every night.

"It means we're pretending to have money that don't rightly exist."

"Well," she said, "we're all doing that anyhow. Don't see the odds in making a fuss of that."

"No fuss at all," he replied. "But 'tis a bad thing, you! The country's in a wicked way."

"Yes, I suppose."

"The Far East's having trouble again." 'Far East'! There was a fine intelligent sounding phrase! And as for trouble—what two words could more suggest trouble?

"What's that?" asked Tansy.

(Why didn't David come in? The moon was high over the moor and the clock ticked slowly round to half-past ten.)

"That's China, that is," explained Arthur. "That's what they call the Yellow Peril." 'Yellow Peril'! The words were like a peach in the mouth!

"Funny," said Tansy. "I always thought the Yellow Peril was a newspaper somehow."

Arthur laughed and clicked his tongue contemptuously. "There's an idea!" he said, and went on reading. When he had done with all the news he would start on the advertisements. Then he would solve perhaps half the crossword puzzle, and promptly at eleven stumble slowly up to bed. There he would roll over on his side, open his mouth and snore invulnerably till morning. Then he would stretch out his arms and wake her just as she was beginning to enjoy and understand sleep. He would get up far too early and make tea that nobody wanted. Fuss the children to school and dribble over his strip of bacon as though he were a turkey-cock. Because it was a Friday, go up to the town to draw his money. Stand about in the square with a crowd of others, discussing greyhounds and the government. Come home to dinner. Suck his teeth as he ate it. Shelve time away in the garden. Drink more tea at four. Then go out, thank the dear Lord—go out to his job of work. Come home at nine with the newspaper. Suck up to Alice; blast David to Hell. Eat supper. Read the newspaper. Ruminate over a political situation of which he had not the faintest understanding. Chutter over a stinking pipe of cheap tobacco. Thrust the newspaper under her nose——

"See that? That chap got fifteen year for arson." She was faced by a large portrait of a suave City gentleman with a crooked nose and a black hat. He was leaving the Old Bailey in a shower of rain.

"Yes," said Tansy. She got up. "I'm worrying about the boy. It's late."

"You said not to worry," he reminded her. "He's able to take care of himself."

"If it was Alice," she returned bitterly, "you'd be mad with worry. But seeing it's only David, it don't matter, of course."

"Well, a boy of that age ought to be able to look after himself better'n a girl of twelve."

He was not in the least concerned about David. Tansy could have slapped his face—wondered what it was that restrained her. "You wouldn't mind if he was brought home dead," she muttered. "You know you wouldn't."

He looked up in surprise, feebly attempting to assure her otherwise.

"How're you saying such wicked things——"

Then suddenly he got what he wanted, for she blazed out

at him. "You wouldn't care! You know you wouldn't care a darn——"

(Upstairs, Alice in bed shivered with delight. David out late; her mother mad. This was life, this was!)

But in a moment the fire died in Tansy, and with a contemptuous little movement of her lips, she turned away from him. "You wouldn't care," she whispered. "You've never cared. And how should you?"

She went to the door, where the stock and thyme were sweet in the night air. The grey ghosts of phloxes nodded a surprised commentary on human affairs. Tansy wanted to cry but could not. Every time she burst out like this she felt driven back upon a wall of solid reason in herself. There was no way through that wall. Arthur was a good husband—so good that her soul sickened at the thought of him. She heard him close behind her— knew that his hand was seeking hers. She smelt his bad breath, a foul antithesis to the sweet stock. He was so useless to her, so insignificant that she could barely believe in his existence. He would try to smooth her over now with lumbering caresses and sticky-sweet words. He would presently claim the right to kiss her lips, to maul her breasts, to possess her in the night furtively, quickly and dutifully. He would eat her up like his food, defiantly undigested. Never had he known, never would he know the rare particles of her womanhood. He would eat her up, leave her exhausted and entirely unsatisfied. Already she felt his arm round her waist, his thick fingers pressing beneath her breast.

... A silver knight under the moon, David ran up the path. He was panting heavily, and stopped when he saw them in the doorway. Arthur grunted and went back into the house. Then David ran up, stretched his arms out to her, and she knew he was afraid of something. She caught him to her, gasping to feel the sweet refreshment of his youth close to her.

"Where've you been?" she whispered. "You're frightened and wet with sweat. I was anxious about you."

He did not answer and she walked him down the path. They stopped by the gate. "Tell me where you've been, son, and what's ailing you?"

"I went to the mine," he muttered slowly. "I got scared."

"To the mine?" And she, too, was suddenly afraid.

"Yes, Retallack. I felt queer about it—felt somehow I had to go looking over there this evening. There's—something that I want to see and—don't like——" He shivered. She could not understand.

"You shouldn't go to such dreary places. No wonder you're frightened. I wouldn't go there, not even in broad daylight."

But she was curious to know more about it, and he began to tell her vaguely.

"I thought about that old man-engine, mother, and all those men caught down in it——"

He stopped and slipped away from her. Then he laughed suddenly and Tansy did not like it.

"Some stupid I am," he said, and did not seem to want to tell her any more.

"What did you do then?" she said.

"Nothing," he replied carelessly.

"But something must have scared you," she insisted.

But he would not say any more about it. His manner seemed entirely to have changed. There was a glee in his eyes, a secret ring of triumph in his voice which irritated Tansy. This was the David she did not like.

"You might think twice," she said bitterly, "before you go giving me so much worry again. And you'd best not tell your father where you've been. He'll be mad."

He chuckled. "Tell him! See me doing that!" He flung an arm to the sky. "Gosh! It's a grand night!" he cried. She was caught by his enthusiasm.

"It is that!" she agreed.

"I want to be out," he went on, "out all night with no clothes to me, and just run wild under that old moon." He laughed again excitedly. His face was satyr-sharp, his whole body alive with impatient energy. "Wouldn't you, mother?" he went on. "Like to be out, instead of being stuffed in a stupid old bed with a man what snores enough to shake the house?"

"Oh, talk proper——" she remonstrated feebly.

"Well, he do snore," insisted David. "If I can hear him, you must be driven crazy by it."

Tansy was afraid lest Arthur should hear them. She begged him to be quiet and come into the house.

"You must have some food," she said, as they went in. But he would eat nothing, and ran upstairs before she could say any more.

Tansy turned into the living-room. Arthur was still bent over his paper, but not reading—she could see that. The air was heavy with his unspoken resentment. She sat down in the rocking chair by the window, secretly studying his face in the rays of the lamp. He had the paper open upon the table and was leaning over it. She saw his smoky blue eyes range a score of times over the same paragraph. His yellow hair sprouted in thin bushy patches, sticking out like gorse. He was getting fat, she saw. The obesity of idleness was beginning to disfigure him. In a few years he would be too lazy even to walk up into the town. He would just eat, read and snore; snore, read and eat. He would even cease to lust after her. That, at any rate, was something to be thankful for. The man Arthur was nothing but a seedy remnant. The man Arthur ... the glorious nakedness of a fiery pool. She sighed, pitying him, therefore despising him. Because she knew she was the reason for his pathetic dissolution. He might have remained a man with a woman who could keep his wits sharpened on the whetstone of her love. But from the moment when he had first slept with her and clumsily fulfilled their marriage, she had known that she could never rouse herself to his heavy love. He was to have been a rock, but he had been a muddy field. When David moved within her she knew that it was Roger Chailey's child who filled her with so lovely and terrible an agony; she knew that no child gotten by Arthur could stir the same burning anguish inside her. She remembered the pain of delivery, sharp and terrible, like a candescent sword piercing through her. But when she carried Alice it had been nothing more than a monotonous burden of spiritual fœticide. Alice, the little pink crab of a child, never uncovered an inch of her mother's love, while before David she felt naked and unashamed. Arthur saw all this and never understood it; only knew that David was different from Alice and that his marriage with Tansy was an utter failure. But Tansy knew that the failure lay in her. In the fibre of her nature was a twisted cord which only one person had ever been able to unravel. And the paradox of Roger Chailey lay in the fact that in unravelling it he had twisted it all the tighter. Living always with the shadow of Chailey, she never dared to examine that memory too closely. For if she did there was always the picture of her Saint, standing where she could not reach him. When she consciously thought of Chailey, she thought of the gold flame in his hair, the compelling harbour of his long arms, the honey-sweetness of his voice. But she never went past the little wood without hurrying and glancing back over her shoulder. She had never heard of him again; did not know whether he still lived. She did not imagine that he ever thought of her. The memory of him was a burden that made life an endless climb to an invisible summit.

She thought of him, and something inside her cried for release. It thrummed in her heart like a devil, mounted to her head and made her close her eyes and hold on to her chair. She wanted to scream out and let it free; she wanted to surge upwards, yet felt chained to her chair. The room swayed around her and became a gyroscope of formless shapes. She held her breath, overcome by a sensuous delight in the physical aeriness of her body—paused on the edge of a strange world. The huddled lump of her husband became the target for her thwarted senses. She wanted to strike him; to beat him and beat again till he was dead at her feet....

It changed and she came back; saw him clearly, still sitting there and reading the paper.

The sorcery of her mind bewildered her. She felt stupid, listless. The room was the same; Arthur there, the children upstairs.

She looked out of the open window. The night was defied by the moon; the air sweet with stock, thyme and camomile. David had said to go out and run naked under the moon. Yes, if she could do that she might find some touchstone upon which to identify herself with the earth.

A pantheistic nocturne flickered its orgiastic liturgy before her. She was trembling now with the burning desire to get out— to find the spell trailing from the cold moon so that it might send her blood running freely in her hard veins; by its alchemy make of her iron a peril of glitter-gold. It was a hunger for adventure in the rotten turning of life.

The clock struck eleven. Arthur yawned, folded the paper and stretched himself. Thank the Lord for that! He looked at her quickly. She knew now that, failing by his silence to draw her out, he was about to plead with her. He would crawl about like a fly with its wings cut off

She smiled a lie at him and spoke in a low, tender voice.

"Bedtime, Arthur, I suppose!"

He was pathetically grateful for the sweetness of her voice. Could she then really love him, he asked himself for the thousandth time? Might she yield completely to him if he seized this moment?

"Yes, bedtime," he echoed. Then, "Tansy, my dear——" He could say no more. Tansy smiled at him, cloudy-sweet in the lamplight. He came over, put his arms round her and kissed her. She did not resist him; even kissed him back with a warmth that was new and thrilling to him. Suddenly he saw that life could be lovely.

"Come to bed," he whispered. "I'm brae sorry we fell out."

"I'll come presently," she murmured. "You go on up, Arthur. I just want to wash these things up."

"Leave it," he urged. "What's it matter till morning?"

"No." Slowly she slipped away from him. Her eyes were shining; her cheeks hectic. "I hate leaving stuff for the morning. You go on up, Arthur. I'll be with you presently."

Still he protested, but she urged him and he went upstairs. She stayed listening till she heard the bed creak under him. Then she went to the door and saw the moon riding like a silver dome above her, racing before the feathery pennons of chasing clouds.

Quickly she took off her clothes and dropped them behind a chair. She found an old raincoat and wrapped it round her. Then she stepped out with bare feet upon the wet grass. The coldness of it shocked her like a knife. She went quickly towards the sea at the back of the house, away from the censure of the open windows, and, climbing nimbly over the wall, ran out upon the moor. She ran faster till she left the house far behind. Her feet were tingling with little thorns, but she did not notice the pain.

The sea was a roadway of little lanterns, jingling in the lustre of the moon. High above it she stood, raising her head to the sky. She pressed her hands to her breasts, gasping to feel the inundation of the air in her lungs. The clouds chasing the moon passed over it, merged into two great arms and mounted above her. The wind, rushing like wings; the penetrating omniscience of a chimney-stack erect out of the head—filled her with fear. Yet without fear the night meant nothing and there was no adventure.

The moon, firing the edge of the cloud-arms with a tincture of dull gold, came out of its black enemy. Then Tansy was consumed, insatiate for the body Earth. Furious, she flung herself face downward upon the ground, incoherent with wild laughter as the drenched grass met her nakedness. She pressed herself into the soil, clutching tufts of grass with her hands. The cloud-arms swayed and hovered to new forms above her; she cried for it to descend and immolate her in the earth.

She ran her hands down her body, turned over on her back and lay with her face upturned to the protean history of the cloud. She strove it into shapes of her will. A cedar tree with old green saucers under the sky; a bearded face; a castle. A ship in a heavy sea; a leaping satyr; a rock. A tongue shot out of it, a phallic fugitive, predaceous above her. She was driven down. The moon went, and in the sudden blackness she was driven down, a trespasser in an unseen place.

Her hands roamed over the ground and she touched something dank and tenacious. She closed her hand over it till it curled itself into a little ball of slime. She picked it up, stroked it and waited for it to probe its head out. Then it extended in her hand, its little sucking mouth fawning at her like a fish in a bowl. She was defiled by its necromancy as it slunk towards her arm.

And suddenly the moon broke through bars in the cloud and looked upon the world like a man through a prison cell. Then Tansy was very cold and fearful to hear a thin voice, high-up, trumpet-true and dreadful.

"Stamp upon and utterly destroy.... Stamp upon and utterly destroy.... Stamp upon ... Stamp upon ..."

... Until the words rocked about the universe and the stars shivered to the sound because there were these thin trumpets, pure as ice, stabbing a long lance into her head. And there was no shield against that lance.

. . . Then, when it was silent, she shook the slug from her and ran over the moor, unspeakably afraid, never stopping until she had reached the house and bolted the door. Exhausted, she fell into a chair. Her body was a dead weight to her. She shuddered, went into the kitchen and washed herself. Her fingers were like icicles; she found it hard to move them in the cold water.

Upstairs Arthur sighed in his sleep, his jaw fell back and a great snore came from his throat.

Tansy Progis heard it very clearly.

CHAPTER III

TANSY rarely passed a week without spending a few hours in her old home. The farm was now completely under the thumb of Bessie, Joe's voluminous and cantankerous wife. Fulfilling an old prophecy of Tansy, he had married her in a great hurry, purely in order to legalize the child he had got by her. Nicolas receded into a retrospective corner, not caring for Bessie's loud voice in a house where women had always been quiet. He often thought rather wistfully of Janet, whose stormy presence in the house of old had urged them all to activity, not driven them to idleness as Bessie did. But Janet had gone to London, and they rarely saw her now.

Joe begat three children by Bessie, two girls and one boy, and then began to have other women. He wearied of Bessie because sexually she was playful and too often evaded him with a snivelling kiss. "Not to-night, Joe," she would say, "I'm not myself to-night." Joe, wondering whether she ever would be herself, could not stand it. Hence the other women. Sometimes Bessie found out; then there was a scene in which she would simulate outraged motherhood, gathering her children around her like a hen with its young. The children implied a truce, and Joe would be received back into her cumbrous embrace. But suffering the customary evasion he would, before long, cast about for another diversion. Thus the sordid farce of his married life.

Andrew kept the farm together for a time, because Joe was lazy and Bessie spent a lot of money on things they did not want. But Andrew, enduring Bessie for four years, suddenly left them all and bought a house and some land miles away beyond Retallack. He had come to hate a farm that would now never belong to him. Evening after evening he had sat silent in a corner, nobody realizing his presence except at those times when he stirred in apocalyptic exposition of their delinquencies. Unmarried and friendless, he had fallen deeper and deeper into his own hard soul, bearing a bitter grudge against the world. So he went, with nothing more than a taciturn shrug of his sloping shoulders. And it was not until the farm tottered under ill-management and the name of Penderil whenever mentioned in the town came to be accompanied by a slight laugh—it was not until then that they missed Andrew.

Tansy was sad about all this, but she could not change it. She came to the farm generally on Thursday afternoons when Bessie was gone to market. The house was easier then. The heavy picture of Emmeline that hung in the living-room seemed to smile an encouragement. And Tansy would talk to Joe about the old days, about the work of the farm, about anything but her own life. Already they courted age by looking back, forgetting the present and never dreaming of the future.

One afternoon, near harvest time, Joe and Tansy walked across the yard together. Joe kicked the old stone trough with a smile.

"D'you mind the time," he asked, "when you and Andrew was struggling over that bit of flower?"

"Yes, I do," she said slowly. "And I'll tell you something I never told anybody yet. When you'd all gone to bed that night I came out and got a bit of that thorn. I've got it still."

"Well, well!" Joe was amused and curious. "What for, then?"

"Somebody gave it me," she answered slowly.

"Ah!" Joe nodded, as he felt, with understanding. "A chap, I suppose?"

"Yes, a chap, as you say. I was—rather a fool about him, Joe. I only saw him three times. He went away and never came back. Not our sort at all." Then she suddenly wished she had told him nothing. "You keep this to yourself," she cautioned. "I don't want for Arthur to know."

"That's all right," he said. "But you didn't have nothing to be ashamed of, did you?"

"No—nothing to be ashamed of. I was just in love with him like any fool of a girl might be at that age, and him a gentleman. That's all."

"Well," said Joe. "Nothing in that at all. It isn't anybody's business how many chaps you had before you wedded Arthur."

"But, you see, Joe," she confessed suddenly, "it isn't the same. With Arthur, I mean. I don't feel for him as a wife ought to feel."

"No?" Joe shook his head slowly. "I understand you, Tansy, and I'm sorry."

"So am I," she said warmly. "Sorry for Arthur. He's a good man. Too good by far for me."

"But you done well by him," reminded Joe. "You've always stood by him straight and proper, haven't you?"

"Yes, I've done that. But it aren't enough just to be faithful to a man. What we've got to do is to get them on fire, as you might say, every so often; to give them all we've got to give and take all, too, so as they can get on with their job the better. It's awful—to live with a person and never love them proper and true. It's wicked. Aunt Janet told me once that when you went on doing a thing you hated it was wicked. And this is like that. It's killing Arthur, Joe. You must see that."

"Can't you ever——" he began.

She understood him. "No, I can't!" she cried. "That's just the trouble, Joe. Every time I see his eyes flare up for me I go all cold inside and feel I want to strike him. I used to force myself to love him, but that was worse. It was—sort of being unfaithful to something inside you. Do you know what I do mean, Joe?"

"Yes." Joe nodded his head wisely. "I reckon I know well enough. You've got something to give and you can't find anyone to give it to."

"That's it," she agreed. "And the longer you keep it, the more dead you get. Mother got like that."

"Oh, I don't know about that."

They were walking across a field towards the valley.

"Yes," said Tansy. "She never loved father—not proper. And the life went out of her, I reckon. It's all right if you don't think much at all. You're happy enough till you see how much happier you might be. Oh, don't think I'm grumbling. I'm only sorry for Arthur's sake that things aren't different. For he's a good man and wants a woman for more than just a pretty smile that's got no bottom to it."

"Don't you fret about him," advised Joe. "He's got the children, anyhow."

"Alice," corrected Tansy, in spite of herself. But Joe took it another way.

"No. He don't care for the boy, do he? He's not like Arthur at all. Strange."

They were standing by a hedge at the end of a sloping field, looking down the valley, thick with bracken.

"We made a mess of things," said Joe, half to himself. Then he changed the subject and pointed down the valley. "That place is teeming with foxes," he said. "Sly devils and hard to beat. They got eleven of our best chicks last week."

"You must make a drive at them," said Tansy, "and beat them out. You'll have no farm left else."

"Andrew was the chap with a gun," said Joe. "He'd go out with old Simon and kill a score. A proper beaut with a gun, was old Andrew. But I don't like killing things much myself."

"When they're doing harm to you, you do have to kill them," insisted Tansy. "Andrew was right. I wish he'd stayed. An old bear if ever there was one, but no fool."

"Like me, I suppose," grinned Joe, with a sudden sad flash of the careless lad of years ago. Tansy dug her fist in his ribs.

"Go on!" she said. "You're no fool. You know how to treat a woman when she want a man, and that's rare seeming. Tell you, Joe—we both got too much guts for what we married, and that's fact."

A lethargic figure called to them from the top of the field. It was Bessie, returned from market earlier than they had expected. "There's the woman," mumbled Joe, as if in apology. "We'd best go in to tea."

"I won't stay. I'll make over the valley this way."

"If you go now," pleaded Joe, "she'll have it all on me later, saying you've insulted her like as not. Stay a bit, anyhow."

"You know I always fall out with Bessie."

"Never mind. It do her good. She's too fond of her own word."

Joe persuaded her and they walked towards the house. Bessie gave Tansy a plump kiss.

"How nice to see you, Tansy! Lor'—but you get thinner every day, I believe!"

It was true, for Tansy was very thin. But she did not require Bessie to remind her, so she said: "Some're born to be fat, others to be thin. And nothing won't alter them, ask me."

They sat down to one of Bessie's artificial teas. There were only the four adults—Bessie and Tansy, Nicolas and Joe. The three children, with David and Alice, had taken their tea to the beach.

Bessie had bought some sticky coloured cakes and grumbled because nobody seemed to enjoy them.

"Don't care for such stuff," complained Joe, as he crammed a pink castle into his mouth.

"Well," retorted Bessie, "it's what the gentlefolk do eat. None of your old heavy bake and saffron buns!"

Tansy was wondering why so large a person as Bessie should have so shrill a voice. When she spoke it was like blowing through a contra-bassoon and hearing the note of a piccolo.

Nicolas, in his chair, was a gaunt, spectral figure, like an oracle who never lives up to his office. He looked at Bessie moodily and said nothing. The three Penderils were bound together in silent hostility towards Bessie. The silence was slow and uneasy. Tansy, remembering another occasion when she had sat in this kitchen listening to the sound of munching jaws and had found it unbearable, thought how much more unbearable it was now. And then she was sorry for Bessie, because they were all silently hating her, although she doubted if Bessie were sensitive enough to realize that. The afternoon sun, tinged with the deeper gold that is the first herald of autumn, sent a long arm through the dairy, resting on slabs of butter and pans of unbroken cream.

Dear Lord, thought Tansy, as she watched the falling of the

slow sun, why do we all sit here and hate that large squeaky woman with her little pink cakes? And immediately she answered herself, because it is something to do. Yes, something to do. Hatred was very important when there were so few people to love. There was nothing else to do. So let us hate; hate with a malignant, consuming hatred in order to pass the time away. And when the objects of our hatred are out of our presence, let us delight ourselves in crucifying them on the cross of our vicious tongues.

Tansy suddenly longed to drag out the goodness from Bessie's torpid frame. Too much of this silent hatred defiled the autumn air. So she said: "How nice you've got the place looking, Bessie! I was thinking, as I came up the path, how nice those cornflowers and marigolds was looking. Mother would have liked that."

Bessie was startled. Her eyes thinned with suspicion.

"Yes," said Nicolas sullenly, "mother would have liked it. You're right there. I thought of her, d'you see, when I planted the seeds. Two penny packets, that's all. But she dearly loved a bit of flower, and the garden's been untidy these many years."

He spoke reproachfully, for he had been proud of his gardening, and was hurt that Tansy should ascribe it to Bessie. But Tansy, inwardly angry with herself, tackled Bessie again.

"Anyway," she continued, "I'm glad you got rid of that old picture what used to hang there." She pointed to the Good Shepherd's vacant place. "Never did care much for it." She forced the words out of her mouth.

Bessie instantly responded.

"I'm some glad you say that," she tittered. The men scowled. "They two cursed and swore no end when I had it took down. Now, I like something cheerful myself. Something with an—appeal."

She was getting kittenish. It was sickening. And Tansy knew now that to try to make a friend of a woman she really despised was only to thicken the poison in the air. Better get her hatred right out of her and have done with it. So she changed the tone of her voice.

"No," she said dangerously, "there aren't much appeal in the Lord for some of us. I grant you that."

Her voice cut into Bessie, sharp as a knife. She had the power sometimes to destroy a person in this manner.

Bessie faltered before her straight grey eyes, deadly sharp and cold. And she knew that in Tansy she met a powerful hostility which was lacking in Nicolas and Joe. She could do what she liked with them. But have this bitch in the house for half a day and she would go to pieces. She knew it. In Tansy gleamed the pointed steel of a fanatic. She looked as though with a gesture of her hand she could invoke a fury to wipe out half the world. And Tansy, enjoying her power, arose and began to play with Bessie like a cat with a mouse. She wanted to toy with Bessie in a corner and make her scamper feebly. It was splendid to hate! Why had she been foolish enough to try to kill it? She searched for a way to assault Bessie.

"I was thinking," she said calmly, "those children of yours are looking sickly to me. Ailing for something, maybe."

Bessie winced and Tansy marked it with glee.

"No, I don't think——" whimpered Bessie, her mouth sticky with pink icing.

"It'd be better," continued Tansy, "if instead of going to town every Thursday and coming back with all this trash"—she pointed to the cakes—"you stayed home and baked some good wholesome cakes as would nourish them and wouldn't turn in their stomachs."

Joe chuckled. It might have been the end of Bessie had there not been a sudden scampering at the back door at that moment. The three children burst in noisily. The youngest, a waxen-faced girl of five, was slobbering into her grubby wrist. Bessie ran up to her, knelt down and put her arms round her.

"What is it then, my pretty? What you crying for?"

She would show Tansy the magnificence of her mother-hood. Oh, yes—she would parade the last most glorious virtue, motherhood and all its fond excesses!

The child, encouraged by adulation, sobbed all the more and whimpered words that nobody could hear. Tansy could have slapped the watery, screwed-up face. Nicolas was uncomfortable. Joe bored. He loved his children little more than he loved the meretricious cakes on the table.

Bessie, failing to get any coherent explanation from the child, turned to Benjamin, her first-born, a spiky lad of thirteen, with a nose quivering into an undying dribble.

"You done something to her, Ben? I'll leave you know if you did! Out with it, now!"

"How should I be doing such a thing, mother?"

How, indeed, thought Tansy—with a face that could only frighten one intelligent enough to desire beauty and strength in the human race? But his next remark was a blow to her.

"It's that David——" he began.

"Yes," chorused Florrie, the other daughter. "Making upon poor Janie something *awful*——" Her eyes and mouth gaped open colourfully at the word. Ben carried on. "Seized hold of her wrists he did——"

"—And glared at poor Janie something *awful*," supplemented Florrie. They rattled off excited descriptions, one after another, Florrie rounding off every sentence with the lugubrious cadence "something *awful*".

If they were to be believed, David had led the others into a deep cave where he said there were seals. It was very damp and slippery, and David took Janie's hand. The others were rather timid, but he made them follow him and clasped Janie's hand firmly. It grew so dark that they could see nothing. Then from a hole above, in the distance, the dim light of day descended; an unearthly subaqueous light. Then David suddenly caught both Janie's wrists, put his face near her and snarled: "That's where they used to drop the bodies of little girls like you who were *afraid!* We're walking over their bones now!"

David may not have meant to scare Janie, but she saw his mouth twisted near her in the wet green lights of the cold place, and she screamed and screamed till they got out into the open again. She sobbed on the way home and clung to Ben, who, angry with David, but very much afraid of him, did nothing but encourage her with uncomforting thwacks on the back.

With many variations, this was the children's account of David's strange behaviour. Bessie, hardly able to keep back a succulent smile, turned to Tansy.

"I always knew it," she said in bitter triumph. "That David's a devil! He may get over you with his cunning smiles, but he's a devil, and you know it."

She patted Janie's head. "There, poor dear! He shan't ever come near you again."

She made as if to enfold the child in her skirts, but finding the gesture, though impressive, exceedingly difficult to execute, she pressed its unwilling head into the irreproachable valley of her bosom.

"He's not a devil!" snapped Tansy, her face very white.

"Yes, he's a devil!" maintained Bessie, standing firm on her words now that she had found where to pierce Tansy. "Everybody do know it. You talk about me and my children, getting big about what I should give them to eat. The idea! Fancy cakes don't make them frighten little girls, anyhow! That boy of yours wants whipping, ask me."

Tansy struggled, because she knew so well what Bessie meant when she said that David was a devil. But she knew also that she had to defend him before this woman.

"I know how to correct my children well enough," she said. "And you needn't fear he won't be properly punished. But I won't have you say he's a devil."

To Tansy it was imperative that Bessie should take back a statement which threatened the very foundations of her life. The whole dispute centered now upon that one point. And Bessie would not move.

"You can ask Joe," she said. "He's too fond of making on little children and scaring the life out of them. He shan't go out with mine again, and that he won't. A hateful, conceited devil of a boy, that had his own way from——"

Tansy cut in. She would not listen to Bessie's invective. She could not face the fact that others were beginning to detect in David a sleeping daimon of abortive power which lay concealed under the rare charm of his superficial manner. She must face this out alone—not with others.

"You hold your words," she snarled, and turning to Joe: "Is it true, you? What she do say?"

"Well," mumbled Joe, "I can't deny but what I *have* found him sometimes making nasty faces at the youngsters. Mind you, I don't say it's more'n a boyish prank——"

"Oh, don't you?" snapped Bessie, enraged by her husband's feeble support. "You know well enough it's a sight more'n that. Why, I've even seen our old bitch run away from him with the whites of her eyes showing! Shouldn't be frightened if the boy's father was a pisgey. I hear tell of such things. Anyhow, there's nothing of Arthur in him——"

Tansy dug her nails into her thighs, burning to tear them down Bessie's derisive face.

"You go to blazes!" she shouted. "You and your mealy-mouthed brats what couldn't say bo to a goose! David's a man and he's going to suffer like a man for behaving foolish to Janie. You needn't think I'm going to stand nonsense like that. But neither am I going to stand you saying things about him as are wicked and a lot of lies. Your sort'd make mischief in a minute——"

"Easy, Tansy! Easy!" fretted Joe miserably. Nicolas bit his lips, resenting this disturbance of his retrospective peace.

"I'm darned if I'll go easy," stormed Tansy. "If anybody's got a devil in them, it's me, not David!"

And she crashed out of the house with a slam of the door. She walked blindly down the valley, a seething cauldron of rage hissing inside her. She felt driven to action after a decade of inertia—driven to action by something stronger and yet the quintessence of herself. And paradoxically, she was happier, like a soldier who has waited tense and nervous in a trench and is at last sent over the top.

She could not define her anger. She only felt certain that out of it some great adventure would emerge. Pressed down for years she had suddenly sprung out of the rotten miasma of her life into a biting country of whips. Possessed by this thought, she never slackened her pace till she came to the gate and saw her son, the devil David, lying stretched out on the grassy wall, his hands making a pillow for his head, one leg thrown over the other. Then she paused as he lazily turned his head and smiled at her under his long lashes.

He had been dreaming of an Eldorado beyond the seas, a place of icebergs and blue-veined shells, of caverns, of ice-coned caverns, of suns that strove in a timeless aura. And dreaming, he saw Tansy through half-wet eyes, for inside he was stirred and the finger of romance, as old as time, traced an uncharted land in his mind. And Tansy was a dream-creature, a shadow in the caverns of his mind, an aery harbinger of fantasies yet to be unfolded. Stirred, his eyes were wet. For in that dreaming moment on the hedge-top he had wilfully sent his mind on to carry him through a lost saga of cold witchery. So his face was dim and lost, his eyes wet.

Tansy saw his long, moist lashes like strands of green weed trailing through a clear stream; saw the liquid haze of his brown eyes cloudy in dreams; saw his long, earnest face flushed with the hectic mark of adventure; his straight inviolable body stretched there in the sunlight. And she felt as though a silver arrow might dart from the skies and transfix him there, to impale him for ever till he might change to a granite figure so that all should see carved in the hedge, a shape of pure beauty, and passing say: "Beware of beauty! This lovely thing you see here was a devil."

A devil . . . and he smiled at her under moist lashes. For fifteen years then, she had worshipped a devil. Her mind twisted and turned, in and out, turned and twisted. And he would not speak. She knew that she was entirely outside him, that in some sort of cosmic design he ventured where she had no place. Upon that wall—the straight shape of a pure devil who frightened little children in dark places . . . caves . . . caves of a mind too deep for her to penetrate. This lovely, lovely shape of her spring ecstasy. . . .

She touched his head in a stupor. She knew that he had conquered her. Her surging anger fell back, died down; she felt numb and powerless. Beaten back again to that nether-world where she seemed to belong. The air was stifling; she could not breathe freely. Above her, so far that she could not strain to see, was a cold unsmiling face, an icy hand. She could not reach. So far above. She could not reach. . . .

David said: "Mother, I was watching that lark. When he stop singing he'll fall like a stone. You see."

She looked at the trembling microcosm of song swaying in the dome of the blue universe. But higher up she saw a hawk, poised like the crook of a palsied hand.

David raised himself. "See that?" he cried. "That's a kestrel! He'll have her! I bet you he'll have her before she drop!"

"Do you want him to?" whispered Tansy.

"Yes, I do!" cried David, his body writhing in impatience. "Oh, come on!" he cried. "You'll miss her!"

And down he came then. Not falling without energy as the lark would have fallen, but swooping down in a great drive of rapacious greed. There was a struggling conflict of wings in the sky, a feeble and a powerful fluttering. Then the hawk flew away out of sight. A small feather floated slowly to the ground. The air was mute with the lark's murdered song. What should never be heard—the last note of the lark—had been heard.

"That was fine!" said David.

"My God!" muttered Tansy. "Do you think it was?"

"Yes, I do."

"And why?"

"Because 'twas well done," said the boy. "The kestrel did what he darn well had to do, and did it well. That's why."

"Why did he have to do it?"

"That's not my affair!" he retorted.

"Suppose," said Tansy, "I had to drop on you sudden like that, would you say the same?"

"But you don't have to," he returned, with the impatient gesture of one who would banish the absurd from an argument.

"Maybe," she said grimly. "But suppose you had to frighten a little girl in a cave, would you say that was well done, too?"

He scowled for a moment. "So they've gabbed about that, have they?" Then he laughed. "If I had to do it," he said insolently, "I'd be proud to do it well."

"And did you have to do it?" she insisted.

He looked her straight in the eye, but she was strong and the rock of her did not move.

"Yes," he said shortly. "I did have to."

She could not answer that. It was a positive affirmation which defied any challenge. She turned from him, her heart like lead, her body a miserable burden to her. He called after her:

"You're not mad about it, are you?"

(Alice sat by the window, listening eagerly to it all.)

"I'm not mad," said Tansy. "I came up here ready to strike you dead, so I did. But I see something more of you now. Something

I haven't always had clear before. It aren't your fault. I'm more sorry for you than anything."

David screwed up his eyes, bewildered by her.

"What do you mean, mother?" he asked. "Sorry for me?"

"Yes," she said, "sorry for you, my dear."

She would not face him and he jumped down from the wall pressing himself near to her. She would not yield to him one inch.

"But why?" he said impatiently. "Why, mother? I'd rather you'd get mad with me than turn away like this, all queer."

"Yes," she said drily, "that's why I'm sorry for you. Because soon I shall lose the power to get mad with you at all. And that's a bad thing for me and you. You don't see it clear, maybe. But when you go behaving like a little sneaking, cowardly bully and I can't even storm at you as a mother should, I say it's a bad thing for me and you."

He put his arm round her waist and pleaded with her, half incoherently. He thought he could not move her, till he felt a warm drop fall on his arm. She was crying.

"When you were on the wall," she whispered, "I loved you. I wish you'd stayed like that and never moved again. Oh, son, I do wish with all my heart that I didn't love you so much. It's terrible to love like I do, hurting you all the time. You can't know. And every time you go and do things like that this afternoon, you just kill a bit of me somewhere. You don't see that——"

(Alice sniggered loudly.)

Tansy pushed David away and went into the house. David, half-savage, half-remorseful, broodily picked a rose to pieces.

CHAPTER IV

WITH the end of August, threshing began, and David spent his evenings helping in the work on the farm. Although some sort of reconciliation had been effected between him and Aunt Bessie, he did not find his position at the farm was very comfortable. She made it quite clear to him that she did not trust him, and the children, as children will, acted spitefully upon this attitude of their mothers. Nevertheless, David enjoyed those sun-cloudy evenings when he worked in the fields with the men who came on the thrashing machine, and he found at sunset that he did not want to return home. He worked hard, more in order to show that he was no fool than because he liked the work. And all the time he thought about his mother, himself and life. There was an estrangement between himself and his mother; he did not understand why. And he knew that without his mother he was lonely, because she of all people could understand him if she wished. He began to long for somebody to whom he could talk; some man older than himself, because he was tired of the company of children, tired of their shallow games. He liked Joe, and although Joe liked him, he was too busy in those days ever to take much notice of him. Grandfather Nicolas was too old and remote. Arthur was obviously impossible. There seemed to be nobody else in his small world.

Until one day, in the middle of harvesting, Andrew appeared out of nowhere, as taciturn as ever, but interested to see how the work of the farm progressed.

He came into the field where Joe and David were working and greeted Joe with a rugged smile. He was then a man of thirty-nine, tall and spare, with hard temples, black hair and here and there a line of grey. Joe was glad to see him. In the last ten years they had only seen him a few times and seldom heard from him.

"How't a-doing, you?" Joe pressed his hand warmly.

"Mustn't grumble. I thought I'd see how things were doing. May stay a day or two if there's room."

"That's proper. Father'll be glad to have you here."

"Good harvest?" asked Andrew. He saw David bending down over a sheaf of corn, brown as a berry in the sun, his eyes inquiringly and half-perplexedly searching out Andrew's. He dropped his head when Andrew looked at him. And Andrew felt a quiver of interest, a warm ripple run over his body.

"Who's the lad?" he asked Joe, not recognizing the little dark boy he had seen years ago.

"Why, that's Tansy's lad. Don't know him now, I suppose? David, here's your Uncle Andrew. Mind him, do you?"

David straightened himself and slowly met Andrew's heavy

eyes. Andrew stretched out his hand, and when they shook there was a strange immediate sympathy between them. "You're like Tansy," said Andrew slowly, "and yet not. Putting in some work here, then?"

"Just for harvest. I come on after school."

They began to talk, and Joe, saying that he must tell Nicolas, walked away. Andrew filled a pipe and walked slowly up and down with David.

"I got a farm, too," he said casually.

"Yes, I know. I hear about you sometimes. You went off on your own——" David hesitated a little awkwardly.

Andrew laughed.

"Yes, I went off. I got fair sick of your aunt and her kids. Couldn't stand it."

"Don't wonder either," muttered David under his breath. He was wondering why this strange uncle of his had always been scathingly referred to as that 'old bear '.

"What you doing when you leave school, then?"

"Don't know. Seems nothing much here for a chap. Dad's on the dole, and suppose I shall be, too."

"Like farming, do you?"

"Well enough. Shouldn't mind having my own farm one day."

"Happen I might start you on my place. Oh, I don't promise, mind you! Times are bad and it's little I could give you. But maybe better'n loafing about doing nothing. That take all the guts out of a man, that do."

David was eager. "Where is your farm then? Oh, I'd love to come. I'm sick of doing nothing."

"It's over there"—Andrew pointed over David's shoulder northward. "Right beyond Retallack, past St. Eile and about another five mile to Rosemulyan. A handsome place for them as wants quiet. Good land, too. Not a town nearer'n St. Ives."

"I went that way once with mother. When I was a kid. We went to see an old woman called Jessie Vean. Happen you'd know her?"

"Yes, I hear tell of her. Saw her years ago at your mother's wedding. A queer old bitch and not spoken too well of. She got a cottage about three miles from me, but I never see her. They say she's going off her head. I heard they were trying to put her away."

"Put her away?"

"Yes. To the workhouse or Bodmin, more likely."

"Oh!" David was silent. Andrew's warm strong arm lay across his shoulders, his fingers pressing into his skin. The evening was declining, the sun rapidly going down over the sea. A swift cleft the air above them, his blue breast flashing in the sun. David was tired and found himself half leaning upon Andrew.

"I should love to go over there," he said dreamily.

He looked northwards. A black fuel in the smoke of the sun's fire, the unyielding outline of the cliff above the pool was shadowed remotely by the shape of a further head protruding from the north moors. The colour of that head was a smoky blue and assembling from the moors, the wind-driven smoke of a heath fire hung in the sky in a strange slowly-moving shape. David was lost in his thought and could not turn his eyes away from that smoke-swept land of purple moors. And Andrew was happy because in and through David he suddenly perceived beauty and accepted it without question.

Joe came up with Nicolas who, chuckling happily, talked to Andrew about the farm. Andrew was aware of Bessie standing a little way off, her hands on her hips, even at his first appearance prepared for hostilities. He laughed to himself.

Leaving David, they began to walk round the fields, chatting to the men and neighbours who had come in. David followed Andrew's slow regular figure and wondered why he liked his uncle so much. There was a spirit in Andrew which he had not found in anybody else.

When dusk came and it was time for him to go, he hated to have to return home. He was jealous of the people who talked to Andrew in the house. But he went home, walking slowly in the chilly gathering darkness.

An unshapely moon rose, orange, through strips of cloud. Over the horizon the last pale green colour of day merged unwillingly into the deep blue of night. A whirling bumbledory accelerating a warning siren, caught David on the nose and staggered off from him like a drunk man against a wall. But David was hardly aware of it. The night was loud with the rattle of crickets, yet David, who so loved the autumn sound, did not stop to hear it this evening. A green-eyed fox that slunk along the path did not stir him. For the adventure of the north was in his mind and he wanted to go with his Uncle Andrew and start a new life of his own with a man who seemed better able to understand him.

His home stood out, carved clear into the sky, and it seemed a cold, lustreless place to him, where he would find no welcome. His father would be reading the paper, would not even look up as he came in. His mother—he tried not to think of her, because every time he did so he was hurt, and in a strange way felt that it was hurting her. He did not want to go in with this new secret burning within him. What did they know of the unhappy loveliness of a secret, who had never had secrets? For he decided that he could not yet tell them of Andrew's suggestion in case nothing came of it. They clearly did not much like Andrew and would not easily sympathize with David's desire to go on his farm.

He paused by the gate, draining in the moist smell of sweetbriar. Through the window in the light of the lamp, he saw Tansy sitting in the old rocking chair and darning some socks. Her head moved very slowly, as though to the rhythm of the needle. Her face was long and narrow, a little cadaverous in the warm light. The light pierced a star in the old lustre of the brooch she wore.

David stayed there watching her, some strange sense of a pre-natal consciousness absorbing him. His mother seemed a symbol, so pacific and monotonous there in the lamp-light. She seemed to him the one immutable figure in a chaotic universe. She was certain, everlasting.... When he looked at her, the association of ideas bred in his mind a picture of a ploughman moving solitary over a black field in February, followed by a score of starlings and rooks. For the first time he saw his mother as a detached creature; consciously he ceased to think of himself as her son, and in doing so he obtained a clearer picture of her than he had ever had. He knew that she was splendid and strong and he did not want to change that picture of her. Nevertheless, he craved for the sweetmeat of her tenderness....

He went in. They looked up, and down again. Alice was

pressed over a book of sums, her brow creased into indomitable erudition.

"Did you have any supper up there?"—Tansy did not look at him as she spoke. Her voice was very low. She spoke as though there were a sleeper in the house whom she did not wish to disturb.

"No, mother. Uncle Andrew's come, and I didn't like to get in their way."

Arthur looked up. "Andrew, eh?" He pushed aside his paper and leant back in his chair. Lighting a pipe long ago dead, he spoke with elementary cynicism of Andrew.

"As cheerful as ever, I suppose? Still smiling sweet and speaking pleasant! But then, of course, I was forgetting you didn't ever really know him. Oh, a nice man! A nice man, Andrew!" He chuckled in the silent room and was not aware that he chuckled alone.

"I like him," said David rather sullenly. He made himself some tea and cut a slice of bread.

"Ah, you don't know him," said Arthur, "like what we do. Your mother'll mind a time when she had a regular set-to with him, and all over a trifle."

David was curious. "When was that then, mother?"

Tansy paused in her work as though trying to remember. Then slowly she said: "I often fell out with Andrew, and never knew a sister yet who always lived at peace with her brother. But Andrew's got good stuff in him and I never denied it. More than Joe, even if Joe's a sight easier to get on with."

David wanted to tell Tansy about Andrew's suggestion, but felt it impossible to speak with Arthur there.

"How's he looking?" asked Tansy.

"Looking well. Straight and——" he searched for a word. "A proper man," was all he could say. But he said it with his eye half on Arthur, and Arthur felt it.

"Oh, it's easy enough to be a man," he commented loftily, "when you spend all your life considering yourself and nobody else. I don't mind that Andrew ever so much as stirred a little finger for anybody but himself."

"Matter of fact," remarked Tansy coolly, "he thinks of a

good many only he don't show it, and you never get any thanks in this world for services rendered save you announce it pretty loud."

"Well, who did he ever help, anyway?" insisted Arthur, not because he had any real grudge against Andrew, but only because he felt bound to stand upon a statement made purely in defence of David's half-conscious gibe at him.

"He thought more about mother," continued Tansy, "than any one of us. Even she never quite realized that. But 'twas he who got her to bed and sent for Aunt Janet."

Alice bit the end of her pencil and waited eagerly for the retort. And Arthur, knowing that he had again engaged in an argument beyond him, said rashly, "He only did that to show off, ask me! Andrew was always like a dog with a wounded paw—mad because everybody else hadn't got a wounded paw."

David was furious. "Don't believe no such thing! Unless he's changed some since you last saw him. He mayn't say much, but he do more."

Arthur, who rarely quarrelled outwardly with David, felt a further taunt he could not pass unchallenged.

"You don't know nothing about it! Hold your tongue! Because you seen a man for five minutes, you have the impudence to tell your olders they don't understand a man they knew before you was born or thought about."

A very bitter serpent uncoiled itself in David. He let it hiss without restraint.

"I darn well won't hold my tongue. Uncle Andrew wants me to go on his farm, so think of that a bit. And I'm going as soon as I can leave school."

He looked quickly at his mother, wanting her support. But although she was stirred inside, she would not show it. Alice's mouth fell open. This was too much for her.

"Talking some big," she gibed, "when all he'll give you to do is feed the pigs and pay you nothing for it——"

"Ah, you hold your silly gab!" snarled David. "You're only a silly bastard of a kid——"

He drew his words back in his breath, frightened of Arthur who had risen and was bending over him. David's words had slipped through the incoherency of his rage. Arthur was white; his teeth pressed together; his knuckles locked on the table.

"I won't have that language to your little sister. You got to say you're sorry to her right here, otherwise——"

"Otherwise what——"

"By God, the cool tongue of you!" Arthur took off his leather belt. "You get out!" he cried, the world a crashing ruin before his red eyes. "You get out—because there's no knowing what I'll do to you. Get out—and away from me, else you want to be beaten till you can't stand——"

David was sweating and trembling. He had never seen Arthur in a rage before. Nor had Tansy save once, when he had beaten a bully who tormented a donkey. Within Arthur at that moment there boiled up all the simmering hostility towards the seed of Roger Chailey, which for fifteen years he had felt but could never name. Never admitting in his mind that David was not his son, his blood knew it of a certainty. His blood, which had never run in the boy's veins, leapt up, carried on like a stream accumulated at a dam and suddenly released—leapt violently forward and threatened to submerge the opposition in its unchecked flow. And David was frightened. There was a burning righteousness in Arthur which shook something very old and inherently weak in David, so that he trembled. Had there been none of Tansy's blood in his veins, he might not have remained standing there.

"You just try and beat me——" he said. His small loose words were like little irritating flies in the room. Arthur veered round the table. Tansy, who had watched all this with silent excitement, suddenly spoke in a very hard and compelling voice. Her lips were curled like a watchful dog; her face, chalybeate. She rose and quickly went over to David before Arthur could reach him. Had she not spoken then, Arthur would have fallen on the boy and killed him. She knew that.

"Go to bed," she said to David. "I tell you to go to bed."

Then David flinched because he loved his mother. Swiftly, without a word, he turned and went upstairs.

Arthur's thwarted rage burst like a flood in his head. He fell down in his chair, gasping a little, his mouth half open, his hands still fingering the belt.

Tansy turned upon Alice, who instinctively recoiled.

"You go up too," she said. "'Tisn't fit as a child should witness such scenes. Go up and forget about this if you can." Alice edged out of the room nervously. Tansy heard her turning about in her bed upstairs a few moments later. She sat down at the table opposite Arthur. She saw that he was heaving in great unbroken sobs of distress. It broke Tansy to see him like that, sobbing there, a terrible distress. She leant her hand over the table and touched his arm. Desperately, like a drowning man, he clutched her hand.

"Oh there," she whispered. "Don't cry, my dear! I know how you felt. I'm glad you showed your spirit. Don't cry so."

She was crying too, so desperately did she want to take the man in her arms and comfort him, and so certainly did she know it would be a disloyalty to herself; a false superficial sweetness. But he seized upon her hand and through the thickness of his throat, muttered, "Tansy, Tansy, you haven't spoke like that for so long. Oh my dear, say you do love me! Just say that and I'll be happy again. I see you all slipping away from me somehow and it's awful to me. Just give me of your dear eyes again and kiss me true——"

Tansy's head fell forward on the table. She felt that her heart was broken and she could not weep as she wished. Only these few bitter tears forced their way through her eyes. The awful long futility of her life with Arthur appalled her and made her want to die and finish it all. To hear his voice pleading like a sick man for water when she could give him nothing that would sustain him, was a reproach too much for her to bear.

"Just say you do love me . . ." and she could have said that and made him think it was true. But all she said was, "Oh, Arthur, I can't—I can't! I do admire you, I'll be faithful all our days. But just that—I can't——"

His hand unclosed over hers. He did not speak. She got up and without looking at him, turned to the door.

"I'm going up," she said lifelessly. "Come soon. Us are tired. You can only want for sleep when you're like this."

She went upstairs very slowly, feeling physically weak and utterly wearied. Outside David's room she paused a moment

with her hand on the latch. She heard him moving about in his
bed. But she would not go in.

CHAPTER V

ARTHUR took refuge in a headache, and Tansy got the children
off to school before he came down. She did not speak much
to either of them. David was morose and only waiting for the
moment to get out of the house. They all bore the self-conscious
expressions of people who try to forget a quarrel, like those
under a black sky who pretend that rain is farthest from their
thoughts. Tansy had slept well and awoken with the immediate
feeling that in some way the course of her life was altered. It
was like waking in an unfamiliar room. Arthur and her children
seemed strangers to whom she need only be courteous. For she
knew perfectly well, as did David and Arthur, that the quarrel
of last night had declared a permanent state of war, hitherto
concealed, but now hideously open. They might talk about gen-
eralities and try to forget essentials, but the foundations of their
family life, never very secure, had suffered too severe a blow for
them ever to stand firm again. The house had been struck and
would never recover.

Early in the forenoon, Arthur went out for a walk. It was still
pure weather and he would have liked to have gone to the farm
to help in the harvesting. But for some reason not clear in his
own mind, he hesitated to meet Andrew.

Near noon, Tansy, drawing some carrots in the garden, heard
a step at the gate and turned round to meet Andrew. She was
very glad to see him. His obtuse strength that had once irritated
her, comforted her now. And she thought there was a warmth
in his manner new to him. They walked into the house and sat
down.

"Alone then?"

"Yes. Children to school and Arthur out for a bit."

"Well, I'm glad to see you alone so's we can have a quiet chat.
How're things, my girl? You're not looking all the world." Tansy
began scraping some carrots into a basin as she spoke to him.

"Perhaps I'm not very grand, Andrew. But I'm not a girl any more and married life wear you out, I reckon. But tell me all about yourself. D'you get on all right over there with no one to tend you?"

"Well enough and a little better."

He was, as always, very guarded in his speech.

"I'm working up slowly, d'you see? Buying good cattle, naught but the best. Reckon I'll show at Exeter next year. I gave up sheep and pigs. More money in cattle, and if you want a good stock you've got to be for ever at 'em. Oh, it's not such a bad place, you!" He was really very proud of it, Tansy could see that. She laughed lowly. It did her good to have Andrew boasting there, the same Andrew with a face like an old prophet, a little warmer, a little fuller, but the same old Andrew for all that. He was like good ground that had been well manured. She studied his clothes. They were good and simple. His white shirt very clean; his socks without any holes in them.

"You have a woman in, I suppose?"

"What do you mean? I don't want no woman and never did!"

Tansy laughed. "No. You're a queer chap that way! I meant to darn your clothes and such like."

"I got the knack of doing such things myself," he said with a slight smile. "Never had no woman in."

"Well, I'm bound to say you thrive on it. You certainly look a sight better'n other members of the family, including myself——"

He was a little embarrassed. "I'm afraid you're not somehow as happy as you ought to be." But he was half afraid to talk of her affairs, and she, although she derived pleasure from his company, did not feel she could tell him much about herself. They had always been apart; as children there had been something in each other which they had never been able to penetrate. Tansy still felt that the barrier of childhood was too strong to break down.

She wondered whether he would talk about David.

"I'm happy enough," she said. "How shouldn't I be? Arthur's very good, though he's had rare bad luck and we've been hard put to it at times, to know how to go on. But I'm content. I've got two good children and that's enough for any woman."

"I saw David. A fine upstanding lad I thought. It must be a sure comfort to you to have a handsome son like that. I wish I had a son like that. A pretty boy, I thought, and plenty of guts, ask me!"

"Guts enough for a dozen!" agreed Tansy. "And more over sometimes. But a fine lad, I grant you."

"I was thinking—only a vague idea, mind you—but thinking he might like a job on my place. I believe I could do with a lad like that. I asked him about it. He seemed to like the idea."

"Yes, I know. He told us."

"He told you? Then why the devil didn't you say something to me about it? Don't you like the idea?"

"Well, he's very taken with you——" murmured Tansy.

"I can't help saying I'm glad," said Andrew a little smugly. "For 'tisn't many as cotton on to me. And I'm bound for to say I was proud to see your lad, and proud to know he was a Penderil. Wouldn't you like for him to come? There's no chance for him up at the farm and precious little doing elsewhere in Penth. If I can give him a start you ought to be glad."

"So I am. And grateful. Though, mind you, if you has David you're getting a good moneysworth. If that lad like you, and seem he do, he'll work hard for you. No. If I'm sorry for him to go, it's no more than a mother's foolishness mourning over a lad she's losing. But I got to lose him one day and I'd rather 'twas to you than most."

"Well, Tansy, I'm glad you do speak sensible like that. I know how a woman feel when her children begin to go. But it's got to come, as you say."

"I shouldn't speak to Arthur about it. You leave that to me. He'll maybe—feel it a bit, him not being able to do anything for the boy."

"Do he like David?" asked Andrew bluntly.

"No, I can't say altogether as he do like the boy. They're different, see? David's different—in many ways. You'll find——" She began to wish she had said nothing. "You'll find queer sides to him. I just warn you he's not all a pretty boy. Older than his years, too."

"What do you mean—queer things?" grumbled Andrew. "The

lad's different, I see that. A darn sight more sharp and lively than most, nowadays. A credit to you, I say——"

"——And his father," murmured Tansy, with a slow smile.

"Yes, I suppose. I tell you what, my girl!" His mind filled with a sudden impulse. "Sometime before Christmas, you and David come over and stay a week-end at Rosemulyan. Then you'll see what it's like, and maybe won't fret so much to lose him."

"Oh, I shan't fret anyhow. If I decide to let him go, go he shall, and you don't see me shedding no crocodile tears! But it's a pretty idea, Andrew, and kind of you. I hardly know what to say——"

She got up and went into the kitchen. She wanted to go to Rosemulyan alone with David. It would be lovely to have David away from the others. But she did not want to make new trouble between Arthur and herself.

Andrew encouraged her. "There's no reason why not. Arthur can easy look after the girl for a day or two. You never had a change these ten years and 'twill do you a world of good. I'd like to see you go about a bit for a change, although, mind you, I'm not one to favour women gadding about all over the place and tit-ivating their bodies instead of their homes. But that don't mean you oughtn't to get a day off every so often."

"Well, I might come," she said cautiously. "Only I don't say I can promise."

Andrew was more enthusiastic than Tansy had ever seen him. "Tell you what," he said expansively. "You come over for Feast at Rosemulyan. Plenty of fun then for you and the lad. And I'll get somebody in, if 'twill please you, to make a bit of Feast pudding and such stuff."

"Feast. When would that be?"

"End of the first week in November."

"A week after Feast here——" she mused. Suddenly she felt much younger. The word "Feast" reminded her of her child-hood. She dug Andrew in the ribs amiably.

"Old chap, you're a sport! All right, maybe I'll come. But no promises!"

It was nearly dinner time, and she got him out of the house

with promises to see him later at the farm. She did not want Arthur to meet him.

"Staying for guldies, Saturday?" she asked at the gate.

"Maybe. But mustn't stay beyond Sunday."

"Ah, well. See you then perhaps. So long!"

"So long!"

He walked across the heath in his slow, precise steps. Tansy watched him for a moment, suddenly rather proud of being a Penderil, then went in.

When Arthur came in a little later, she decided to approach him immediately on the subject of Andrew and David.

"How's your head?" she asked, as a smooth preliminary.

"Fair. But still a bit heavy."

"I expect you're hungry. Shall I take you up some of this stew?" She paused with a ladle in her hand.

"Yes, I dare say I could eat a little."

He was rather too obviously poorly, thought Tansy, but still, it was better to humour him.

"Andrew been here," she said quickly, glad to get it out.

"Oh?" He came over to the table with not the slightest sign of interest.

"Yes." Again she paused. Then: "Arthur, I'm real sorry to talk about what pains you, maybe. But best to get it over and have done. He really do seem to want to give the boy a chance. I think we'd best not stand in his way at all. It's soon time he was earning a living and this is his only chance, seeming."

"That's all right," said Arthur, chewing stewed steak defiantly. Tansy was impatient with his dogged attitude.

"I'm not standing in his way," he added.

"Aren't you glad at all that he's found a job?"

"I'm not glad. I'm not sorry. I don't feel somehow that it concern me at all." He went on eating loudly.

Tansy could not speak. It was a shock to her to have to realize so acutely that Arthur would be a happier man if he never saw David again. She wondered what he would say if she went, too. Cry a bit, likely, she thought, and then snore again. The sympathy she had felt for him the night before was rapidly giving way before the old irritation. She saw him again as a useless clod of a creature, utterly valueless to her, glad to get rid of the only thing in life she really cared for. She felt she would like to keep David back just to infuriate him.

"Another thing," she said coldly. "Andrew's asked me and David to go over there for a week-end."

"You'll go then?" Arthur looked up quickly.

"Yes, I reckon we will. You can easily manage for a day or so."

"As you please." In his anxiety to show that he was unmoved he jabbed the fork in his lip. Tansy laughed.

That afternoon she went into the town to do some shopping. She did not take the direct path that ran past the farm, but went along the valley towards the Vicarage wood, a way that she loved and could not forget. The hedges were luscious with blackberries, and where the thorn had blossomed was now the sloe. It was a quiet day, with the quietness that the earth has when old age begins to creep over it. There was a sense of order and restraint. Tansy felt that the world was like a house that had been scoured, and waited now for the coming of some honoured guest. But she could not name the guest, unless it was winter. Opulent as a sententious alderman, a robin flaunted himself on a twig, reminding her of winter. Time was when she might have welcomed it, but now the seasons all seemed much alike. Except that now the sloping fields of the valley-side were dotted with mowies of wheat, like a courtly assembly of grand ladies in crinolines—and that in a few weeks' time they would be hard and black under the plough—it was all much the same. The birds had found their voices again, but they were sombre comments upon the passing of summer. Soon, there would only be the robin to sing.

She stayed a moment by the stream-side, standing where Chailey had grasped her hand years ago. The old cottage by the little wood was falling down, but nothing else had changed. Except herself. Nobody had built any houses; none had been taken down. The mines along the valley had reached a state of decay where seemingly they would remain for centuries, for the crumbling of a ruin cannot be noticed in a life-time. Nothing had changed—and yet, she thought, all had changed. There were different flowers, different trees, even different water flowing to the sea.

She saw an old man walk slowly across a field with a bundle of blackened gorse-stumps on his back. He passed over that field very slowly because of his heavy load; each footstep a labour, each footstep nearer home. In a few days' time he would pass over the field again with another load. His labour would not reap him a release from further labour. The monotonous engine of toil going on and on, with never an end in sight, filled Tansy with sadness. The man passed through that field and left no mark more than the print of his feet in the soil; something had set him in motion, and without question on he went, on he would go, until his body drooped with the weariness of death. And other things than this old man . . . the blue star of speedwell in spring, the grasses that withered sweetly into hay, the swallows that made movement an endless design, the cuckoo who sounded the end of the year in his first note. . . . These were the same as the man. Even the sun, in his continual march up and down a changing but immutable sky, was going somewhere to his long home. And she, too.

Oh, my dear Lord! thought Tansy. What are we all here for at all, if it's nothing but a long walk from cradle to grave? But being something of a humorist, although in these days a grim one, she laughed and walked on. She always imagined that God must laugh a lot. . . .

In the square she found the customary band of idlers lounging by the Bank. Some of them were squatting on their haunches. Idly discussing the vices of their neighbours, they seemed exceedingly happy. They were like the granite houses of the town, thought Tansy; just as much a growth.

She went to the baker, the grocer and butcher. Then to a crazy shop where an old woman sold little more than sticks of liquorice and bottles of rennet. Tansy often bought things here that she had no real use for, because she had known the old woman from her earliest childhood, and in these days it was hard for her to make a living. The little dingy place was red with the fire in the room beyond; the window so obscured by notices and grimy bottles of sweets that little light could penetrate.

"Well, Mrs. Nankervis, I've come to buy some—" What had she come to buy? She did not know. "—some sweets for the children."

The crooked yellow face cracked above a row of glass jars. Two eyes, like hat-pin heads, pierced the gloom.

"Is it you, my dear? My Tansy, then—well——"

She heaved a curiously high-pitched sigh that fell from her lower and lower, spreading like the ripples of a pebble in a pool.

"I was just a-going to snap you up and say no to you. Thinking you was the minister with another notice for the window-pane. Humbugging crowd! In here every minute saying will I put up this, will I put up that, and never so much as buy a toffee-apple. Mean old stinks, I calls 'em! Come to the Lord's house, they do say to me, some soft." Mrs. Nankervis spat. "And praise the Lord with a psalm and a trumpet—and humbug, says I. Well, I can't go a-doing of it, Tansy, my pretty, and no good saying I can. What'll you have?"

Tansy bought some liquorice all-sorts. The old woman had to thump the bottom of the bottle to get them out.

"I hear from my boy," she croaked with harsh joy, "in—where do you call it—where we do get that there tea from. Lyons, is it, you? I can't tell his writing, my sight's getting some bad. Here's his letter. You read it. Read it aloud, there's a dear." She folded her hands on her wiry bosom and waited proudly.

Tansy read: "Dearest Mother. I'm in Lyons now, that's France. Some handsome place with pretty girls, too many of them, you might say. Our boat sets off for Gib to-morrow. . . . Well, mother, hope as how you're prospering and not getting a lot of that rumaticks like you had when I was home. Seeing you soon. Keep the home fires burning for your son what always thinks of you and says a prayer. Your loving son. . . ."

"Ah!" Mrs. Nankervis heaved a sigh of lachrymose satisfaction. "A good boy! And fancy—he'll be getting his promotion soon!"

A good boy. . . . Tansy walked down the narrow street with its serried line of grey, formal houses. A good boy . . . with a prayer for his mother every night. Oh, yes, a good boy . . . so they were, all good boys when they left home and wrote smarmy letters full of humbug to delude a poor woman who had nothing else left in the world. Good boys . . . they took the heart and the soul out of you, then went off, only thinking of you when they wanted something that nobody else would give them. The gay, brave, good boys and their poor fools of squashed, deluded mothers. Wasting their love where it was not wanted. She suddenly realized what a drag upon a man a loving mother must really be. She remembered Emmeline's benign detachment from all of them. Tansy would be the same; never crave from David what was not hers to have, the complete fire of his love. She would let him go to his own life. It was right that she should. Years later, when she was dead and he an old man, he would remember and know that she had been a wise mother. Years later ... David grown up. She could not imagine him as anything but the stripling she now knew. What would he do with his life? Where was the woman he would bewitch? God help her, she muttered, and as she said the words, found that she was passing by the church gate. The worn old clock hung unwillingly back, ten minutes behind the correct time. Ten to five, it said. She wanted to go in the church, for she rarely came now except at times like Easter.

She went in, half afraid of its emptiness and the hollow sound of her feet over the tiles. She went up to the Sanctuary. To-morrow, she supposed, they would be decorating the place for Harvest Festival. She wished her old Parson was still alive. They had a new Parson now, young and athletic, who shouted so much from the pulpit that it made one ashamed. His favourite word was sin; he seemed to spit it at them in letters of blood. It was a word which, far from reminding Tansy of the error of her ways, set her mind upon a conscious train of perverse thought. So she gave up coming to church. But as she stood there, she wondered why she had not been at times like this, when it was empty. For it was very lovely and peaceful; full of comfort in a queer emotionless way.

The sun came through the west window, streaming over the dark walls of the belfry, travelling in avenues of golden dust along the nave, and striking, as it always did, a rich orange patch on the left of the altar. She felt it streaming over her like the lustrous caparison of a Saint of God. It was so beautiful, so nearly tangible, that golden path, that she wanted to gather it in her hands like pollen and fling it over every dark and sooty thing she could find.

She looked up to the east window, where, above the sunlight, very cold and grey, the mournful George stood, with his sword, his face heavy and remote under the silver casque. She wanted to pray, but she did not know for what. Perhaps for rest. She only knew that she stood outside the Saint's benediction. He was above the sun; she glowed in it. She was not strong enough to exist without the sun. There was a shade of contempt in his fine features. He did not seem any more to want to look down. How stupid I am, muttered Tansy, to make up such nonsense about a picture in a window. But she knew the Saint was not nonsense; that what the old Parson had said in this place so many years ago had never been nonsense. And very quietly she said the only prayer she could think of, pausing at the end and repeating it. Deliver us from evil. Deliver us from ... She turned, startled out of herself. The new priest, tall, red-faced and angular, with a cassock and a biretta, stood behind her. "Ah, a newcomer, I imagine?"

He spoke like a magistrate in a court of petty crime. Tansy stared at him with a shade of insolence.

"Lord bless you! I should think not! I knew this church before you was born, I reckon." And with a malicious twist of her lips, she went out.

The priest went into the vestry, muttering crossly: "What can one do? These people have absolutely *no* spiritual outlook whatever. . . ."

CHAPTER VI

THE gramophone blared a cacophonous summons to Georgia where, with a peach, days were apparently easily beguiled.

Joe, containing far more beer than he could balance, lurched towards Bessie. She caught his arm and shook him. "You're stupid with drink," she muttered angrily.

"So I am, you!" he cried in her face. "And if only I had another pint I might be kissing of you and never know it!"

He fell into a chair beside Nicolas and John Stone. John was now so old that he was incapable of uttering more than three consecutive words. But with remarkable tenacity he still maintained his ability to appear at festivities to which he had not been invited.

They looked at Joe sourly as he lolled up against them. Nicolas sniffed. "Get away," he growled, "you're drunk."

"So Bessie was telling," rumbled Joe. "I got a pain." He rubbed his stomach like a cake-stricken child.

"I hear tell"—began John Stone in a voice that shivered high up amongst the cobwebs in the beamed roof—"I hear tell——" But the only word he could produce was "tin". He slavered over his naked gums with secret satisfaction.

Joe stumbled to the door, and standing on the high steps of the barn, watched the yellow moon sailing up over an ocean of crested cloud. Or was it the sea? Joe did not know. There were far too many moons sailing about for his liking. His stomach heaved and he brought up his beer with a tremendous belch. Then he felt very stupid and didn't want to go back to the barn.

Bessie's vigilant sister, a spidery argus of a woman with a dewdrop on her nose—Joe called it the family dewdrop—was peering round the door at him. She prinked back into the barn and told Bessie.

"That man of yours, he been sick, you!"

"Dirty beast!" said Bessie loftily. "What you might expect of a Penderil. Thank the good Lord my children aren't Penderils!"

Tansy, who was talking to one of the guests just behind Bessie, overheard the remark and resented it.

"We always knew Joe couldn't be their father." She snapped the words and walked over to the other side of the barn before Bessie could say anything.

"Did you hear that?" she breathed. "Did you hear what she said? Darned bitch of a woman and I don't care who hear me say it. Now!" Nevertheless, she had whispered the words.

Somebody put on another record and they began to jog along the floor with an amiable disregard for one another's feet. The gramophone, nearly as old as Tansy, belched amorphous music through a bellicose and indomitable yellow horn.

Arthur was sitting on a bench next to Tansy, smoking his pipe in a dogged attempt at jollity. But Tansy, whether she wished it or not, was a constant deterrent to the emancipation of whatever gaiety he wished to express. Whenever he ventured upon a slightly rude story or tickled one of the girls in the ribs, he was sharply reminded that Tansy might disapprove. Actually Tansy would not greatly have cared had he taken down his trousers and danced a jig. She might even have commended such an exhibition.

He looked along at the crowd of noisy people, thick figures in the smoky light of the lamps and lanterns. They had decorated the barn with coloured paper streamers and decadent bits of evergreen.

"Pretty sight," he remarked to Tansy, in the tone of one who had been responsible for it all.

"Yes, pretty," she agreed. "Though it's not like the guldies we had when we were kids and used to dance to Uncle Jim's concertina and Willie's mouth-organ."

"No, I grant you. Don't care for these gramophones myself. Nothing but tinned music, ask me." Tinned music! A lovely phrase that was! He had recently acquired it from the correspondence columns of the *Radio Times*.

Bessie flounced before them, determined to get the better of Tansy. But it was unfortunate for her that she chose a method most likely to amuse Tansy.

Bessie's pale blue satin frock was swathed so tightly across her belly that Tansy wanted to jab her finger in her navel to see if she could squeak.

"Well, Arthur—coming to have a go round with y'r 'umble? I'm sure Tansy would not mind?"

No, indeed. Tansy would not mind. She would be glad. And Arthur, with a rather furtive glance at his own woman, led Bessie into a tempestuous valeta. Tansy followed them with amused contempt. She thought they fitted each other very well. They might have married and been very happy.

With a detached air she looked at the dancing figures. She did not feel in the least supercilious. But they were waxen, she thought, like marionettes in the blurred light of the smoky room. Alice was dancing with the boy Benjamin. They were exactly like a couple of starlings, thought Tansy, mincing about over a field of dung with an air of smug fastidiousness. Florrie, the sister, was chasing around with some other children, in and out of the legs of the dancers.

The room was pretty full. The machine men had come, and there were neighbours and many friends of Bessie. Tansy wondered where David was; then she saw him talking to Andrew in a corner. They seemed to have been together all the evening.

They caught her glance and seeing she was alone, came over to her.

"David wants you to dance," said Andrew.

"Yes, come on, mother," said David a little stiffly.

"Well, what about you, then?" she said to Andrew. "I haven't seen you go round once for the evening yet. David can take me, if you'll come round afterwards."

"Maybe," said Andrew. "But I'll only tread on your toes. You go on."

David took her hands and awkwardly trotted her round the barn. Then he grew more certain of his steps and held her tighter, his hand pressing more firmly into her back. He was very hot and did not much enjoy the dance. "Afraid I'm stupid at this," he muttered. "Never know which foot goes after which."

"Oh, you're all right," she said warmly. "You got your hand in the right place anyhow."

He was silent. Tansy felt hostility in him. When she had wanted to rouse him, she had only succeeded in subduing him. She was angry at that. There was a young man in her arms—whether her son or not did not matter—and he was unmoved by her bodily contact. She felt the insurgent tide of her blood rush up against him. But he was stiff and cold. Somehow she had offended him. The colt—she thought; but maybe he's just shy.

She remembered him down at the pool when his young life had stirred to flame at her touch. And she pressed her hand tight into his waist, feeling the slim circle of his loins through the wet shirt. It was beautiful, the flow of his loins; an immediate sustenance to her who had for so long been starved of a man's body. And this young shooting flame started the old agony, the buried questing deep inside her.

Then she hated herself and wished she had never danced with him. But as she touched his loins a shudder went through him.

His face was tormented, his eyes like those of a beast driven into a corner. He was stricken dumb by her touch and stirred in spite of himself, so that he felt the old trouble of desire against his thighs. He loathed the woman's hand that could so easily search out his secret burden.

When the dance was over, he stood restless and sweating before her, not daring to meet her eyes, the slate-grey eyes that half contemptuously probed into his.

"Do he dance well?" asked Andrew.

"Well enough for any maid!" laughed Tansy flagrantly. Andrew saw that David was uneasy, and scowled. But his attention was diverted by the adventurous figure of Joe, who with greedy eyes and an uncertain step was fluctuating from group to group.

"Where's Bessie?" he grumbled. "Where that woman to?" But nobody knew or much cared. (And where's Arthur, thought Tansy.)

Somebody put out a foot against Joe and he tumbled over on the ground amidst roars of laughter.

"He's some soft," cooed Alice, pulling at his coat. "Uncle Joe, bet you can't catch me!" And, with an entirely unnecessary display of feminine bravado, she ran away across the room. Joe sat up and tumbled his fingers through his hair.

Old John Stone grizzled with inept laughter. "Could tell you——" he began, and the cobwebs quivered, the spiders shook and curled up, ready to drop. But John Stone could tell nothing.

Nicolas was angry with Joe, but he said nothing because his word was no longer respected.

"Where's Bessie?" (Where's Arthur?)

The humid atmosphere of the barn sickened Tansy. Where's Bessie? she heard them ask. Where's Bessie? She wanted to scream out and tell them—not because she envied her Arthur's wet kisses, but because neither of them would have cared had the other died to-morrow. Men and women, thought Tansy, behaved in much the same manner as dogs—only with this difference, that dogs never approached their pleasures with a furtive eye.

The gramophone blared out a waltz in a palsied fever of strident notes, a crapulent torrent of sound masquerading as a tune.

Tansy remembered that she had claimed a dance with Andrew, but when she looked for him she saw that he had moved to the other side of the room with David. Nicolas came over to her. He was smiling, an old cracked smile of sympathy.

"All alone, child?" He sat down.

"Why, yes, father; just for a minute or two. Enjoying yourself?"

"That Joe"—Nicolas shook his head sadly. None of the air of a denouncing prophet was left in him.

"I know," said Tansy. "Sickening, I say. But there—poor Joe was born with all the silliness of men and all the charm too. It often go together, so don't blame him."

"They're not the right crowd somehow," he said mournfully, voicing her own thoughts. "I think of your mother. She'd have sat on some of them. So quiet like, you wouldn't hardly know it. But she'd have done it proper."

"She would that. Aunt Janet, too. I wish we had her here. She'd show them up. Not that there's much, maybe, to show up."

"Ah! You know I never fully approve of Aunt Janet's tongue, as you might be saying. But Lord, she's got a brae good heart, bless me, she has and that!" He changed the subject. "Old John Stone going home rapid!" He chuckled.

When a man is getting old he likes to remark decrepitude in an older man. And Nicolas derived great satisfaction from the fact that his own faculties were in better working order than John Stone's.

They were dancing wildly and blindly. David and Andrew stood against the wall on the other side.

"I'm sick of this," said Andrew. "Let's go and take a turn outside."

They could not get to the door opposite through the swirling couples. "There's a way up here," said Andrew. "Maybe you've not been. Down the loft steps and into the cow sheds. Come on."

David followed him to the far corner near the gramophone, where there was an opening in the floor leading down a ladder to the shed below. Andrew swung down, groping in the darkness, and David followed. They landed in a bundle of straw. The sweet smell of it revived David, who sighed with relief. The air was cool and moist.

"Better strike a match," said Andrew, "against there be any calves we can't see."

He fumbled for his matchbox. There was a rustling in the straw, an uneasy whispering, and Andrew stumbled over a man's body.

"What the hell!" he cried.

David shivered with excitement. The match flared up. Andrew caught Arthur's hot, frightened eyes in the quick light; saw the bundle that was Bessie, lying below him.

"Who is it then?" whispered David.

Andrew spat on the match and dragged David unwillingly to the door. "Nothing for you to see," he snarled loudly. "Only a lout making a fool of himself."

He almost pushed David outside, and breathed with relief as they came into the utter purity of the night air. David was startled and a little mortified.

"I'm no baby," he said savagely. "Couple canoodling, I suppose?"

"Yes," growled Andrew. "They ought to be ashamed——" He stopped awkwardly.

A slender tabby cat rushed up out of the shadows and brushed against David's legs. He picked her up fondly and they walked over the yard.

"I hate all that," muttered David. "Don't know what they do see in it." And in the savagery of his heart he pressed his nails into the cat's side till she scratched and bit him with the pain. Then David got in a rage and held her paws so that she could not move. "Think you'd bite me, do you?" His eyes were sunk deep back in his head, seeming to meet above his nose until they concentrated into one dark moving pool of malevolence.

"What in hell's name're you doing to the brute?" cried Andrew.

"Making it squeal," replied David tersely. "Look!" He caught hold of her tail and swung her in the air with a high laugh.

Andrew wrenched the animal free, struggled with David and found he had to use all his strength to keep him firm in his grasp. For a moment the boy was a writhing fury.

"You little devil of a boy," panted Andrew. "My gosh, if I ever see you doing that again I'll thrash you till you're blue. I'll show you what 'tis like to be hurt."

He held David's arms firmly. Then David was utterly broken and wept in Andrew's arms.

"I'm sorry. I—didn't know as I was doing anything. It got me mad I suppose, and I lost my head. Don't be mad with me, Uncle Andrew. Don't be mad, please——"

The boy's face was a pale line of anguish. Andrew softened. "There, boy. I'm not mad. I'm never mad. Don't you cry. You're a man now, and men don't cry." He patted his heaving back.

"I can't bear you to be mad with me," whispered David. "I wish I could be with you always——"

"So you shall. Though it's good-bye for the time. Your mother'll bring you over in November, then happen after Christmas you can come for good and all."

"It's some queer to me——" murmured David.

"What? What's so queer to you?"

"You," he said. "How I like you more'n anybody else——"

Andrew's eyes were heavy. "I feel as though you was my own son," he said.

"I feel as though you was my father."

Andrew thought of the crouching shape on the floor of the cattle-shed, and wanted to laugh.

They stood quite still there for a moment. Then the door at the top of the barn steps opened and they heard laughter.

"They're coming out," said Andrew. "We mustn't stay here, they'll think we're mad."

"I shan't see you again then?" David clutched to Andrew's coat. His body was limp.

"No. Not until November."

"Write to me, please write. I will if you will."

"Yes, I'll write."

David suddenly ran away. People were coming down the steps, speaking in raucous voices. Andrew hated them all and hated mankind. Because of secret happiness within him he was unhappy. And he felt he wanted to stop all these loud people and tell them something new and lovely. But he was not at all sure what he wanted to tell them.

CHAPTER VII

OCTOBER saw the beginning of wild stormy weather. The country scowled under skies piled thick with rapid grey clouds. In a single night when the south-west gale tore at the windows of Boscedjack, the little stream of summer music in the valley was changed into a roaring flood toppling over the boulders, furious to spend itself in the sea. A few bedraggled yellow leaves fluttering from naked branches were all that remained of the rich fire of autumn. Ravaged by heath fires the hillsides were a black waste of rotten gorse roots, sodden in the twisting streams of rain. The arm of grey roofs sloping along the carn, seemed to press more deeply into the sky.

In a few days a new land came into being. Locked under swirling skies and beaten by rain the panoply of summer withered into the threadbare shroud of winter. Doors were locked again; fires lit; the smoke of a hundred solitary chimneys scattered over the moors, drifted into the sooty sky. An agitated shape in the filament of mist, a man with a sack drawn over his shoulders, stumbled over the moors gathering kindling.

No lovers wandered down the Penth valley; there was no twilight but the twilight of day. The pool was silent except for the roaring of the sea at its walls. The cattle were sent back into their long sheds; horses, glistening and steaming with moisture, hung their troubled heads morosely over the stone hedges. A thousand starlings swarmed on to the Chapel roof, chattering like a dissenting jury.

All over the land was a sinister pride—a thievish spirit picking the bones of summer as a vulture on a lovely corpse. A buried voice of man rang through the hollow hills—a voice that uncovered decades of man's adventure with the world and revealed him as no purer a creature than the Celt who had squatted over his camp fire. All that had passed seemed to revile all that was passing. Because another summer had gone, the rock of time

never swayed. And around those infrangible coasts where the
beast of the sea leapt and fell back, leapt again and fell back, man
was no more than a trumpery marionette of God. Stripped of
the comfortable vestments of what he called culture, he was
driven back nakedly upon the fact that the final culture might
disregard him altogether.

Late one afternoon near the end of October, Tansy projected
her individual thoughts into the long silence of the still scene
before her. She was sitting on a jutting rock immediately above
the little channel where the sea pressed into the core of the cliffs.
The weather had driven her out; the tattered lamentation of the
hanging skies made her sick of the cottage. The first time for
many weeks she had come down the valley and climbed above
the black channel to a point where she could sit poised over the
gathering gloom of the sea. A motionless ship hung before her, a
black phantom with a meagre yellow eye. The sea was calm, for
the wind had dropped and a yellow mist pressed over the land.
The angular rocks slanted down to the sea, oblique knives upon
shifting iron, cutting the water and carrying their foundations to
a distorted reflection. Minute by minute the silence was broken
by the subterranean rush of the sea as it surged into the hollow,
met its enemy the earth, and fell back again, reverberating like
the laboured retort of a distant gun. It was a warfare in the earth.
Thwarted, the sea fell back. Yet inch by inch it weakened the soil,
driving as certain a destruction for the land as the slow crumbling
of the mines in the valley.

Tansy was fascinated by this ponderous march of the sea upon
the land; this ceaseless invasion, day in, day out, with never any
spoil of victory save perhaps one shattered rock rumbling to little
pieces down the hillside inland. She sat there with her chin on her
hands, gazing down, as still as the rock on which she sat. She felt
alone—more alone than she had ever been. And here above the
arctic chastity of the endless sea, the terrible truth of the unremitting culture of the universe caught her mind and held her in
thought. The Parson spoke of the soul and a loving Father who
was God; of gentle Jesus with his lambs. But here there were no
lambs, and if Jesus stole over those hills what would He find but
the ruthless logic of His Father?

And what would the Father do if she were to throw herself down into that menacing channel? Would He part it asunder as He had done for the Jews? A pretty story! The sea would go on, still tormenting the wounded side of the earth. Go on, like a demented fool who bangs his obtuse head on a padded cell. And yet the very certainty of this icy logic contained for her the germ of the love of God—a love so powerful that it must destroy to create anew—so terrible that it needed the gentle Jesus and His lambs to assure a frail world that there were mansions in Heaven.

Tansy sighed deeply. She was alone and she lived. She wondered how that could be. To be alone in your soul and to live. This was a wonderful fact that filled her with a contentment deeper than anything she had experienced with any human person. For to be alone was the ultimate adventure. And to-day she felt that the heavy load which had always hung upon her, had dropped in the material certainty that she would somehow have to change the course of her life. She did not seek to let the springs of her body run free again; she was content for them to dry up so long as she could be alone.

David would go soon. This would end a phase in her life. Then she knew she would leave Arthur because it was a ceaseless mockery to her soul to be with him. The knowledge that she would have to leave him, go somewhere alone, lightened the load on her tired body. Yet a voice told her that in running away she would not obtain the freedom for which she yearned. Something more had to be done. She did not know. But only up here in this graven moment in time's long monument, she found a truth. The truth of the icy love of God, never propelling her this way or that as He propelled the sea to its thwarted goal, but leaving her free to travel where she wished.

Tansy thought: only once had she obeyed her heart, yet it had led her into a prison from which she never seemed able to escape. What would she have done with life had she not married Arthur? If she had done always what she wanted, would she be any happier now? She could not answer these things. She knew that now she must obey her heart; that God having left her free, she would cease to reason with her instincts. Free. Yes, she was alone and free. God left her to do as she chose. She could direct her life as she pleased, take this path or that. And she saw a path she would follow. It would lead her—God knew where, but somewhere—somewhere in His ruthless universe.

Somewhere . . . some far oblivion. Out there, where the thousand voiceless ghosts that made the sea, ceaselessly turned in and out upon themselves, an infinite convolution of unreasoning energy. She shivered, frightened momentarily by the occult inundation of the yellow sea.

She rose and turned towards the valley. It was almost dark now and she had to choose her footholds carefully. Half-way down the slope was a mine shaft, narrow and deep, covered over with a layer of grey rubble. It was an easy trap for the unknowing, for at the side was a gap large enough to take a man. An absurdly easy trap. Tansy avoided it carefully. She passed over the mound of slag, then on to the little rocky path leading up by the stream towards the town and her home. In the falling gloom, the windows of some distant cottages opened their red eyes. The lamps of home were lighted. Man took refuge in his little hut, kindled warmth for himself and his own and forgot he was nothing in the world. He built and planned and believed he would endure, even if only in a gravestone. His last forlorn prayer that he might rest in peace.

Tansy overtook an old man carrying wreck-wood along the path.

"Coming in stormy again, I reckon," he cried after her.

"Yes, I suppose. Good night."

"Good night, Mrs. Progis."

Mrs. Progis. Tansy laughed. She rarely heard herself called that, except in a few shops. It was quite unreal to her, as though she had been cast in a play. Mrs. Progis going home to her family . . . it was a joke. Somehow: a tremendous joke.

She jumped back. A donkey with ears like long carrots was hanging his head above her up the side of the valley. He let out an agonized shriek of homesick dismay—an appalling declaration of lost dignity. And sounding a thousand times through the little hills another answered him from the other side, the cry falling to a cacophonous flutter of nostalgia.

"Poor thing," said Tansy. "Poor, chained, stupid thing!"

She turned where the path branched off to Boscedjack, walked quickly to the house because she knew they would be wanting their tea and the habit of having their meals punctually set before them was too strong to be broken. Tansy was a creature of habit; perhaps this fact had kept her world together. The ordered cleanliness of her home was a pride to her; to destroy that had always seemed impossible. So even now, with her mind set upon a new life, she was slightly irritated by the fact that she had kept them waiting and hurried up the path half angry with herself. She smelt the wet sickliness of a veronica bush as she pushed open the door and went inside. To her surprise the tea was laid on the table and the kettle rattled on the hob. They were apparently all in a very easy mood: David reading a book one of the schoolmasters had lent him; Arthur helping Alice at a crossword puzzle. It was a scene Tansy had neither expected nor wished to see. When she had decided to forsake her world it suddenly turned on her a comfortable and self-righteous face. This was a home and as she looked at it she knew she had made it, built it slowly, year in, year out. Yet it looked to her now like the disposed work of an artist; an early picture hanging in a friend's room. And when they all looked up and stared at her, she felt she was a trespasser. She was not wanted. Barren inside, feeling utterly unable to smile upon them, she forced herself to speak kindly to them, to try not to break the lovely ancient security of a home in winter. But when she spoke she heard her voice, harsh and cold, seeming to sound from another place.

"Who got tea all ready then?" She sat down.

"I did," said Arthur. And there was even no pride in his voice. "Alice helped. Seeing as you'd be tired after your little walk, thought as we'd better have tea waiting for you."

"That's very kind, Arthur. And you're a good girl, Alice."

"Ah. She'll be looking after me soon, won't you, Alice?"

Arthur smiled and tweaked the girl's nose artfully. Tansy was startled at his remark.

"Why, what do you mean? Looking after you——"

"Only that she'll have to look after her dad when you and David go over to Rosemulyan." But there was pride in his voice this time.

"Oh, I was forgetting——" Tansy smiled weakly. Forgetting. Yes, they were to go to Rosemulyan in a fortnight or so. It would be a very nice change. And after that . . . meanwhile Alice must learn how to cook and darn and scrub floors . . .

She spoke hurriedly, bringing a nervous irritability into the room. "Yes, Alice is getting handy, I must say. And a proper thing. I'll be able to leave things to her soon. Why, we'll have you doing the baking and all in no time, won't we, Alice?" Alice tittered.

Tansy made tea and pulled her chair to the table. David was deep in his book.

"Tea, David," she said. He reached out a vague hand for the cup and nearly upset it, his eyes still on the book.

"Stupid!" she cried. "Now put your old book aside and come to your tea proper. 'Tisn't polite to read at meals." But why shouldn't he, she cried to herself? Why in Heaven's name shouldn't he if he wanted to? By what right did she shut the dam of her reason on the flood of his instinct?

She half hoped he would defy her, but he came to his senses and said he was sorry. She saw that he was merely taking the easier course. Refusing to question authority as she had done with her father, because it saved so much energy. Yes, there was no doubt that she was breeding a secret life in him. A year ago he would have shown her the book and told her about it.

"What're you reading then that's so interesting to you? Not trash I hope?"

"No, it isn't trash. It's a poem about the sea." He took up the anthology eagerly. "Listen to this bit. It's fine!"

He read aloud in a strange trembling voice.

> "The very deep did rot, O Christ
> That ever this should be!
> Yea, slimy things did crawl with legs
> Upon the slimy sea."

He paused. Arthur scowled. Tansy felt hot and a little sick. Alice's mouth gaped open. David read another verse, his voice smouldering in a low blaze of vitality.

"About, about in reel and rout
The death fires danced at night;
The water, like a witch's oils
Burnt green and blue and white."

The wind swirled in the chimney. The old man had been right; the gale was rising again.

David seemed about to read more, but Arthur's hand closed over the book.

"That's enough," he said quietly. "It's trash. Your mother's right."

"No," said Tansy quickly, "it aren't trash, Arthur. But I don't like it for all that."

David's searching eyes burnt into hers. She felt them, but would not look at him. And David, furious with Arthur for disapproving of the poem, drank tea down savagely, scalding himself and provoking Alice to a snigger.

The evening set in. Again the house had been threatened. They did not talk much, for anything they touched upon seemed to provoke argument. The fire crackling made the only sound in the room as Arthur bent over his paper, Alice over a new puzzle, and David over his book.

Tansy sat near the window in her chair listening to the high wailing of the wind. A gust of smoke blew into the room, and rain suddenly whipped against the window.

Arthur objected. "As if we hadn't had enough rain! The country's rotten under it."

But the gales of a rural winter are no more than a rustic melodrama. They do not touch the sententious divagations of the sons of Westminster. Arthur was assured of that from his newspaper. The country was in a bad way and demanded his sympathy.

"This National Government'll be the ruin of us," he predicted gloomily. "They cut the dole—they cut the teachers' salaries. If they cut much more it'll be their own throats, ask me."

Arthur, who had always nailed his political hopes to the Liberals, could only see in the emergency government a new and sinister party. Arthur was Liberal because of Mr. Runciman; and Mr. Runciman was Cornwall. No further argument was needed.

"I reckon the King had a lot to do with it," echoed Tansy with sudden sapience.

"What—with the cutting of the dole?"

"No," replied Tansy, as though she were explaining a lesson, "with this here National Government or whatever they do call it." She had overheard the remark in a shop that day, and felt that it would impress Arthur.

"Well, the King do more than what they tell," he admitted sagely, and went on reading.

Alice went to bed. "Can I read in bed, mother?" she asked.

"Till half-past ten," said Tansy. "No longer."

"Chap here got ten years for setting fire to a house to get the insurance money," remarked Arthur. Tansy murmured incoherently. She looked at David, who seemed to be asleep. His head had fallen forward and the book had slipped from his hand. His cheeks glowed in the firelight, his cheek-bones carved out of his face, accentuating the depth of his closed eyes. The firelight fell over his body, and in the flickering movement of the flames he looked unreal to Tansy. She swayed her chair slightly to and fro. Save for the occasional remarks of Arthur, the silence of night began to change the spirit of the house. A coal fell out of the grate, sizzled in a sharp flame and then went black. Tansy wanted to sleep. Her lids fell heavily over her eyes. She yielded her spirit and felt easier. Sleep was lovely and she could rest.

... Arthur's voice sounded through the long, strange corridors of the sub-conscious.

"A nasty business here, you." Unwillingly Tansy opened her heavy eyes. "What's that, then?"

Arthur looked at David strangely.

"He sleeping?" he whispered loudly.

"I think so. Why?"

"Well, there's a queer thing here. Not quite fit for him to listen to, I think."

Tansy was interested, for Arthur did not often consider David in this way.

"Show me," she said.

But he had to read it to her. "Another sort of Jack-the-Ripper, seeming," he said slowly, relishing his words. "Listen. 'Amazing series of crimes baffle London police. Hampstead Heath murders. The third of a series of foul crimes, rare in the annals of criminology in this country, was brought to light early this morning, when Mr. Howard James, of Well Walk, taking an early morning stroll before breakfast, was horrified to find the mutilated body of a young woman lying near a shrubbery not far from the Vale of Health. One of the arms had been severed and could not be found in the——' "

White with anger, she snatched the paper from him.

"How can you interest yourself in such filth?" she muttered savagely. "They only put in that sort of stuff for such as you to read."

He was bewildered. "I'm sorry. I didn't mean—I didn't know as you'd take it amiss. After all it's nothing new. A lunatic, I dare say."

She stifled her words, remembering that David was in the room. She looked at him. Then she knew that he was not asleep. She felt certain of it. She went near him and knocked the breadboard on to the floor at his feet. He quivered, but did not open his eyes. She knew then that he was acting and she shook him roughly. He stumbled carefully to life.

"You're never sleeping," she said harshly. "Go to bed."

"All right," he mumbled. "No need to go on like that."

She knew there was no need, and the logic of it infuriated her.

"I was sleeping," added David. "How should I close my eyes otherwise?"

"You were shamming," she challenged.

"I tell you I was asleep till you came and shook me."

"You were listening to we talking here and pretending to be asleep. You needn't lie to me. It don't work, for I always know."

Arthur was blowing out his pipe with an ingenuous attempt at casual indifference.

"Have it your own way," said David carelessly. He yawned with loose insolence. She saw that he would not trouble to argue with her. She wanted to force him to lose his temper, anything but this contemptuous indifference, this arrogant disregard of her anger. But she knew it was idle to fight with him over nothing. What was it all about? She hardly knew. Her head was suddenly thick with old words, her eyes streaked by a bloody vision. A whirlpool of dark, muddy water swirled round and round in her head. She saw David through it leave the room; heard him go upstairs.

The fire was dull; the lamp dying for lack of oil. Arthur rose and yawned. Tansy was mad again; best to go to bed and say nothing about it. He shambled to the door with an apprehensive glance at her. The clock struck eleven laboriously.

CHAPTER VIII

THE last day of October was the Eve of Penth Feast. It was, everybody said, typical Feast weather. All the pent-up fury of the gale that had waited under the yellow skies the afternoon Tansy sat above the valley, seemed to accumulate and come to a head on Feast Saturday. But the people of Penth were accustomed to this. Years ago they had always had a fair in the market place and Feast had been something to talk about. Late into the night the town would echo with the slow urge of the miners' voices singing old tunes over their tankards, their heads falling on each other's shoulders, their eyes closed. Then one year the old woman who travelled from town to town with her crazy Fair quarrelled with the district council, who suddenly and foolishly decided to demand a fee for the use of the town's market place. They were financially embarrassed, and it was a way of obtaining a little money. But the old woman, though she paid that once, would not pay again. Moreover, she was a witch and had an evil eye. The council had forgotten that. So that when she and her assistants stored up their caravans on the Tuesday morning, she roved her bleary eyes over the sleeping town littered with the evidences of festival, and said in a firm voice: "Come every Feast at Penth from now on, 'twill rain till their hearts are heavy." The curse, supported perhaps by some meteorological whimsey, had its desired effect. The Fair never came again, but the rain did. In the course of years, too, the population of the town dwindled owing to the emigration of many miners who were thrown out of work. More and more mines closed down; the town grew sombre and retrospective.

So Feast was a bedraggled remnant of what it had once been, though there were still many families who observed it conscientiously, planned for it as people up country would plan for Christmas, ceased their work, put on their best clothes and made merriment out of the few flapping booths and stalls that some adventurous mendicant now erected in the market place. The observance of Feast would start on Saturday evening, when all the lads and girls would walk up and down the one street of the town, cracking their bawdy jokes and waging their old wars of youth. Sunday was a day when people from miles around who never went to church or chapel at any other time, clamoured piously into the religious buildings. The military had seats reserved for them in the church and blinked obtusely at the Anglo-Catholic contortions of the ardent new Vicar. They had always been used to Morning Prayer with a hearty *Venite* to set the ball rolling, and were piously insulted by this Romish succulence. But the Vicar said: "If they come, they must come to the Lord's own service, whether they understand it or not. It is the faith of their fathers." But since most of their fathers had never had any faith worth speaking about, unless a fervent belief in Mr. Wesley as the bellicose evangelist leading them into the New Jerusalem, the Lord's own service, with all its mellifluous accompaniment of acolyte and ciborium, did little more than open their lurid mouths upon the ever-engaging subject of the Pope and his satellites. They would have preferred Mr. Wesley's own service. But the Vicar thought it was very inspiring to see them all sitting there following the mysteries, and he took the precaution of preaching to them on one of the more pugnacious texts of the Apostle Paul.

The local and extremely doubtful Saint of Penth having been duly honoured, Monday opened upon a meet of the Hunt in the square. The Hunt was followed by an incredible number of hangers-on mounted on every type of steed, from a disguised cart-horse to an elongated donkey masquerading as an incipient mule. Tally-ho meant quite a lot to the people of Penth, who, swayed by the press, still firmly believed that the gentry were not real gentry unless they could kill a fox. Put Colonel So-and-so in a pretty pink coat, and he was undeniably a Colonel. The people were very pleased even if they were well aware that the Colonel had no bluer blood in his turgid veins than anybody else in the town. But they were pleased; it gave them a sense of feudal stability to see the Colonel in his pink coat, stuck on his horse like a spruce tin soldier. So they all turned out for the meet and followed it as far as they could.

In the afternoon were clay-pigeon shoots and a football match; concerts and dances in all the religious halls in the evening. So that Feast still meant something to Penth, was still picturesque even if somewhat self-consciously.

Tansy had happy memories of Feast when the farm, her home, had stood on firm ground, and she and Emmeline used to make quantities of Feast pudding, cakes and pasties. But the decline of the town's industry had depressed her more than most, and she found it hard now to enter into a spirit which was a shadow of what it had been, even though the children enjoyed it well enough. And Arthur was one of those who took pains in observing it, believing in it almost as a duty. He liked to go to church, to patronize the Hunt or the pigeon shoot, to take them all to the church concert on Monday evening.

More than usual this year he made a pathetic attempt to uphold the festive standard of his ancestors. Without ever referring to the scene he had had with David, he had made it painfully clear to the boy that he bore no grudge. It was a valiant attempt to step over the breach, and David, touched against his will, half-heartedly tried to behave naturally to him. So in a strange deluded atmosphere they forgot their differences and called a truce in honour of the Feast. Tansy, braced by the prospect of the coming trip to Andrew's place, partially succeeded in fooling herself. She saw that it rested with her to keep the old life together; that it might go on smoothly if she chose. Then she remembered that David was going. The old life could never go on. She might delude herself before the others, were he present. But with him gone, what was there to sustain her? Watching the hidden questing in his eyes, studying him when he thought she was not looking, she saw day by day that he was establishing something within himself that did not include her in its scheme. What that was she did not know. Always there had been a secret side of David which she had not understood; this was the side which grew more and more like the spreading branch of a tree which overshadows the old trunk. He resented her thoughts turning upon him; she was a torment to his conscience as a son. And she herself, in those dead moments when she had turned away from him and killed the flood of tenderness that rose in her—she herself had caused this change in David. He did not speak much of his going away, but she knew that it was always in his thoughts. She never imagined him as a farmer; could not believe that he would stick to his work. She realized that he only wanted to go because it was a chance of getting away from an atmosphere that stifled the rising life in him; that the deadly hostility between him and Arthur, though cloaked in smooth words, had reached breaking point.

Now, for hours, David would sit in his room reading books that Tansy did not like. They were ghostly and bloody stories that he cared for. And she left him alone, believing it was right he should have a place of his own, as she had had as a girl, where he could retreat and dream his own dreams that were not for her. She left him alone. Loved him and hated him for taking so much love from her, for drying up the springs of her love towards anybody else. She loved him, hated him and was frightened of him, frightened of the silent intensity of his eyes, of the careless contempt of his loose shoulders.

Sometimes she wanted to tell him that he inherited something richer, if more disturbing, than the sluggish blood of Arthur. But she could not part with her secret. Neither was she certain of what he had inherited from Roger Chailey. It was a power, that was certain. In all his gestures, so opposed to the lethargic movement of her own people, there was the compelling appeal of Chailey. The same bewildered anxiety that sometimes clouded his eyes. The same moodiness and impetuosity; the same reaction to lovely things. It was a strong flow of blood in him, a vital heritage if a frightening one.

But in spite of all these doubts and fears she gained a superficial enjoyment from Feast time. It was like welcoming an old friend ignorant of her troubles.

On Monday morning she prepared a good dinner for them

while they went up to watch the Meet. Joe had given her a duck, and she enjoyed roasting it and watching its ample breast turn a rich brown in the oven.

Near one o'clock she stood by the window wiping her hands, the dinner all ready, the plates hot. She looked out of the window. The rain had ceased and the sun was trying to pierce through some muddy clouds. But there was rain in the air and the wind was still powerful.

She saw Arthur and Alice coming across the moor.

"Dinner's all ready," she said briskly, as they came in.

"That's right, mother, that's right!" Arthur rubbed his hands together, the clockwork gesture for the particular occasion. It was Feast and a duck for dinner; one rubbed one's hands together. It might have come out of a book on etiquette.

"Where's the lad, then?" asked Tansy.

"We lost him somewhere in the crowd up there. But he'll be back presently, I dare say. I think he went after the hounds."

"Was there a good crowd?"

"Oh, just as usual. And the sun come out as it belong to, just as they were getting away. A pretty sight as you know."

He threw the folded newspaper down on the window seat. He would not look at it now. The affairs of the great world must wait upon Feast Monday.

"I got four tickets for the church concert to-night," he said. "Thought it'd do us all good to go out for once."

"Well, I hope it don't rain, that's all. Because there's nothing I hate more than sitting in that stuffy old hall with wet clothes up to me. But, after that, it's kind of you, Arthur, I'm sure."

They did not know whether to wait dinner for David. "I told him one o'clock," said Tansy, "and it's a pity to keep stuff hanging about when 'tis cooked."

"Well, he know and it's his own fault," said Arthur.

"I say we start. Alice is ready, I'm sure."

"Oh, yes, dad, always ready for a bit of duck. My, mother, but it do look lovely!"

Tansy put the duck on the table.

"It's not quite what Joe's ducks usually be," she remarked. "Bit scraggy like. But there, good enough for we."

They sat down.

"Why, the Parson couldn't be doing better'n this," said Arthur, smacking his lips in another acquiescence to the clockwork of Feast. "And speaking of him," he continued, "I hear tell that he's having the old Vicarage repaired and moving in there so soon's it ready. Foolish, I say, for 'tis a dark old place, as anyone do know."

"Yes, 'tis a gloomy place," she said. "Too many trees."

"They're cutting some of them down—making a clearing round the house so's more light can get it. Firewood for somebody, I suppose."

"It's time they were cut down."

David burst into the room, out of breath with running.

"Sorry," he panted, "forgot as dinner was earlier. Gosh, that's looking grand! I'm some hungry, too."

"Well, now, where did you get to?" asked Arthur, heavily humorous. "Up to some mischief, I suppose."

"No," he said, helping himself to potatoes and speaking quickly. Tansy saw he was excited about something. "No mischief at all. I been helping that Sammy Stiles cut down trees in the old wood along Turnpike. Vicarage, I mean."

"That's funny," said Arthur, surprised. "I was only speaking about that place when you came in. Case of—telepathy, that is. Nothing less. What made you go down there?"

(Tansy cut some more duck for Arthur and served him with potatoes.)

"Oh, I dunno," said David. "I reckon I was always a bit partial to that there wood somehow, though I don't often go there. But I come along Turnpike after I left the hounds, see, and got in with Sammy Stiles. You know he live just over by the edge of the wood?"

"I know," said Arthur. "Felling trees was he, then?"

"Just going up there. He said would I like to go along and see a big tree go down, so I went. 'Twas that big spiky sort of tree he brought down. Don't know what you do call it, but tall and no leaves. It was some grand sight to see it topple over into all the smaller ones, though I was sorry somehow to see it go. I had a shot at it myself, but Sammy got more muscle than me, and it soon took the guts out of me." He paused reminiscently, a forkful of food held before his mouth. Then he crammed it in and munched hungrily.

"What sort of state's the house in?" asked Arthur.

"Awful," replied David. "Roof leaking, rats everywhere. He took me inside."

"Oh, you went in, then? I thought 'twas all boarded up."

("Have some more potato, David," said Tansy.)

"Thankee, mother. . . . Sammy said they always used to keep it boarded against the kids and canoodling couples what used to go there one time. But now they taken down the boards, and Parson been down and seems he's going to live there."

("I got a nice pudding for you——")

"Handsome," said David. "Sammy said there'd been a murder there years ago. He said——"

"That's true," said Arthur, a little sourly, who hated talking of horrors when Alice was in the room.

"Yes," continued David, heedless. He was obviously very interested in the story. "He said about the old Parson's son what got his throat cut by a madman——"

Alice, who had never heard a story that was now almost legend, writhed with nervous excitement.

"Tell us about it, David," she said. "Was he really killed there, then?"

But Arthur broke in before David could speak.

"You can leave it to another time. We don't want to go talking about such unsavoury things as murders on a day like this. Quite enough of that in the paper."

"All right," replied David. "I'm only telling you what Sammy told me. I never heard much about it till this morning."

"Here's some pudding for you, David," said Tansy, quietly. He took it and looked at her.

"Did you ever go down there, mother? To the house, I mean. It's strange—some strange down in that long room at the back——" He mused silently.

Tansy looked at him steadily. "I went there once," she said. "But I never care for it at all. I shouldn't be going there if I was you."

He immediately knew he would have to go again.

"Well, he won't be able to go if the Parson's going to live there," said Arthur. "And a good thing, too."

"What're you going to do this afternoon?" asked Tansy of Arthur.

"Thinking to go to the pigeon shoot. But if it rains again, and seeing as we're going out this evening, I may stay in. That was a brae good pudding, mother. I know a good pudding when I taste one."

Feast. Clockwork.

"Glad you like it. Looking plenty of rain about to me."

"We going to the concert this evening, then?" asked David.

"Yes. I got four tickets."

"Will there be a sketch?" asked Alice. "I like a sketch better'n all songs and music."

"There always belong to be a sketch," said Arthur. "Can't call it a proper concert else. And I suppose Parson'll be giving a speech."

"What time is it?" asked David.

"Seven-thirty."

"Well, I'm going to the football match, rain or no. It looks like being a good game to me."

David rarely took any interest in football.

"We'd better have tea at six," said Tansy, "and don't you be late, David, because we ought to leave here at seven."

... The sky was all cloudy again. Tansy made David take a coat, although he did not want to. The others stayed in—Arthur, after a cursory glance at his paper, falling asleep over the fire. The day was very short. Tansy lit the lamp about four and tried to blot out the murky gloom outside. The rain fell in fitful gusty showers. She sat in the rocking-chair and picked up the paper. But it did not interest her, and she threw it down. She only looked at the pictures on the back page. She wondered whether Arthur would read the news aloud this evening when they got back from the concert.

Drip, drip, drip down the pane went the water from the gutter along the roof. She could hardly see out of the window now. Alice was working at a jig-saw puzzle her father had bought for her. Her frowning face strained over the coloured pieces in the lamp-

light. Arthur was snoring. His mouth fell back and the engine of
his sleep began to work. Feast Monday. Tansy swayed her chair
backwards and forwards. She wished she could sleep as easily as
Arthur. Half, more than half his life was an easy dreamland.

Drip, drip, drip went the rain. A grey waste outside, the moor
seemed to want to invade the house like a long creeping army.
The wind made a scuttling sound through the house and rattled a door upstairs. It was very warm in the room. Yet to open
the door would be to adventure something. Across the moor
. . . an old song came back to Tansy, like the scent of a pressed
flower between the pages of a book. "He went away across the
moor . . ."

"I can't do it, mother," grumbled Alice suddenly.

"What? Can't do it——"

"The puzzle. There's one piece I can't find."

"Oh, you leave it to your dad. He's good at puzzles, he is."

Arthur's jaw looked as though it were about to fall off its
hinge. His throat was loose and skinny like a bird's. His hands
were clasped over his belly, his head lolling like a doll on one side
of his chair. Poor Arthur, she thought. Beaten back upon sleep,
sleep, sleep. No wife to love. So sleep, sleep, sleep and drip, drip,
drip of the rain. It was an anodyne, this rain, hard to resist. It
needed a tremendous effort to rise from her chair and put a kettle
on for tea. Another meal, when only a moment ago, it seemed,
she had washed up the last one. Nothing but stoking up the
engines. When one stoking is finished, lay the fuel for another.
That and sleep and the drip, drip, drip of the rain. Energy wasted
on energy; nothing accomplished; nothing created but the way
for the expenditure of more energy.

Outside, the skeletons of some elder trees rattled their bones
together in the wind. The monotone of the moor pressed her
into herself. She wanted to be out, but knew she lacked the courage to go. There might be something across the moors to release
her from drip, drip, drip and sleep, sleep, sleep. But where she
looked lay Retallack, all that she could see of it now, nothing but
one faint thrust of a stack in the veiling afternoon. Nothing but
the ghosts of men at Retallack. Better stay inside and go down
deeper into herself, nodding to the rhythm of the rain on the

window and the snores of Arthur. And while the kettle hummed she dropped her eyes, might have slept had not David returned, dripping wet and miserable.

"You were stupid to go," she said. "Now you'll have to change your clothes come evening. You don't mean to tell me you've been watching football all the afternoon? Shouldn't have thought they'd have played in such weather."

"No, they didn't," he muttered gloomily. "They put the game off. I wish we hadn't got to go to this concert."

Arthur was still asleep. David made a wry face at him, and for a moment there was sympathy between David and Tansy. Then she asked him where he had spent the afternoon. He hesitated. Alice waited curiously. He shook his coat in the passage, humming a tune maddeningly.

"Went for a walk," he said.

"Alone?"

"Yes, alone."

He went upstairs to change his trousers. Sitting on the bed he rubbed his damp legs with a towel. He had wanted to tell Tansy about his second visit to the wood and the rotting vicarage, but Alice's watchful eyes had made it impossible. He half resolved to tell Tansy later when they were alone. But he could never tell her quite how the place had thrilled him, very much as Retallack had thrilled him. About it, was the rotten odour of death and mutilation. The house was hollow with silence, as ghostly as the man-engine where the men had crashed to their end. It made him afraid, and because of that, he had to venture there alone to find out what it was that had struck fear in him.

Sammy Stiles had said that the place was haunted and that nobody had lived there for well over thirty years. David thought he would live there if he had the chance. He wanted to see a ghost and because of that he never did see one. And there was something terrible and alluring about the story of the madman cutting the boy's throat. He shivered, and gloated over the bloody story, dimly aware that he felt as sorry for the murderer as for his victim. Because when you were mad you didn't know what terrible things you did. Like this fellow in the paper who was cutting up women in London.

He found a copy of the Sunday paper that he had taken from downstairs and read again of the further discovery of another horrible murder, a servant girl in a dark alley late at night. The police were following a clue and seemed confident of an arrest. David read the heavily-coloured report; read it with a beating heart, a finger knocking, knocking in his brain, knocking like a bringer of ill news at a happy man's door. He read and re-read till he was sweating and sick, and threw the paper down in horror. It was like coming upon the corrupt entrails of a bullock in a slaughter house. He could not bear to look, but he had to. And having looked he was sick with loathing, yet knew that he would look again.

As usual he had to be called down to tea. Then, when Tansy had cleared away and washed the things, they smothered themselves in coats and scarves, took a lantern and began the long walk into the town. For a moment the rain had stopped and they pressed on quickly before it should come down again. They did not go along the bed of the valley, but crossed over the little bridge, decaying now with age, and thus past the farm and into the town. There was a light in the kitchen at the farm. Nicolas would be alone, for the others had gone to spend the evening with Bessie's sister. Tansy felt she would have liked to keep her father company; sit by the fire silently with him under the picture of Emmeline.

The wind was behind them and the walk was easy. An impatient chattering mob of people pressed at the door of the church hall. Acquaintances hailed Tansy and Arthur as they joined the crowd. Arthur was jovial to everybody and cracked his Feast jokes. But Tansy, shrinking as always from a crowd, was ill at ease and hoped they would find seats away from anybody they knew. But when they got in and struggled into some seats, she heard a hoarse whispering behind her.

"Oh, 'es, you! She got a brother, Andrew Penderil he's called, what live over to Rosemulyan in the moor. A queer chap, I hear. And the boy's going over there to work, so they do say——"

Tansy was too wise to try to identify the speaker. She strained her ears, impatient when Arthur or the others passed a remark to her and she missed part of the conversation.

"—Oh, he's a pretty boy, mind you, but a sight too big for his shoes. Bessie Penderil was telling of me only the other day how he——"

"There goes the Parson." Arthur nudged her arm. "Now we shall soon get going."

"—She always was a bit strange as you might be saying. I mind the time when her mother was living, and she a glum woman that you could never get to know. And that Andrew's another deep one. Oh, straight enough, mind you! I never hear nothing against them, not as I can recall, that is. Though there be those as do say——"

"Mother, when will the sketch come?" asked Alice loudly, sucking a sweet in the middle of each word.

"Oh, hold your tongue, can't you," muttered Tansy.

"—Mind you——"

"I suppose Miss Clotworthy'll be at the piano," said Arthur.

"—And nobody knows whether they're married or not!"

They were obviously talking about somebody else. It was not easy to apply the rumour to any of Tansy's family. She turned round carefully to catch a sight of the speaker, but the lights were turned off suddenly and she could not see.

The curtains parted upon a drab stage looking like pasteboard and hung at the back with moth-eaten brown draperies. On the stage were a few derelict pitch-pine chairs, heavily marked with white numbers; a card table; and a walnut piano, peeling with corruption, stretched above the keyboard with red plush, and already creaking with apprehension. Right in the middle of the stage hung a dejected gas-globe, dependant upon a long rod of rusty iron and adorned with two chains. Feebly it spluttered its reluctance to do anything more than make the performers look as sickly as a miller in a snowstorm.

The Vicar mounted the squeaking steps at the back of the stage, smiled in exactly the same way as he did when he announced his text and spoke to them in the contemporary Parsonic manner, that is, as a man-of-the-world-who-has-knocked-about speaks to his fellow men—sinners all. Briefly he announced Miss Connie Clotworthy, their organist, who—in the Vicar's own manly words—would start the ball rolling with a piano solo enti-

tled—what was it entitled? Here there was a hurried confabula-
tion with the lady at the back of the stage, and some considerable
delay occasioned by the fact that Miss Clotworthy's pronuncia-
tion of French differed appreciably from the Vicar's. But presently
it appeared that Miss Clotworthy was to start the ball rolling with
Brise d'été.

There was a thunder of applause as Miss Clotworthy, bobbing
like a clever jackdaw, took off a ring and placed it above the keys.
A lady with a goitre and a pendulous yellow jaw appeared as out
of nowhere and sat by Miss Clotworthy to turn over, entirely
overshadowing that worthy lady. Then Miss Clotworthy started,
piano, very *piano*, because the soft pedal most efficiently prevented many of the notes from sounding. It was a very good soft
pedal indeed. However, presently the pianist pressed down the
loud pedal and the effect was instantaneous, for the piano jangled
to life like a gipsy's tambourine. Where one note had sounded
before, a score sounded now; half-tones, quarter-tones, eighths
of tones. It was all very weird and made the piece sound oriental
and exceedingly difficult of execution. The audience was spell-
bound.

"She's a beaut, boy!" commented some youth at the back in a
loud whisper. "See her hands flying away like lightning?"

Miss Clotworthy sweated away valiantly and pressed the
breeze on to a hurricane. A page of the music dropped, but she
was equal to all emergencies. Fumbling on an opportune domi-
nant, she assumed a rapt expression, while her partner reassem-
bled the yellow copy.

"See that, boy," said the youth. "She goes on a-doing of it, telling it all off proper, even when the book drop!"

The hurricane died suddenly as the soft pedal came down
again. The quarter tones scrambled back hastily to the diatonic.
Three *p*'s, and Miss Clotworthy with a deftly muffled flourish of
naked arpeggios, put on her ring, stood up and bowed. There
was tremendous applause as they walked off. Miss Clotworthy
whispered to her accomplice: "I didn't do that *crescendo* too well,
Amy. It's a good thing nobody here understands much about
music, proper music, that is!"

The concert went on. There were songs, duets, glees and

banjo solos; then more songs, duets, glees and banjo solos. Alice got very impatient.

"When's the sketch?" she kept asking. And when Tansy assured her it would come at the end, she said bitterly: "Well, when's the end, then?"

A bent old man with a drooping moustache climbed up on to the stage and was a little scared by the amount of clapping he got. It was Jimmie Blackmore who had been in the church choir longer than anybody cared to remember. Everybody was fond of Jimmie, and old people would speak of the days when he had filled the church with his voice. A pretty singer in his day. And there was still life left in him even though he must have been over seventy.

The hall grew quieter and old people's eyes very soon clouded with mists of memory. Miss Clotworthy played admirably, and always knew exactly how long Jimmie wished to stay on his high notes. And Jimmie liked singing in the church hall because the piano was down a tone and made it easier for him.

He sang *My Pretty Jane* very slowly in a thin, long, wavering voice—the attenuation of a melody. When he had finished it the audience stamped on the ground and demanded another. They had heard his songs a thousand times and could hear them a thousand times more. So Jimmie came back and sang another—a song yellow, yellow with age. Jimmie struggled to the top notes as though his soul were at stake, and perhaps it was. *Faithful I'll be to the colleen I adore! Eileen Alannah! Argus Astore!*

Tansy was moved to hear this broken old man singing of the colleen he adored. What buried love did it revive in his heart of a lad so far distant as to be legendary? She knew the song as everybody knew it. The old man closed his eyes, for with open eyes he could not deliver to them his message. In the dim, smoky hall, hovering over the laboured heads of the people, a forgotten spirit came, timeless and powerful as a cromlech held fast in the wind. It beat upon the people like the rushings of great wings and forced out of them something old, elemental; an anguish, a burden, a heritage.

They were the people of the earth, lost in racial memories, brother and sister, mother and son, man and lover, brother and brother. One by one, slowly and unconsciously, with their eyes closed upon the visible evidence of their progress upon the face of the earth, they began to sing in low vital voices, adding their own crude harmony to the chorus of the song. The attentuation of a melody became the structure of a tribe. The hall filled with sound, was a burdensome wail of sound.

Tansy sang with the rest; she could not, if she wished, resist the song. *Eileen Alannah! Argus Astore!* Her eyes were thick with tears; she was a brooding mourner of the past. All that had passed, and every note she sang now was passing. Where to, O God, where to?

The song ended, and the world changed slowly. An unwilling rustle of dresses and stiff legs, and the people thundered their applause for Jimmie. Thereafter the concert settled down to more flippant items to which Tansy did not want to listen. She could not listen to anything after that old man's song. But it went on and approached an interval while they made preparations on the stage for the sketch. So Alice got her moneys-worth, and afterwards on the way out, gabbled incessantly about the antics of the local comedians.

It was pouring with rain and the walk back was a dark, driving adventure. They did not talk but forced their way along the black path, guided by Arthur's lamp. The moors were black as the sky so that it was impossible to tell where the line of the land ended and the sky began. They stumbled down into the valley, Arthur clutching Alice's hand, Tansy behind, then David. Up again on to the moor, where the gates of the gale had been flung open. Tansy tasted the bitter refreshment of salt on her tongue. Her body was stirred by the tearing ravage of the gale and she did not want to go into the battered house that awaited them. She wanted to stay out in this and hear the wind sing *Eileen Alannah* in a thousand swelling voices rushing over the black land in a never-ending whirlpool of sound.

They barred and bolted the door; lit the lamp.

"My gosh! Some night!" exclaimed Arthur. They took off their wet clothes and Tansy put a kettle on the oil stove.

"I wish we'd built up the fire," she said. Her words were fresh and full of life. She felt a vigour in her blood, a strength new and invigorating to her. Arthur saw her flushed, excited face and remarked on it.

"Why, Tansy," he said, "I believe this evening's done you good. You're looking quite a girl again."

David looked at her. Yes, his father was right. Tansy seemed years younger.

She laughed. "Well, I enjoyed the concert and that's a fact. And the walk home too. The wind gets into me somehow. Reckon you forget how to mope when there's all this howling wind about."

They talked about the concert, discussing the merits of all the performers. Then they drank tea and warmed themselves over the lamp in the hearth. The wind was like a sullen beast who could not get what he wanted. They taunted it behind their locked door. The house on the moor had fulfilled its purpose. And Tansy was happy. Even if only for this hour she was happy and young again, ridiculing her foolish fears as she ridiculed the wind.

"Well, it's been a rare good Feast," said Arthur, a trifle smugly, as though he had invented Feast.

"It has that," sad Tansy. "More like the old days." David took the newspaper idly from the window-seat. Arthur had hardly touched it for the day, and it was still folded up. David opened it.

"Mother, that there sketch," said Alice, "did they have a real fowl or did they make one special?"

"Made one, I suppose. Though I must say 'twas well done."

"That Miss Clotworthy play well," said Arthur. "I hear she got a gold medal for it."

"Yes I daresay," said Tansy. "She certainly do make the old piano shake. I wish we had a piano, then we could learn Alice. I must say——"

"I say!" burst in David. "They got that man——"

"What man?" asked Arthur.

"Haven't you seen this, then?" said David. "The man what done all those murders! There's a picture of him here. Strange, quiet looking chap called—Charley. I can't read it, you. No—Chailey——"

Tansy took the paper from him with a taut hand. She saw

immediately the twisted smile of Roger Chailey. She got up quickly. Her mouth fell open.

"I'm sick," she said quickly. She went to the door and struggled blindly with the chain and lock.

Arthur hurried up to her.

"Tansy, my dear, what's amiss?"

"Just sick," she muttered. "Open the door. For the Lord's sake open the door. I want the air. I'm all right. Too much excitement. Just—sick——"

Arthur got the door open for her and she staggered out weakly. He tried to follow her but she pushed him back. She leant against the wall of the house and retched so that it tore her inside out. She was violently sick. Then an absolute emptiness of spirit overcame her so that she found it hard to think of anything. She was conscious of Arthur helping her in, giving her water and leading her upstairs. She knew that she was in bed. Almost immediately asleep.

CHAPTER IX

SHE did not wake from a heavy sleep till after nine. Then Arthur brought her a cup of tea which she drank eagerly, because there was a hard, dry feeling in her mouth and throat. Arthur was anxious and pressed her with questions. In all his time he had never known Tansy sick as she had been the previous night.

"How do you feel?"

She answered with an effort. It was as though she controlled her movements by the pulling of a stiff lever that set her muscles in motion. "I'm quite all right, thankee Arthur. You no need to worry."

"But last night," he objected, "you was—awful. Never seen you go so white and stiff, to say nothing of bringing up all your food. You better stay in bed."

"Oh, no." Already she was half out. "Don't be so stupid. I aren't ill." She was sponging her face in the wash basin. Arthur had a vision of Tansy's mother, remembering the stubborn will that had resisted all who might help her until the final collapse came.

"Are you sure," he said firmly, "as there's nothing you're hiding?"

"Hiding?" she repeated quickly.

"Yes. I mean you haven't got something wrong with you like your mother and afraid to see a doctor?"

She forced a metallic laugh. "My Lord, no! I tell you there's naught wrong with me. I eat too much all day and that's all there was to it. Duck don't agree with me and never did, though I didn't say so."

"And you really feeling all right now?"

She faced him and pressed her lips together in a thin line.

"I'm feeling proper. And if you worry any more, I'll be mad, though it is kind of you."

More or less reassured, he went grumblingly out of the room. She was not alone a moment before he returned with a letter. "I forgot this," he said, and went out again.

It was from Andrew. Her mind wandered and she had to read it three times before she could grasp it.

". . . Better come Friday night instead of Saturday morning. Give you more time and make it worth while. If you catch the 5.30 bus from Retallack Corner I'll meet you Rosemulyan Cross with the trap. That means you leaving home about 4.30, and if you walk along the cliffs through the mine, 'tis quicker than going along the main road."

"Along the cliffs . . . through the mine . . ." Yes, it would be much quicker and David would like the walk. They need not take many clothes. One small bag would be enough. And it would be a nice walk for David. Yes, it would be much better to go on Friday night. It was Tuesday now; only three days. How time did fly to be sure! Feast over and the long anticipated visit to Rosemulyan nearly over. It would not be long before David went; Christmas, and then he would leave school. Seven weeks to Christmas; yet it seemed a long time. But it would make a nice break, this little holiday at Andrew's. Nice for her and David to get away together, alone. The walk through the mine to Retallack Corner would thrill David.

She felt sick again. She pressed her hands to her throat and battled wildly with the window to get it open. The bright sun of a rain-washed morning streamed in, and the breeze flapped the curtains in her face. The air was wonderful to her; she absorbed it half drunkenly, holding on to the window because of the rocking world in her head, a crazy kaleidoscope of contorted images, sounds, sentences. A thousand burning memories flocked wildly in the tumult of her mind. The room was covered with pictures of naked people who mocked and tormented her. Phrases rang in her ears.

"... I would cut off the limbs, but the trunk I would keep ... poor twisted devil ... poor twisted devil ... you have a lovely ear, I feel it belongs to me ... I would cut off ..."

She was hemmed in by great trees towering so high above her that she could not see the sky. A woodcutter was lopping the branches, crying with insensate mirth as one after another they crashed to the ground, leaving but a naked army of stripped trunks standing solemn like mourners at a requiem. She was in a hot, shadowy room pressed down on a bed, gloating in a fever of desire. An old man with the fierce eyes of a warrior sent out against the devil, flung his passionate words from a church pulpit.

"... Stamp upon and utterly destroy ... utterly destroy ..." She leant on the sill and held her head in the boisterous child of last night's gale. Her palm closed over a grey slug. The loathing and dread went through her soul. Then she pressed with all her strength until her hand was foul with its squashed body. She kept her hand there till she felt the soft death yield in her flesh.

Now suddenly she felt that something unspeakably light and sweet, yet possessing great power, had touched her for a moment on the forehead. So that where the corruption of memory had rotted the fibres of her brain and sickened her rising stomach, there was now nothing but cool purity of feeling. What had assaulted her in all its malignancy, seemed then to depart from her, so that immediately she felt free again. Like an arrow released from the bondage of the bow and delivered into the bondage of an enemy, quivering still in the stiffening flesh of an enemy. There, for a while, she waited, and as her normal world came back to her it seemed to her a thousand years since she had woken up. Because suddenly, in one fierce flood of comprehension, she lived through the past fifteen years and saw quite clearly what it was that had pressed her down until she felt she could never rise again. And after the first overwhelming shock of this discovery, when she fully realized what it was that David inherited, what sort of blood it was that flowed in his dark veins, she was able, like stepping out of a tunnel, to see clear daylight before her. She had to redeem something that she had sold fifteen years ago.

And now that she knew the truth, redemption seemed possible, even easy. She found it possible to bring back to her mind the twisted smile of Chailey; found it almost pleasurable to indulge the panorama of her memory, detached, now that she knew why his brown deep eyes—the eyes of David—had burnt into hers with such force. And thinking of David, she loved him as terribly as, that yellow afternoon above the sea, she had felt God must love his children. She knew that her love must preserve him and guard him for ever. She felt the coldness of the purpose of God as an astringent covering upon her body; through his messenger, the graven George, she asked him to keep her eyes hard and clear.

The awfulness was over. She took her hand away from the sill and quickly washed it. A sudden thought urged her to go to an old trunk that stood in a cupboard on the landing outside. In it was a motley collection of household oddments. Folded up in a old black skirt she found the twisted little piece of blackthorn, kept through all these years. Often she had wanted to destroy it, but always something had prevented her. "Because of this evening which was lovely ..." Was it? Yes, O God, it was ... Again she could not destroy the thorn. It meant too much, that little twisted tree stuck with drab ghosts of a blossom. So she put it back in the trunk, closing the lid upon it as one who would never look there again.

When she got downstairs Arthur was washing the breakfast things. She remembered Andrew's letter and told him they would be going to Rosemulyan on Friday night.

"You don't mind, Arthur?"

"No, I don't mind, of course not. Glad for you to have the change. But I must say, Tansy, my dear, as you're certainly not looking slight at all. Perhaps a bit thin, but you've got more colour in your cheeks than you belong to have and your eyes are some bright."

Tansy smiled, the sort of smile he seldom saw. "Yes," she said. "I had to bring something up and I got it up and now I'm all right. So don't you go fretting no more."

She started to bustle round and clean up the room, never pausing for one moment in her work. She felt possessed with the idea that a complete scouring of the house was necessary. Above the stairs was a line of sooty cobwebs; the stair carpet was grey with mud and dust; in the scullery where Arthur ponderously washed-up, and got in her way, was a collection of jam-pots, tins, worn-out saucepans, all of which she collected together in a pile outside the front door.

"Arthur," she said, "the place wants a proper clean-up. Now you be useful, my dear, and just take all this rubbish down to the shaft and get rid of it. You can use the wheelbarrow."

She was bright-eyed and red-faced. Her sleeves were rolled up, leaving her strong capable arms bare. She moved about the house quickly, like a cat who jumps on a table of dinner things and touches nothing with his feet. Arthur, glad to see her so happily active, willingly carted away the rubbish. When he came back he found her in the scullery with a broom. Everything had been taken down, every shelf carefully cleaned. There were black corners where the lamp had smoked and Tansy was impatient with them.

"This place wants a good liming to make it sweet again." She frowned. Then she dumped a blackened kettle into Arthur's hand and told him to take it outside and make it shine. After a while she had the scullery spotless, with the little window open to let in the breeze. Then she started on the living-room. Before Arthur knew where he was, most of the furniture was out in the garden. She chucked pleasantries at him and he grinned amiably. This was a Tansy of another decade. Every minute she gave him a fresh job to do. Then about twelve she sent him up to the town with a list of things they wanted for the house.

Left alone, she worked all the faster. Once she paused when she came across yesterday's newspaper. She held it in her hand as one might hold a dead rat. She did not know whether she wanted to read it or not. But presently her curiosity made up her mind, and opening the paper she saw again the picture of Chailey, a picture taken as he was being hurried into the police-station before a group of excited people. He was smiling and seemed to be able to ignore the police and the hostile crowd. She read:

"The atrocious series of murders that has lately alarmed the public and baffled the police, was brought to a dramatic climax last night in the sensational arrest of Roger Chailey, described as a gentleman of no fixed abode who had taken rooms in Hampstead. Mrs. Trull, of Turner's Green, who had for six weeks harboured Chailey in her house, later told our representative that he had never given her any trouble. She had not seen very much of him. Apart from the murders of seven young women in North London alone, it is believed that Chailey has been associated with a number of similar outrages that have occurred up and down the country during as long a period as the last ten years. When he was arrested Chailey made no protestation, but smiled and allowed himself to be led away. His trial will be awaited with keen interest. A full report of the arrest and Chailey's subsequent statements appears on page ten. . . ."

She did not turn to page ten. She was not interested in the picturesque details of his arrest. All she had wanted to know, she now knew. She wondered vaguely whether they would hang him or whether he would get off on a plea of insanity. She had heard that such people often did; that if it could be proved you were insane they could not hang you. But she hoped they would make an end of him. She hoped that for his own sake. Because so clearly she saw that what he had done he had been compelled to do; that what she had shrunk from fifteen years ago was the beginning of the dry-rot that had now resulted in his downfall. Yes, she hoped they would hang him. She would rather be hanged herself were she in such a position, because to her mind an asylum was worse agony than the gallows. How else could the disease of his mind be cured? Death was his only chance of safety. Put him in the hands of the icy loving Father and he would be safe for ever. That was the only certain harbour for him, the poor twisted devil. And there lived in her at once, an intense compassion for him, for the God in him that had turned devil. "Because of this evening which was lovely . . ." Yes, it had been lovely. Even if he had pressed her down and down, it had been lovely. Now he could never touch her again. He would go to the frozen bosom of the Father. In that icy agony of love the devils would droop and die, and the poor torn soul of man that remained would find a pure place somewhere in the universe. She would be free again. She did not think of the material future now; did not reckon up the manner of her life with Arthur and Alice. But the fire of her love fell upon David. There was no other vision in her, except the ultimate certainty that she would reach the Saint's immaculate resting place and feel the timeless pressure of his cool hand dispelling the fever of her life. Heaven, the Heaven of her infancy, grew large, terrible and sweet before her. She was small and fearful before the throne of the Lamb and felt all about her the rushings of angels' wings. She felt as Magdalen might have felt when the devils were driven out; was aware of a slow expurgation taking place inside her, an expurgation which she herself would finally have to consummate.

The world was sweet, clean, new as a young lamb or the first celandine. Through bleary eyes she had seen it for so long. She stood at the door now and saw it all as a new place; the quintessence of joyous cleanliness. The wind blew upon the faces of the rain-pools and shook the grasses; far across the moor it was clear, the hills sharp and the sky no more a covering upon the earth, but an adventure away from it. The lovely earth filled her with exultation. She saw herself now as part of it. She did not desire any longer to express her love for it. She saw that the only perfect expression lay in utter loyalty to her own soul; that only thus could she give back to the earth what it had given her. And the cold, chaste sunlight streamed down into her bowels, moved through her veins, stirred a glacial tide in her blood, so that she was hard as a rock inside, and as still, as everlasting.

She moved and went on with her work. Finishing downstairs she went up and turned out Alice's room and their own, putting clean sheets on the beds and brushing the floors. But she would not go into David's room. She could not change anything in there, did not want to touch any of his things.

Arthur returned and the day passed rapidly. When the children came back at tea-time, they ran up asking if she were well again. She said she had never felt better; nor had she. She joked with Arthur and Alice, gave them their food, and did all the work of the house quickly and efficiently. But to David she spoke very little. Once she told him they were going to Rosemulyan earlier than they had originally planned. He received the news with careful indifference, because he did not want to show them how he looked forward to going. In truth he was counting the hours to the visit and thought of little else.

When all the work was done and evening came, Tansy sat in her old chair feeling tired in her limbs. The others were silent. The room, soft in lamp-light, unbeaten by wind, reminded her of the farm, years ago when it had hung upon the strange silence of her first spring day. Still it seemed that they were waiting for spring. She found herself looking at David secretly under lowered eyes. He was reading. She thought he had never looked so utterly beautiful, so strong a spear of boyhood. There was nothing she could ever love more than this. And she studied every detail of his face and supple body, attempting to grave it on her memory as a living picture she might always carry.

But then he looked up and she dropped her eyes.

"Mother," he said in a queerly muffled tone, "have you yesterday's paper anywhere about?"

"Somewhere. What you want it for, then?"

"I—was doing the crossword puzzle," he replied.

"Here it is," she said. "But I shouldn't waste time over the puzzle if I was you. You'll never work it out right."

She gave him the paper and watched him under half closed eyes with amused detachment, as he made one or two desultory attempts at the puzzle. But it was not long before he stretched himself, yawned and rose to go upstairs. He folded the paper and took it with him. As he passed her she pretended to be asleep.

"Good night, mother." But she did not answer.

Alice had gone to bed. Arthur nodded over the paper. A foolish man. A happy man. She was glad he loved Alice.

Presently, before Arthur had much chance of commenting on the day's news, she too went to bed and was asleep long before Arthur came up.

CHAPTER X

"MOTHER, why've you been so strange to me of late?"

"Have I been strange, then?"

"Yes, you have. You know you have. Never seeming to want to come near me. I don't know a bit what's happened."

"Sometimes, David," said Tansy quietly, "you're strange in yourself and don't realize it. Then you think it's the other person who's queer."

"You mean that I'm queer and thinking you're queer?"

"Maybe."

They walked on in silence for a few minutes. The short afternoon, white with a moveless mist, was darkening to night. They were nearing the Retallack mine. David, wearing a scarf and a mackintosh, walked in front of Tansy, carrying a small suit-case. The path was too narrow for them to walk abreast.

"How am I queer?" asked David after a pause. And Tansy did not immediately reply. When she did so they came on to a wider stretch of the path and she was able to walk beside him.

"However it is," she said, "it's not your fault. And maybe it's me who's queer and seeing things wrong."

"No," he insisted, looking on the ground all the time. "No, mother. You just said——"

His words were drowned and lost in the reverberating siren of the lighthouse northwards. The sound echoed through the hollow countryside every minute—a long lost cavernous diapason. And answering it, many miles south, they heard the double report of the Longships gun. The sea was lost entirely in the mist, and all they could see of the land were a few chimney stacks looming up suddenly in the grey pall. When the siren, ending on a dissonant low growl, like the echoing crash of a gong, died away to its silence, David continued speaking.

"You said I was strange and you must have some reason for

saying that. Tell me, mother, because it's some miserable us not being ourselves."

He turned an appealing face towards her, but she only smiled secretively and would not meet him.

"I think we are ourselves, boy," she said. "I think you're just growing up, growing away from me and trying not to show it. That's all 'tis."

"But I'm not," he cried. "I want to be with you and tell you all the things as I'm doing and thinking, but when you never smile and speak soft as you used to, I can't—I just can't. You freeze me all up."

"We freeze each other up," she said in a stony voice. "Or we burn each other. It come to the same thing in the long run."

"Well," he reasoned, "I'd rather be burnt than frozen."

"I'd rather be frozen," she said, and stayed her next words on the siren which broke again from the mouth of the northern caves.

Presently she said, "You're glad enough to go to Rosemulyan— glad enough to get away from me——"

"No, that aren't true! Not a bit!" he cried. He stopped for a moment in his path, his face heavy with pain. "It's not you I ever want to get away from. It's—you know——"

"No," she maintained. "'Tisn't only Arthur, though you disagree with him enough and it's natural as you should."

"Why do you say that?" He pounced on her words. "Why is it natural? Other fellows can get on all right with their dads, and 'tisn't as though he was bad, or cruel or anything."

He still stayed in the path. She hedged her reply. "Well, you're—just different. You don't see eye to eye on nothing at all. But lately you've come to—to live a life of your own that I don't know about, and p'raps as well. You're going your own way and I reckon I'm leaving you to it. That's all. I don't care for these interfering mothers. Never did."

She began to walk on. "Come on," she said impatiently. "Else you want for to miss the 'bus."

He dragged on behind her unwillingly.

"You don't care for me any more," he muttered, "and that's where's to."

Then she stopped, turned round and faced him.

"David," she said, "you're all I have in the world and you're all I do love. Whenever you get doubting me, think of that. For I'm not in the habit of saying things like that twice over. 'Tisn't easy and you ought not to want it said."

He advanced to her impulsively. "Oh, I do know it," he said, "but——"

"Us don't need to talk about it now," she said. "We're going to Andrew's for to enjoy ourselves. And if us stay talking now, us won't get there at all."

So they went on again in silence, entering now upon the shattered remains, the mounds of slag and toppling chimneys of the mine.

" 'Tis a wisht old place!" Tansy shivered. "And I don't wonder with all that happened here"

"I haven't been here since that night in August," he said.

"No," she retorted. "Other hunting grounds now, I suppose?"

"What do you mean?"

"I mean the Vicarage." She laughed somewhat cynically, and he was hurt by it.

"Well, what of it?" he said, "if I like it, what of it——"

"There you are," she said. "It's your own life you're living. Something you don't care to tell me. D'you think I can't always see through your deceptions?"

"When do you mean?" he mumbled reluctantly.

"I mean Feast Monday, when you spent the afternoon down in that dark old place and only told me you'd been for a walk. As if I couldn't guess from your eyes what tell everything! Why didn't you want to tell me?"

"It was father being there," he explained, eager to exonerate himself. "And Alice. That's all."

"You've had plenty of time since then," she said. "Why didn't you want to tell me? Not only that but other things."

Then he flung a challenge at her.

"You know why. Just because you don't want to know and I know it. Because every time it's on my lips to tell you about—about such things, you freeze me all up and I can't part with something—something——" he hesitated.

"What?" she urged. "Go on. Get it out, my son."

"Something—that gets hold of me," he blurted half incoherently. "You don't know. You'd never understand at all."

"I reckon I do know and understand more'n what you do think," she said. She ceased speaking as the siren filled the land. She was a few feet in front of him, a faint traveller in the mist. David felt as though he were following a ghost. And suddenly he, too, grew hard inside and would not speak any more. His efforts at reconciliation had come to nothing. He was furious with his mother, even after her cold protestation of love for him, feeling certain that she no longer cared for him. He thought of Andrew and the new life that he would lead away from the leaden weight of his family. He began to build a new world for himself; all the formless aspirations of his boyhood mounted up in him and began to take tangible shape. He would make enough money to enable him to live alone. He did not want to be with people. He would dream and dream again and find out the secrets of the moors. He would eat sparingly and simply, wear light loose clothes, and in summer go naked under the sun. He would write great, strange poems, fiery and bloody, drawn out of the smouldering castles of the sunset, poems like the Ancient Mariner. He would learn the darkness of night, would adventure to tractless, unheard-of places. The life that he would live! The lovely, lonely adventure he would make of life . . .

A little gust of wind swirled the mist around them in eddies. He saw that they were now walking along above the dilapidated workings of the mine. A platform bearing a great wheel stood near the cliff. There were little interwoven streams of thick brown water running in and out. A long low building stood on their left, heavily boarded and shuttered. It was the power house of the old man-engine. And near to that, laid over the gravelly soil, were a number of boards, all rotting away with damp.

David remembered the cries and echoes of the lost place, the gaunt land of a dead industry. The boards covered in the shaft where the men had fallen. The last time he had been here, in August, he had grown afraid in the shadows of a summer moon and had run home sweating and trembling into the arms of Tansy. He had wanted to peer down through the cracks in the boards, to the long tunnel that pierced its way towards the sea. But he had never got as far as that. A fox had slithered noiselessly along the path; a bat had veered round his head; a donkey had outraged the silence. And the night had broken upon unholy things, too much for him to bear. Like a coward he had run home, knowing as soon as he fell into his mother's anxious and too easy arms, that he had come away before he had dared the place to yield up its secrets to him. The dead secrets of thirty men, crushed and torn in the dissolution of machinery . . .

Now, as he passed the place again, the old sickening dread, the old morbid craving for horror overcame him. He could not, would not pass it this time without standing for a second on those boards. Immediately he resented Tansy, yet was glad of her presence as otherwise he might have been afraid. He called out to her:

"That's the old man-engine——"

She turned round and looked in the direction of his pointing hand. "Yes it is," she said slowly. "I remember, just such a day as this and about this time of year, their bringing body after body away from here. They never found some till days after. Arthur used to come home sick as death every night. It was an awful time and there wasn't a man or woman in Penth as could find the heart to smile for weeks afterwards."

David's eyes burnt eagerly.

"Did you come up here, then?"

"Yes, once," she replied. "To help an old woman whose son had gone down with the others. She came to claim his body, y'see, like scores of others. But they never found the body. They only found——"

She paused and looked straight at him.

"Go on," he muttered. "What did they find?"

"His head."

"Oh!" David was horrified by the brutal coldness of her tone. But he forgot it in a minute.

"Did you ever come again?" he asked.

"This is the first time I been this way since then," she replied. "I—was frightened, and no wonder. No one ever come out here much save they've a reason."

She spoke very slowly with emphasis on each word.

"Aren't you feared now?" asked David. Still she looked at him with a directness that troubled his soul.

"Somehow I'm not," she said. "I might-a been a week or so ago, but somehow I'm not now."

"Let's go and look at the man-engine," he said. "There's lots of time for the 'bus."

He dropped the bag by the wall and began to walk down the slope. Tansy followed him mechanically. He was surprised that she did not protest.

He peered through the cracked windows of the power house, could faintly discern in the gloom the shape of the great boiler. He beckoned to Tansy to come, and she too peered through.

"There's the old devil," he said, "what really did all the mischief. It's strange to think that a lump of iron could do all that."

"Not half so strange as men killing each other," she said. "They know what they're doing. The engine don't."

"They don't always know what they're doing," he objected.

"What d'you mean, then?"

Slowly they walked over the boarded shaft.

"Why," he said, "sometimes they can't help it, I reckon. They're mad and don't know what they're doing, any more than the old man-engine did. Poor devils!"

"Yes. Poor devils!" she echoed drily. Her words seemed to hang on the sparse wintry air like the notes of a summoning bugle.

"Take that chap in the paper," continued David. "I reckon he didn't know a bit what he was doing. And they'll put a rope round his neck likely as not and never think how he must have suffered."

"Who do you mean?" It amused her to ask.

"Why, that Chailey fellow. You read about him?"

"Yes, I remember. You sorry for him then?"

They paused just by the boards of the shaft. His long, narrow face cut into the gloom and he spoke in a mournful voice.

"Yes, I am sorry for him. Something went wrong in the poor devil, you might say."

"How d'you think it happen? A man going wrong in his mind like that?" They had forgotten their differences and were almost in sympathy with one another.

"I dunno. Unless it be in their blood. I expect you'd find he was—descended from another such."

"Yes, I suppose," she murmured. Then David's sad, reflective manner changed.

"Look," he cried, "we're almost standing on these rotten old boards and never thought about it!"

"I didn't forget——"

David knelt on the ground looking through a crack in the boards to the blackness of the shaft. A thin, cold blast of sea wind pierced up from it. He shook the board with his hands.

"This board's loose," he muttered to himself. "If I can get it away I'm going to drop as big a stone down as I can find." He exerted his strength and tore away the board, which suddenly snapped off in the middle. The smell of damp earth and rusty machinery blew up through the gap he had made. For a moment he felt dizzy and sick as he felt the rush of deep air upon him and realized that he had only to take a step forward to crash headlong to his end. Then he jumped up, the fever of nervous excitement in his eyes.

"I've done it!" he cried. "Where's a stone?"

He ran to a pile of stones near by and stumbled over with one the size of a football. He held it over the hole.

"Now listen!" There was a crash and the crumbling echoes of a thousand smaller stones that the large one had dislodged. Tansy stood behind David and strained her ears to catch the final thunder of its fall. But it was a sound that seemed to go on for ever, and before she could tell whether she heard the end of it the siren began to send its querulous complaint over the land. When it had died away, David flung out his arms wildly.

"My gosh!" he cried. "That's some depth! Think of all those bodies falling and falling like that stone! Oh, my gosh, what a sight it must-a been!"

He shuddered and put his arm over his eyes as though to blot out the picture he had created. Then he ran for another stone. This time it was a larger one, and he had difficulty in carrying it. He bent over the opening, balancing the stone on the edge, ready to let it fall. He was crouched on his haunches above the black hole, his feet on tip-toe.

"Be careful," warned Tansy, just behind him. She bent down on his right so as she could the better listen to the falling of the stone.

"I wonder how a body would sound——" muttered David. She did not hear his words, for her eyes were fixed on a long grey slug crawling over the stone towards David's left hand. It was the last time. It must be the last time.

"There's a slug crawling to your hand," she murmured through a narrow mouth, a thin edge of a voice, sparse like the air. "Kill it, David, for I hate slugs."

He looked at his hand in surprise, then laughed. "I'm glad you told me," he said. "Otherwise it might have gone down with the stone. Who'd be killing a harmless old slug? They bring you good luck, they say."

With his right hand he pinched it up and laid it on the wet grass by the boards.

"Now for the stone," he said. "Listen."

But as he was about to release it upon its dark journey the siren pierced the air again.

"Darn!" he muttered. "Must wait for that, else we'll never hear it at all."

But Tansy did not want to hear it. Standing a little to one side of David, for a brief second she absorbed all the beauty of his eager, wild face. The note of the siren sank, grew louder and more compelling in her ears.

"Hurry!" it cried. "Hurry ... hurry ... hurry ..."

The word grew longer, more laboured and drawn-out, hung in the mine-pitted hillside.

"Hurry ... hu-rry ... hu-rry ..."

The dynamic force of it broke in her head, generated to a blinding flash of fire in her head, so that her veins seemed to burst in her and her blood stream down blackly before her eyes. Her vision was streaked with blood, so that the smooth, sticky world around her became dead and unreal. She was driven forward. Her hands, cold and taut, like the steel girders of a great machine, were not her hands. She did not feel the pressure of his waist meeting her palms, as in one violent attack upon his crouched body, she sent him down his long home. The stone crashed after him. She did not hear him cry, heard nothing of the unending crashing down the shaft, of the little stones that rained upon his body. For thick in her ears were the last hollow echoes of the siren, a sound inexpressibly mournful, yet a sound she hoped might never stop. And when, after an infinity, the siren died away again and the place was silent; when she stood there above the long black mouth of the shaft, alone, where a moment before she had stood with David, she could not believe he had gone, that she had stamped finally and utterly upon the poor twisted devil of her son and sent him to the icy bosom of his God. She could not believe that. Indomitable in her purpose, now that it was done and she stood alone in this ghost-locked land with never a voice to say it was well done, never a hand to touch her burning forehead—she got back her human reason and became a woman, alone and horribly afraid.

She called, knowing he was not there.

"David—where are you——? David—David——"

And then she wished she had not called, for to break a dead silence with one's voice is to send sound back and back upon itself, crying for more and more sound, a lost sound finding itself in tractless silence. So her words came back to her again, poor outcasts in a place where words were unknown, and clamoured for her to send out more words to company them in the long adventure. Of all things dreading this silence, she cried again. Her words begat words till it was unbearable to stay silent, and she began to scream out a gabbling torrent of incoherent words into the derisive mist. She longed for the sound of the siren again, and when it came, for a moment it comforted her. But it was for a moment only, and the silence following was a thousand times worse. She stumbled over the rocky ground and ran up to the path where they had left the bag. She did not know where to go. It was almost dark. Where had they been going? To Andrew. Yes, she must get to Andrew. He would understand. But he had loved David. . . .

She screamed in a frenzy and ran along the path backwards and forwards, demented in the quick darkness that fell around her. With all her power she cried into the air. But no answer came back except the loathed sound of her own voice. She started to run wildly along the path they had been taking northwards. She had no light and could see nothing but her own coat flapping against her legs. But she was driven on, away from the foul place of her triumph. She did not think of anything save getting away from that place. Impelled by this thought, her body assumed greater strength and she dragged every inch of energy out of her limbs. Soon she got very hot and, throwing off her coat, left it on the path. She lost the path and came on to open moorland. By the sound of the siren on her left she judged she was making inland. She went on running till her heart throbbed up in her throat and her mouth was sticky, her limbs burning with pain.

Gasping, she fell down upon the moor. Slowly her breath returned, and with it a fuller realization of her position. She did not think once of David now. She only knew that she must find somewhere to go for the night. There came over her suddenly the overwhelming realization that it did not matter where she went; that this material consideration no longer had any bearing upon her life. That in the last few minutes she had ended her life and already started a new one. Where was the new life to be? There was no compassion in the licking menace of this crawling mist. No light shone anywhere for her; no grave face smiled solemnly for her; no clear voice called her.

With a slight shock of amusement she realized that her life had ended, and that four miles away Arthur and Alice were washing tea things. Everywhere, all over the world, life would go on the same. The ploughman march again over his black fields; the celandines spatter the ground with their yellow stars; the swallows flash their way into another spring; the cuckoo drive its insistent message into the languid hearts of lovers; the thick green fields wither to the hay harvest; the black field, where the ploughman drove his team, spring to another sheen of gold corn. Another harvest and another winter. The sea would beat up the little channel with no change in its reasonless rhythm. God would not alter that, nor anything. Why should He, she asked? He Who struck down a million birds and a million flowers every day, why should He incline His head when she, no more than a bird or a flower, had herself been struck down? Even now He would not give her a glimpse of His messenger. He would not

stir an inch to help her, till she had reached, through aeons of
tempering, the blinding throne of His glory. Then she might cry
out: "O God! I have come through. Keep me." Not until then
would He listen.

She was very cold, for the mist had pressed through her
clothes and her body was damp with the sweat of her running.
She got up and began to walk, not caring now what direction she
took, only knowing that morning must come, and that when that
happened she must give herself into the hands of the first person
she saw. She walked very fast, to keep warm. For two hours she
walked, sometimes straining her eyes for the light of any cottage.
But she saw nothing to relieve the blackness. Once she fell over
some sleeping ponies and stumbled, terrified, to her feet as they
scrambled together and whinnied with alarm. Then she ran, the
fear of the moor gathering in her soul—the numbing hand of
the senseless moor threatening to assault her and beat her down.
Because she feared to fall, she ran to keep her body alive.

A little point of light glowed in the far distance. It seemed suddenly to rise out of the darkness. As she ran, it grew larger, the
lovely friendly eye of a cottage. The benison of home overcame
her, even though she knew that home no longer existed. She
longed to drink cold water and lie upon a bed until the morning.
The lovely thought of sleep was too much to bear. Frantic and
desperate, she came to the garden gate; opened it with her last
strength and stumbled up the path. She slipped down by the door
and could barely summon enough strength to knock. But when
she did so, weakly and impatiently, she heard after a long silence
the sound of slow uncertain footsteps and a groping hand fumbling for the lock.

CHAPTER XI

A GNARLED yellow hand shook with a candle lantern. A cracked high voice broke the silence.

"Who is-a you? Who is-a come to make an old woman open the door? Me bones are weary with opening and shutting, opening and shutting, letting of 'em all come in. Who is-a?"

She dangled her lantern guardedly over Tansy's head and would not open the door more than a few inches. Tansy caught hold of the door, pulled herself up and struggled to get in. But the old woman had her foot pressed against it, and Tansy was too weak to move it.

"Tell me, who is-a?" Little cracked pipes of a voice. "Then maybe I'll open."

Tansy knew then. All the horror of her journey passed away in the limitless dimension memory makes of time. She slipped back a thousand years and was standing here on an autumn evening with David, a little boy; further back still, was crying in her old bedroom, hearing the faltering notes of a withered old song.

"'Tis Tansy Penderil," she said slowly, "and I do know you. You're Jessie Vean. Let me in, Jessie, for it's cold and I come a brae long way."

Jessie hovered a moment above the door, the shadow of her spreading over the ceiling like an eagle. Then she gave a long, scuttling laugh—a laugh that sent a thousand whimpering little spirits whining through the walls of the house.

"That Emmeline's baby," she wheezed in her throat. "Who'd-a thought! Come in. Come in, you!"

She opened the door wider, let Tansy in, and immediately bolting it, replaced the sacks that kept out the draught. Tansy stood blinking in the passage, where the walls rattled with little pieces of rotten plaster released by the gust of wind through the door. She was uncertain. This was to dream a dream again, a dream with all the details gone, but the same dream.

Jessie pushed her into the living-room with a harsh, half-pleasant cackle of amusement. In there, the fire winked in the slab, the lamp crouched under a tent of shadows, the great grey tabby cat, half blind with age, quivered in a muffled wave of pristine contentment. Jessie's supper, a bowl of bread and milk, stood steaming on the table. A heavy red curtain covered the door; an orange blind, the window. Insidious in the room was the fœtid smell of rotten walls, unwashed clothes, stale food, and the smoke of a thousand lamps. But to Tansy the place was a magic sanctuary of old dreams. She fell all a-crumple into a high wooden chair by the fireside. The cat feebly stole round and round her ankles.

Tansy felt thirsty. "Give me some water," she murmured. Jessie grumbled and took a pitcher from the pantry at the back. There was very little water.

"Ye'd much better have tea," she said, "for there aren't but a drop of water till morning."

But Tansy begged for a sip, and the old woman poured out half a cup. Tansy drank eagerly as the water searched for the starched avenues of her body.

Jessie sat opposite her, clutching a thin, straight stick and groaning a little.

"Me pipes," she moaned, "not what they was. And the house full-a people upstairs. Falling over each other like ninepins." She reached out and poked the curtain with her stick. "Dost-a see anybody there, you?" Then she called out in a harsh croak: "Who is-a? Who is-a, you?"

Tansy half heard her, half heard the evil little wind hissing at the window. Jessie fell back very weakly in her chair. "You see," she said to Tansy. "You see, my dear, see if there's anybody there, there's a little dear. For I'm too old to move all that way. And I do like to let 'em in when I've got the place all ready and they've come for to wish me well."

"There's nobody there," said Tansy. "We're alone. There's nobody else in the house."

"Nobody else!" Jessie squealed angrily. "Hark then! Hark to 'em upstairs! A-coming and a-going like flies, thicker than flies. I can't go up there. I never do go up there. I can't abide stairs. So I let 'em all stay and do as they've a mind."

"Who are they all?" asked Tansy, the deep peace of the fire stealing the coldness from her heavy limbs.

"Ah, ye may well ask, for I do hardly know. There's me brother. And me three sisters, Rebecca, Susanna and Loveday. Pretty dears. And all their men up there too, so many, so many—I can't tell 'em proper. Then there's father—ah, poor father! Poor dear! Him's dying, y'see. Him's on the bed pretty near done. Go up and see un, my dear. Go up and see un. You was from the farm across the moor, wasn't-a?"

"I'm Tansy. Emmeline's Tansy."

"Emmeline! There's a saucy maid if ever be! How is-a? How's mother doing now?"

"Mother's dead," she murmured. Jessie was only a heavier shadow in the room; the drone of her witless voice only a closer song of the wind.

"Mother dead! Oh, you don't say! Oh, there's a thing! And I see her last week, spick and span as could be. There's bad news you do bring me. But go up and see un, my dear. Go up and see un. And how're ye here so late? Courting?"

"I lost my way. I was going to Rosemulyan."

"Rosemulyan," echoed Jessie darkly. "A wisht sinful place where there be devils and things done against the Lord. You'll not be getting there to-night."

"I want to stay till morning," said Tansy. "Jessie, let me stay just till morning."

"I ain't got no beds," she complained. "For they took 'em all away. But ye can sleep on the sofa down here if ye've a mind. What'll mother say?"

"Mother's dead——"

"Ah, to be sure," muttered Jessie. Suddenly she seized her spoon and began sucking up her supper. There was silence. The cat, tired of Tansy's ankles, sat hunched up sullenly, its back a potent arc of contempt. Tansy did not move. The heat seemed to forge her limbs to the chair. Presently, when Jessie had finished her supper, she spoke again.

"That old cat," and she flicked him with her stick, "come Michaelmas'll be sixteen year old. The little dear. I don't mind a time seeming when he weren't with me." The cat still sat solemnly resentful, because Tansy had not yielded to his overtures. "I keep un in," continued Jessie savagely. "I do hate un to go prowling o' nights. I hate un!"

She spat fiercely. A door rattled upstairs. "There's father," she muttered, "turning and twisting on his bed, poor dear. He eat his food some eager. I don't like un, don't like un when they do get that rawnish they pull at the bedclothes. Go up and see un, my dear. He'll be glad for you to see un."

But Tansy, reaching her hand up to her neck to loosen her dress because she was hot, pricked her finger on the warm gold points of the brooch she wore. She remembered, and unpinning it, held it out to Jessie. The small gold word coiled and uncoiled its letters before her eyes. Jessie glared at it, then snatched it eagerly.

" 'Tes mine!" she cried. "I lost un these twenty year or more. 'Tes mine and you had un."

"You gave it me," said Tansy. "You gave it me on my wedding day. Now you can have it back, for I done with it."

Jessie's suspicious eyes drew to a narrow thread of light. "I gave un you?" she muttered doubtfully.

"Yes. And you said you hoped as I'd live up to it."

"Well, did-a?" snapped Jessie with a soft click of her hard gums. "Did-a live up to un, you?"

Tansy did not answer, and Jessie, in impotent rage, tapped her stick on the floor, and repeated: "Did-a wear un true and proper?"

"Yes, I did," said Tansy. And she felt she wanted to sway the hard tall chair backwards and forwards, but it would not move.

"It was me mother's and her mother's before that," rambled Jessie. "But it never brought no good to me. Ye can keep un!" She thrust it out before Tansy. But Tansy would not take it, and it fell from Jessie's hand on to the floor, gleaming dully under the fire.

"I had a lover once," came Jessie's shadowy voice. "I had a lover like no maid ever had, I do believe. But he went away and wouldn't marry me. That's why I do hate wedduns and such trash. He went away over the moor and I never see him again. But he's here, you. The pretty dear he was. He's always here." She clawed at her heart. The lamp was burning low and she grumbled at it. "They take all the oil, the darn crowd up there, and don't leave a drop for a poor old woman."

The shadows thickened to grey shapeless masses like gale clouds. Tansy was moving in a silent cold sphere, felt as though she were floating effortlessly over a land of icebergs. The ancestral twilight of her soul closed slowly round her. There were bells clanging in her ears, the deep bell-roars of the sea in a cavernous Arctic world. She experienced the same delight as a child who puts his ear to a sea-shell and is flooded by the sound of ageless seas. The veil between things seen and unseen was threadbare. And when she spoke, it was to play on an instrument of speech, controlled still by her, but entirely outside the adventure of her mind. Her voice was like a minstrelsy of old sweet pipes, moving in grave rhythms.

"He went away," she said. "Across the moor——"

Jessie nodded. "And never come back. Never come back to me. Oh—a pretty man too! I wrote a little song about un, but I can't tell it right now. I can't sing me notes true."

She fell to humming the melody, but could get no further than the first line. The lamp was lower, quick towards its death, like the sun over the sea. Then it spat and died out. So there was only the fire to send moving, dying shadows up the wall. Jessie sat back in her chair, alert to the sounds of the wind-rustling house. The door banged again and she twiddled her stick impatiently.

"Dost-a hear un?" she said. "Dost-a hear un tossing about up there, poor soul? Go up and see un, there's a dear."

The door rattled again and a mouse scrabbled. Jessie looked quickly around her.

"Go up and see un——"

BOSCEAN 1933
GREENFIELDS 1934